JIM
in 1
Esse
and
a yo
build

He later moved to London to study journalism and publishing. Around this time, he dabbled in poetry, and one of his poems won a BBC Reggae Writing Competition. He also wrote lyrics, and performed regularly with Colchester art punks, Maniac Squat.

While working the nightshift at a media monitoring company writing summaries of newspaper articles, he took an MA in Fiction at Middlesex University. He currently lives with his partner in Bethnal Green, East London. *Penknife* is his first novel.

Visit www.penknifenovel.com to find out more.

JIM WESTOVER was born in Kent in 1968 and grew up in Brightlingsea, Essex. He left school with one O Level and fell into labouring work, including a year spent renovating old farm buildings in France.

He later moved to London studying journalism and publishing. Around this time, he dabbled in poetry and one of his poems won a BBC Magazine Writing competition. He also wrote lyrics and performed regularly with Colchester art punks Atlantic Squat.

While working the night shift for a media monitoring company writing summaries of newspaper articles he took an MA in Fiction at Middlesex University. He currently lives with his partner in Bethnal Green, East London. Twinkle is his first novel.

Visit www.xxx.xx.com to find out more.

PEN
KNIFE

JIM WESTOVER

SilverWood

Published in 2022 by SilverWood Books

SilverWood Books Ltd
14 Small Street, Bristol, BS1 1DE, United Kingdom
www.silverwoodbooks.co.uk

ISBN 978-1-80042-222-3 (paperback)

British Library Cataloguing in Publication Data
A CIP catalogue record for this book is
available from the British Library

Page design and typesetting by SilverWood Books

To my mum, Belinda Birch.
Also to the memory of my old friends, Paul Ford and Stuart Jay,
and my brother in law, Jesús Diez.

Part One

Part One

Chapter One

It was a scorching hot day in early May and the sun's rays coming through the windscreen of Mum's old Renault 12 were making me sweat. I took off my tie and stuffed it in my pocket, where it bulged on my thigh and left a stripy trail down my leg.

I didn't need it now anyway. Oakbridge was a council school, not private, so it weren't like the old school tie was worth anything. Especially not mine.

I tried again to placate her. 'We all make mistakes, Mum!'

She turned sharply towards me, with her chin jutted out accusingly. She was wearing a crumpled red beret, and her eyes were obscured by large round frame Reactolite glasses.

'A *mistake*. Is that what you call it? A bloody tragedy more like.'

'They said I can still go back for the exams though.'

'Oh, don't talk wet. How are you going to get there?'

It was a fair point, cos Oakbridge boarding school was in the middle of nowhere. 'I'd probably fail them all, anyway.'

'Oh, well that makes it all right then.'

She pushed in the car lighter and reached for her Rothmans.

'Anyway, that's not true, Jarrod. You're good at English, aren't you? Your teacher said once that you had a real flair for writing poetry and stories.'

It was decent of Mr Griffiths to tell her that, and I knew it would have cheered Mum up on one of those long journeys home on her own from parents' evening; it was probably the highlight of all her parents' evenings at Oakbridge. My highlight was the night she swore at my housemaster while tearing into him publicly for writing in my report that I thought of myself as a "simple clown".

A "flair for poetry" was being generous I reckon, but it was true that English Language and Literature were the only two subjects I was good at - though I'd failed them both badly in my mocks a few months earlier. What I'd never told anybody, cos it would have sounded like an excuse, is that I couldn't write down my answers fast enough against the clock. After about the first hour of each exam, my hand would run out of power, and I wasn't able to form legible letters unless I went really slowly. There was no point in swotting if I couldn't pass an exam.

Mum took an angry drag on her fag. 'What a bloody idiotic thing to do, getting expelled just before your O-levels. You only had to stay out of trouble for another six weeks.'

'I wasn't expelled, I was asked to leave.'

'Don't be *ridiculous*. It amounts to the same thing, doesn't it?'

I couldn't resist: 'Yeah, well it's funny how I got asked to leave when nobody asked me if I wanted to go there in the first place.'

'I'm glad you think it's funny.'

'It's true though. You and Adrian forced me to go there.'

'We were only doing what we thought was best for you.'

I scoffed. 'More like the best thing for him.'

In theory, Adrian was my stepfather. But he'd never tried to be my dad. Mum married him when I was three and then he'd legally adopted me, and this meant I now shared his surname, Brook, though I couldn't remember him ever calling me Jarrod.

It was always *Brat*. Brat this and Brat that. Brat written in permanent ink in a sleeping bag, before we left for one of Adrian's camping holidays. *Brat* until he decided I was old enough for *Yob*, or *Yobbo*. All my friends were yobbos too. I preferred Yob to Brat cos it sounded more rebellious and threatening. I wanted to feel threatening to him. But I never understood why he didn't try to win me over. I don't remember trying to convince him I wasn't a yob either. I reckon I'd have had to give up on pop music and football and only play chess and listen to classical.

10

Eventually something had to give, and someone had to go, so I was sacrificed to Oakbridge to help save their marriage. It wasn't enough. When I came back for the holidays, Adrian would loudly chant down the days until I left again. Then, when Mum finally left him, we moved into a semi next door but one to the Colne High School, the school that she wouldn't let me go to.

Now we were on course to arrive home during the school lunch break, and as I dragged my heavy suitcase from the boot of the car to the back door of the house, I'd be exposed, and caught bang to rights in the act of being different, by the hard nuts who'd already left the Colne but still loitered around the phone box and by some of the actual pupils, like the girls I used to fancy at junior school who'd be sitting on my neighbour's front wall.

A road sign flashed past us on the A12, revealing we were nine miles from Colchester. How long would that take? I wondered. Well, if Mum was doing sixty and... it sounded like one of those maths questions I wouldn't have to answer now. Or something off *Ask the Family*. I used to fancy going on *Ask the Family*, but you never saw a family on the programme without a dad. I didn't even know who my dad was.

One freezing evening, when we still lived in a cottage in Tollesbury with no central heating, Mum brought me a cup of cocoa to bed. And then she told me that Adrian wasn't my father. It explained a lot about his behaviour. But it still left some big questions, like who is my dad then? She told me his name was Nicky, and it had happened at a party. I took comfort from this story, cos I associated parties with people being happy, but I didn't have any understanding of the fact that I was born out of a one-night stand. Afterwards, she gave me a kiss goodnight and told me I could always ask her anything else I wanted to know and then she left me, with a crinkly layer of skin on my cocoa. I didn't ask her any more questions though, cos I never felt like I was missing out by not having a dad. I still don't, I just wish she'd left Adrian much earlier.

I reckon we'd both been stewing, cos she suddenly glared at me so ferociously that I had to look away, out of the passenger window onto the annoyingly quiet dual carriageway. 'You can drag up the past all you want, Jarrod, but you can't blame anyone else for the fact that you and

11

your moronic friends sneaked out of school in the middle of the night to burgle the village pub.'

Moronic was one of Adrian's words to describe me. And her, come to think of it.

'We didn't *burgle* anybody, Mum.' She'd made it sound like I'd climbed through someone's window and rummaged in their drawers. 'We just helped ourselves to a barrel of beer from the back of the pub.'

'And siphoned it into squash bottles and sold it to twelve-year-olds and made them ill!'

'*I* didn't sell it.'

'Oh, *come on*, Jarrod. I'm not talking about the ethics of it. The fact is, you've fucked up your life and you're only sixteen. What are you going to do now, without any qualifications?'

'I'll get a job, Mum.' What else could I say? What other options did I have?

'You and three million other poor bastards. Who's going to employ you now? You'll be lucky if you end up in a factory.'

'I don't want to work in a factory, I'd rather be outside. I'm going to get a job on a building site.'

The previous summer, Mum had a boyfriend who was a general builder and I'd done a week's labouring for him. It was only sweeping up and mixing muck and barrowing rubble into a skip, but I'd got the hang of it, and as work goes it wasn't too bad. I hardened my biceps and accelerated my tan. I couldn't imagine many builders would care whether I'd taken my exams.

'I don't know what the hell you're going to do...but you'd better think of something, because I'll tell you what, I'm not having you and your mates dossing around the house all day doing nothing.'

'What mates?' I only had one mate left in Brightlingsea, and he was bound to be working already.

The other two had melted away during the Easter holidays. Pilkie was getting serious with his girlfriend and already had a job lined up at the office where his mum worked; Kevin had moved to Clacton and started as a groundworker with his uncle. That just left me and my oldest mate, Colin.

Our friendship started the year I moved to Brightlingsea, on one of those Sundays when Adrian paid me 50p to stay away from the house until it was dark.

The worst part of the day came when everybody else went home from the Rec for their roast dinners. They'd always go at the same time too, and nobody came back for at least an hour. I would play football on my own: keepie uppie and smashing in the winner for England on the half-volley. I'd seen Colin and his brother, Ryan, playing on the other side of the Rec a few times, and then one Sunday Ryan shouted me over. He went in goal, and I played against Colin, who was more skilful than me and took it really seriously. Afterwards, I went back to theirs, and we watched a Western on the telly. Then, Colin cooked up bangers and mash and onion gravy. I was amazed: we were only eight, I didn't even know how to make a cup of tea at that time.

Me and Colin would spend every weekend together: playing football, hanging around the swimming pool and the prom, going over the humps and bumps on our bikes. Colin's dad was hardly ever around cos he did night shifts driving a forklift and when he wasn't working, he was sleeping or fishing. Sometimes other people hung around with us too. But when it came down to it, we played by different rules to them. I didn't have a dad, he didn't have a mum, and neither of us had to turn up for meals or be home at a certain time. Then one day, I told him I was being sent away, and we both knew that he would need to find some different friends. Colin took the news almost as badly as me, though he blamed Mum, not Adrian, for separating us. Adrian was my enemy, so it was to be expected, but he thought that mums were supposed to protect you, despite what had happened with his.

We stayed best mates and I caught up with him in the holidays, but our new situations had diluted the closeness of our friendship. I couldn't get him interested in my stories from boarding school, and I felt left out when he talked about people he knew from the Colne or at work.

Colin had always been a grafter. From the age of eleven, he had at least one job on the go: a paper round, or washing up at a pub, or cleaning his neighbours' houses. I'd never been a grafter. But now I needed a job in a hurry, and I hoped that he could give me a clue what to do.

We'd come off the A12 and joined the long tailback of traffic on the approach to Colchester. The danger was almost over, cos the Colne High kids would soon be back in their classrooms and the hard nuts would've drifted away, to do whatever they did for the rest of the day. I unclipped my seatbelt so I could loosen the strap, then stretched out my legs and began to relax. Well, sort of.

Mum switched on Radio 4, and they were reporting on the miners' strike. Talks had broken down because officials from the Coal Board had refused to discuss pit closures.

Some of the kids at school had assumed they were striking over money, but I'd tried to put them right. Thatcher planned to close a load of pits cos she said they were uneconomic. What she really wanted, Mum had told me, was to destroy the miners' union in revenge for the strikes the Tories had lost in the seventies.

If I tried to start a conversation about the strike, I'd be able to gauge whether Mum was willing to talk about anything else yet, apart from me being expelled.

She surprised me by mentioning it first. 'They've been bringing coal in through Wivenhoe and Brightlingsea. Did I tell you?'

'No. Bringing it in from where?'

She turned down the radio and explained that scab coal was being sneaked into small ports from Eastern Europe to boost stocks and undermine the strike. Some miners from Kent found out what was happening and had come to picket locally. Mum told me she was on the committee of the Miners Support Group in Brightlingsea. 'We're organising places for them to stay.'

'That's brilliant, Mum.' It sounded like socialism in action - backing each other up. Solidarity. My favourite group, the Style Council, were already playing benefit gigs for the miners; I'd read about it in the NME. Sharply dressed socialist, and poetic and political lyricist, Paul Weller was everything I wanted to be. But I didn't have a group, or any money. Or even a decent haircut.

For the first, and perhaps last time that day, Mum smiled at me. 'I'm glad you approve, Jarrod, because Tony has been sleeping in your room and I don't think it's fair to ask him to move, just because you've been kicked out of school.'

'Who the hell's Tony when he's at home?'

'A striking miner, from Kent. He's going to be staying with us during the picketing at Wivenhoe.'

'You could have given me a bit more warning, Mum!' Then I remembered that I wasn't even supposed to be back for another six weeks.

We were already in the shadow of the overhanging trees next to the old church on the way into Brightlingsea. As we came round the tight bend and back into blazing sunshine, the only sound I could hear was the car engine. And the scene was so still and familiar; it felt like we were bursting through the middle of a painting.

She watched over my shoulder while I dragged off chunks of potato skin with the bread knife.

'Come on, Jarrod, do it properly. Here, use a peeler, you're wasting half of it.'

'I can't use a peeler, I'm left-handed, remember.'

'Well use a more suitable knife, then.'

'I am trying, Mum. You know peeling potatoes isn't one of my strong points.' Though apart from a knack for making perfect boiled eggs without a timer, I wasn't sure what my strong points were.

'Well try a bit harder!' She sighed, and then muttered, 'How did I manage to bring up a child who can't even peel a potato?'

'Cos cooking's just a chore to you.'

'Oh, perhaps you think I should have baked a cake to welcome you home? I'm not a bloody housewife you know. Who do you think pays for all the food in this house? I don't think you appreciate that I've had to take on three part-time jobs to support this family. I've got Adrian mucking me about over Lucy's maintenance and...shit!' She rushed to the cooker to turn the mince, which had already stuck to the pan.

I jolted upright when I heard two sturdy raps on the back door.

'Come in,' Mum called, switching smoothly to a more welcoming tone.

He was probably no taller than me, but his presence in the doorway made the small kitchen seem crowded. He looked normal, like he could have been one of Mum's least embarrassing boyfriends. I don't know what I was expecting, I'd never met a miner before. He had short thick black hair, which was streaked with grey at the sides, and he wore a gold sleeper earring.

'Ah, hello Tony, I was just… we were…this is my son, Jarrod.'

'Good to meet you, Jarrod. Angie said you were coming today.'

Had she told him why? I shook his outstretched hand but was too shy to look him in the eye.

'I'm just baking a shepherd's pie, Tony. It should be ready in about forty-five minutes.'

I don't think I'd ever heard her sound so much like a housewife.

I sat on the other end of the settee from Tony, watching *Anglia News*. I guessed he wanted to see if there was anything about the local picketing. Me too: but the biggest news was about a baby rhino born at Colchester Zoo. Tony spent the whole time scribbling in a notebook, so I didn't try to start a conversation.

Mum called through to the living room to say that dinner was ready. 'Jarrod, can you bring the bread and butter from the kitchen, please?'

I thought I must have misheard at first, but there it was on the side, a plate piled high with wholemeal bread, thickly smeared with margarine. This must have been for the miner's benefit, cos I couldn't remember us having bread with dinner before, unless dinner was something on toast. It was the best way to cope with the Oakbridge food though: coat it with salt and hide it between folded slices of Mothers Pride.

'It might be easier if I take my piece first,' Mum said, before explaining that she'd built two walls of mash to isolate the corner of shepherd's pie made with soya mince.

I studied Tony's bicep vein as he leaned in to scoop from the tray. If I worked on building sites, I could have muscles like that one day. He placed a half-slice of bread and marge on either side of his plate, and so I did the same.

My sister, Lucy, usually ate in her bedroom whenever she was allowed while watching the colour portable Adrian had bought her for Christmas. But today she had honoured us with her attendance.

'How was school today, Luce?' Tony asked. 'Did you have that maths test you were telling me about?'

I never called her Luce, not even when I was trying to be nice to her.

'I think I just about passed,' Lucy said. 'But I won't find out the mark until Friday.'

'Well done, Lucy!' Mum said. She asked Tony if he had any plans for the evening.

'There's a pool and darts competition down the Yachtsmans. Locals against miners.'

'Oh, that'll be fun. I'll try to make it down for last orders if I'm not too tired. I've got a huge pile of marking to get through first unfortunately.' She shot me a look like this was somehow my fault.

Lucy cleared the table and then disappeared to her bedroom. After we'd done the washing up, Mum got on with her marking. Tony went to the phone box outside the school to make a few calls. The miner had found his way in this house and this town; now it was time for me to find mine.

Chapter Two

Colin didn't have a phone at home so I never knew when he might turn up at my door, or if I'd find him in. I'd tried knocking round a few times but then I finally bumped into him one morning on the High Street.

He was dressed like a poor man's casual, in old bleached jeans, scuffed white trainers, and a yellow Gemelli cardigan, which was slightly darker than his shoulder length hair.

'Fucking hell, Jarrod. Why didn't you tell me you were back?'

'I'm back for good, mate. I got kicked out.' Then I laughed, I don't know why. Cos it wasn't funny really.

'You fucking idiot. What you done now?' He liked to think he was more sensible than me. But he'd left school at Easter without any qualifications either, so I didn't think there was much difference really.

An old granny needed to pass with her tartan shopping trolley. We stepped off the pavement and moved around the corner into Sidney Street.

I told him it was a long story, cos I wasn't prepared to rush through it when I could see he was in a hurry. I could tell him later, over a fag and a cup of tea. I asked him what he'd been up to.

His eyes were naturally narrow: when he narrowed them now against the glare of the sun, they were like slits between the slats of closed blinds. 'Not a lot.' He leaned over and gobbed on the pavement. 'I'm just doing a couple of bits and bobs.'

'What you going to do now, Jarrod?'

I looked down at the two heavy carrier bags at my feet. 'I've just got to nip to the baker's and –'

Colin was shifting from foot to foot, all impatient. 'Nah, what you going to do about work?'

Trust him to bring that up already. He was on my case quicker than Mum.

'I dunno. I'm thinking of maybe trying to get a job as a building labourer,' I said.

'I know where there might be some work coming up.'

'What, on a site?'

'Potato picking, in St Osyth. It don't start for a few weeks though.'

'How d'you hear about that?'

'Dennis done it last year. He reckons it's good money an' all.'

'Dennis who?' But as soon as I said it, I got a sinking feeling in my guts. We only knew one Dennis in Brightlingsea.

'Who d'you reckon?'

'Have you been hanging around with him, then?' My voice gave away my sense of dread. Things were changing quickly: Colin had got a new mucker, and I had a miner kipping in my bed.

'Don't worry, Jarrod, he ain't like he used to be.'

'What do I have to do to apply then?'

'I can bring him round yours tomorrow lunchtime if you want. He usually goes up the school anyway to meet his bird.'

'What are you up to now?'

Colin looked away, like he didn't want to answer. And then a flash silver motor came round the corner and pulled up opposite us.

The driver had a long fat face, which filled the frame of the open window like a portrait. 'Are you still planning to come and do some work today, Colin?'

Colin looked awkward, like he'd been caught between two worlds.

As I watched them drive off, I was already fretting about whether I'd done the right thing, putting my job prospects in the hands of Dennis Winch.

Two things Colin had said kept repeating in my head – *it's good money an' all* and *he ain't like he used to be*. But what did that actually mean? He was no longer a bully? Or he was less of one now?

He'd moved down from London at the start of the final year at juniors and sat next to me on his first day. We were both outsiders, and we both stood out in our school clothes: Dennis, because his trousers were too short, and his shirt was too tight, and I wore an embarrassing jumper that was knitted by Mum. It was green and speckly and Dennis nicknamed me *Bogie,* which stuck like dried snot in the winter.

Dennis would knock round for me every school morning at twenty past eight, even though the school was only a ten-minute walk away. Like me, he needed to escape from his stepfather. Adrian nicknamed him *Jarabah* cos of the way he asked, "Is Jarrod about?" in his cockney accent.

Before school, we would play with our catapults on the waste ground next to Hall Cut, or nick sweets from the newsagents in Victoria Place. Sometimes I'd buy us a quarter of aniseed balls or bon bons if I'd managed to nick any money from Adrian. Dennis's stepdad used to beat him with his belt and his fists while Adrian's viciousness mostly came out of his mouth, and in the ways he treated me so differently to my sister.

They had a game, which they played in Lucy's room before she went to bed. Once I'd clocked the door ajar and managed to peek in. Lucy was bouncing around on her bed and there was lots of laughter and shrieking. I was jealous of all the fun they were having and the next evening I asked if I could join in. But like the big kid he'd been playing, Adrian took a spiteful delight in excluding me.

I wasn't allowed to use the toilet in the bathroom, only the tiny bog next door. Adrian said it was cos I splashed piss on the floor. I also had to clean my teeth in the sink in my bedroom, even though the tap was really stiff. If Adrian ever saw it drip, he would dock 5p from my pocket money on the calendar next to the fridge. Sometimes he'd chase me round the house and then attack me with slaps, but they didn't sting as badly as his insults. He used to say I was an imbecile and a cretin; he would call me an amoeba and a unicell, cos he reckoned I only had one brain cell. His favourite line though, was to tell me that I needed a lobotomy. I didn't know the exact meaning of all his names for me until I was at Oakbridge and had my first dictionary. Adrian probably didn't realise this, but he was softening me up for the treatment I got from Dennis.

After school, we walked through the Rec, which was on his way home but not mine. This was when Dennis would be at his most dangerous and cuntish and usually he would rope in at least one accomplice. Though he never did it when Colin was there, cos he knew that Colin would refuse to join in.

Dennis would drag me around the park by my arm for a laugh or get people to pin me down while he dangled a lolly stick dipped in dog shit over my nose and mouth. Or they'd throw me over hedges and garden walls. The next morning on the way to school, Dennis would usually act like it hadn't happened though occasionally he'd apologise, and then if I was lucky, he'd treat me well for a while.

It was after one of these bullying rituals that Mum told me I was being sent to boarding school. She was waiting in the kitchen and there was a Mars Bar on the table, which was suspicious, cos normally we were only allowed sweets at the weekends. I yelled at her that they would have to drag me there in handcuffs, then legged it upstairs and sobbed on my bed. All I could think about was that Adrian had won, and of the gloating expression on his face when I next saw him. Once I'd run dry of tears, I didn't want to think, so I went to the corner of the room and scrubbed at the grass stains on my school trousers in the little sink.

Mum couldn't have been aware that at least she was saving me from Dennis's bullying, cos I never said anything, and I was always careful to clean up the evidence. I didn't tell anyone, not even Colin, though I reckon he must have known something. I was too ashamed, but I was also confused, cos I didn't have an answer to the obvious question: why was I putting up with it? I was behaving like Adrian's fantasy had come true, and I'd had a lobotomy, and it had brainwashed me into believing that I deserved to be abused.

I never saw Dennis at weekends, cos he always knocked about with his brother, Greg, and the older kids who lived on his street. After I'd started at Oakbridge, we only ever bumped into each other if he saw me first. Now, five years after he'd helped to make my life a misery, I'd agreed to Colin inviting him round.

The next day at twelve, they were at the door. I led them into the front room, where I now slept, and Dennis quickly spread out across the middle of the settee, with his legs wide apart and his arm around his girlfriend, Sian. He wanted to know who else lived here. Whose is that suitcase? And where's your old dear?

He asked these questions in a friendly tone, but I still felt like I was being unsettled in my own home. It was almost like the years had disappeared, and we were back in the playground at juniors. Almost. But Dennis wasn't the only one who weren't like he used to be. This was going to be a new start for me in Brightlingsea. I wasn't so naïve that I'd believe Dennis didn't still flip, but if he flipped on me, I swore he would only do it once cos this time I wouldn't be coming back for more.

Sian's friend, Verity, was sat on one of the flowery armchairs next to me. I reckon we were one of the only families in the town that didn't have a matching three-piece suite. There was a Tupperware container open on her knees; she said she hoped I didn't mind but she was really hungry. Then she took a bite from her cheese and tomato sarnie. She had pale skin, thick blonde hair, and a couple of zits on her chin. There was a grey canvas bag at her feet with pin badges on it.

Sian asked me why we had a rug on the wall. I didn't know. Why *did* we have to have a rug hanging on the wall? Why couldn't we be more normal? I wondered if they thought this was a hippy house, with the flowery armchairs and all those books, and the Russian dolls and joss stick holder on the mantelpiece. In Brightlingsea, a hippy was one of the worst things you could be. Mum got called a hippy cos she had a 2CV – you could get away with that in Paris, but not in Brightlingsea. And it had a *Nuclear Power – No Thanks* sticker in the back window. So that was two marks on her card in the spot-the-hippy bingo. Still, they never said it to her face though.

I'd tried to make the front room more my own by putting a Style Council poster above the stereo, and a *Victory to the Miners* one next to the wall-mounted bronze plate with the French writing on it. I'd also put away Mum's hippy and classical LPs and displayed mine more prominently.

Colin was knelt in front of the breeze block fireplace, flicking through my records on the shelf. He didn't have any records of his own anymore, not since we went through our heavy rocker phase when we were twelve and thirteen. He relied on the radio and chucked his money in fruit machines. He put on one of my UB40 LPs, *Labour of Love*.

Dennis sat forward to get down to business. He had broad shoulders that were fit for a hod and a flash haircut, which was long at the back, shaved at the sides and spiky on top. From the neck up, I reckon he could have been on *Top of the Pops*. I liked the tattoo of a tiger on his upper right arm, which had a banner with *Dennis* underneath, but I was less keen on the scrappy green ones on his hands and wrists.

He lit a Benson and slurped his tea, and said he'd had a word with the head farmhand, Wurzel, and he could get me on the firm if I still wanted to be. If I did, I'd have to give him a fiver as a finder's fee, but that could wait 'til I got my first wage packet.

He was squinting and shielding his eyes as he spoke, cos the sun was pouring in through the windows behind me. Mum didn't believe in net curtains.

I said, 'I know its potato picking, but what do I have to do?' I glanced at Verity, cos her quietness intrigued me, and I didn't want to give her the impression I was slow on the uptake. But Verity didn't seem to be listening to the conversation, she was gazing up at the bookshelves.

Dennis said I didn't need to worry; the job was a piece of piss. 'Are you up for it, Bogue, or what?'

I said I was, cos he clearly weren't going to hang around for a decision, and I couldn't afford to be picky about the ins and outs of potato picking or even who I'd be picking with.

Dennis rubbed his palms together, as he always used to do when he got excited. 'That's it then, Col. We've got our little spudding crew sorted.'

They came round mine every school lunchtime, except for Thursday, which was Mum's day off. I always offered them a cup of tea, and Verity would volunteer to help me. I tried to make the most of each second we had alone in the small kitchen while I dragged out the process of preparing us a brew. I would think up questions the night before and then try to slip them naturally into the conversation so it didn't sound like an interview.

I was curious about her friendship with Sian, cos they came across very differently. Sian seemed to say the first thing that came into her head; Verity appeared to only speak when she needed to. She told me they'd been next door neighbours when they were little and had stayed mates ever since. I also got the feeling she had other friends, and different interests but she wasn't going to give them up to me in a hurry. It was easier to talk about music, at least at first, cos she wore her tastes on her bag.

One day, Verity was studying the postcards pinned to the cork board while I washed up some mugs and put the kettle on. Above her head was a poster showing women toiling in a field, below the slogan, *Boycott Products of Apartheid*.

She turned to me. 'Is your mum a feminist?'

'Yeah. She teaches it up the Adult Education Centre in Colchester.'

'I didn't know you could do courses in feminism.'

'I think they call it Women's Studies. What about your mum, is she a feminist?'

'Nah, but I am.'

'Good for you.' I wasn't sure what to say. She clearly wasn't the sort of girl you could meet every day. Certainly not in Brightlingsea.

She turned back to the postcards and giggled as she read one aloud. *Marriage starts when you sink into his arms and ends with your arms in his sink.*

I laughed too. 'I help out with the washing up every night. And I do the shopping and hoovering.' Though I didn't admit it was cos I'd been expelled.

'Good for you,' she said, slightly sarcastically, but she balanced it out with a mischievous smile. It was a smile that provoked a prickly twinge in my chest. She was bold, and that boldness encouraged me to be bolder. I looked at her like I wanted her; well, at least that's what I was feeling inside. Then, my eyes dropped to her shoulder bag, and I noticed a new badge: *Coal Not Dole*.

I came closer and touched it and said that I liked it. I couldn't wait to tell her all about Tony, but, not for the last time, she went one better than me. Her dad was a communist, so they had two miners staying at their house.

Chapter Three

I didn't tell anybody I was planning to go to the picket line, in case I ended up losing my bottle. It wasn't like I had any friends who'd go with me. Colin was working for Skully, the fat bloke with the flash motor, at his restaurant down the Hard, though I doubt I could have persuaded him anyway. Henry, my best mate at Oakbridge, would have been an outside bet, but he was still at school. Maybe he'd be sitting an O-level at the same time I was taking my picketing practical. I wanted to see what it was like with my own eyes and to have a good story to tell Verity.

Every dinner time, I asked Tony how the day had gone, but he never took the hint and invited me along. Perhaps he didn't want the responsibility or always had a car full. So, one day after the school lunch break, I took the bus to Wivenhoe on my tod. There was picketing at the wharf in Brightlingsea too, but from what I could gather, Wivenhoe was where the action was. Except it wasn't, not on the afternoon I turned up.

I guessed I was too late, cos when I wandered down to have a look around by the port gates, the only people I saw were locals walking their dogs and a couple of coppers, who looked like bobbies. On my way back through the village, I couldn't spot anyone I thought might be a picket, so I went and bought some chips and sat on a bench and stared out at the estuary. It was a clear and calm sunny day, and the chips were lovely, but that wasn't a story I thought worth telling Verity.

The following day, I forced myself to get on the bus by eight and was rewarded with the sight of a few small groups of blokes milling about by the port. There was even a geezer selling the *Socialist Worker*. I bought a paper from him, so I could start a chat about the picketing, but he didn't know what was happening either. Though he did invite me to a branch meeting that evening in a room above a pub in Colchester.

I hung around for a while until people started to drift away. I found out later, from listening to Tony, that there hadn't been a shipment of coal in that day. Most of the pickets had gone to Rowhedge instead.

I kept schtum about these anti-climaxes and didn't plan any more picketing trips until the following Wednesday, when I heard Tony tell Mum that the next day was going to be the biggest picket yet.

I arrived in Wivenhoe by 7.30 and was looking forward to spotting Tony and surprising him. Maybe he would introduce me to some more of his comrades. But as I looked around at the crowd gathered by the passenger bridge, which led across the railway track to Wivenhoe port, the only person I recognized was matey with the Karl Marx beard from the Brightlingsea health food shop.

I watched two blokes nearby unfurling a banner. The lettering became clear as they pulled it taut: National Union of Seamen – Harwich Branch. This was the sort of solidarity I was hoping to see. The solidarity that was needed. If all the unions got behind the miners, then surely they would win. I reckon the geezer from the health food shop would have agreed with me that the workers of the world really needed to unite.

We were led up the metal stairs to the bridge by six blokes carrying 'NUM – OFFICIAL PICKET' placards. One of them started the first chant of the day:
What do we want!
The right to picket.
When do we want it?
NOW!'
I joined in from the second time around, and as the chant gathered momentum, each rendition was louder than the last. The stamping of feet and pummelling of the bridge became more frenzied; a quiver numbed my cheeks and a shiver went through me. I was already thinking of how to describe the atmosphere to Verity.

'It's always the same old fucking rigmarole,' a geezer shouted behind me. 'We go through the formality of telling them we're entitled to have six pickets on the gate to speak to the drivers and they tell us we're not pickets we're demonstrators.'

'*Demonstrators*,' another bloke spat, like he was reading out some bullshit headline from *The Sun*.

I didn't know if I was a demonstrator or a picket. Did I need to be a miner to be a picket? Or was anyone who turned up at a picket line automatically counted as one? I'd been on a few CND marches with Mum, but this was already rougher, and the people around me looked tougher. I couldn't recall seeing any women yet at all and there were no peace signs, or signs that this was going to be peaceful. I also appeared to be the only one who was supposed to be at school.

We shuffled forward, half a boot at a time. Midway across the bridge, I peered down and saw a sea of black in front of the train station: rows and rows of dark helmets sat on white faces; hundreds of silver nipples twinkling in the sun.

I heard somebody saying in a Yorkshire accent that they'd brought in the heavy mob from Chelmsford. 'Those are the *bastards* that don't even wear numbers.'

My nerves gave me a coughing fit. Why would they hide their identities unless they wanted to lash out with impunity? Or worse? Cos from what I'd seen on the telly, they were lashing out already.

I felt my guts rumbling, thought I could hear them too. Suddenly I really needed the bog. I twisted round to look over my shoulder, but the bridge was packed tightly behind me. There was no going back, even if I wanted to.

We came to a halt when the pickets at the front were held up by coppers at the bottom of the stairs. From this position, I could see over the port wall. There were cranes moving around between what looked like huge sheds, and at least three massive black piles on the ground.

Two trains clattered past on the line below while we were still stuck on the bridge. There was an outbreak of sarcastic cheering when we finally got moving, then the chant I'd heard on the news: *Here we go, here we go, here we go.*

On the other side of the bridge, we were released in small batches and made to walk in single file through a corridor of coppers onto the grass verge at the left of the port gates. I kept my head down, so I wasn't able to clock if they were wearing numbers or not, but I was convinced that this lot were the heavy mob. They were wearing boots with more holes than any punk or skinhead I'd ever seen. Were we being lured into a trap? Well, it was definitely a sun trap, cos the back of my neck was roasting. It seemed to have got very hot, very quickly.

I smoked one of my last three Bensons as the grass verge filled up slowly around me and I carried on looking out for Tony. I remembered what he'd said the previous night about stepping up the pressure over picketing rights. By hook or by crook, by coach, car or foot, they were coming to North Essex from all over. Kent had got here first, cos they found out about the scab coal coming in from Poland; then, a few weeks ago, Derbyshire had started arriving in Brightlingsea. Now there were Welsh miners holed up in Wivenhoe and I could hear Scottish accents behind me. But I still hadn't spoken to anybody.

I looked around to see if I could catch someone's eye, but everybody else was busy chatting, or reading the papers: *The Miner*, the *Mirror*, and the *Socialist Worker*. Everybody was waiting for something to happen.

It all changed when we heard the first lorry rattling down the road towards the port. I imagined this was what it was like to be a film extra. After hanging around for hours, you suddenly had to be ready to spring into action and do another take. Except this was going to be my first take, and nobody had shown me the script.

I followed everybody else and pushed into the geezer in front with all my strength. When I pressed my palms against the back of his T-shirt, it was already soaking wet. The scent of our collective sweat was pungent, but not unpleasant. It smelled earthier than the sickly sour milk odour the kids gave off at school. I wanted to believe the difference was because they were miners, but I guess it was really just cos they were men.

A new chant started, which we grunted in a low hypnotic hum: *Heave...heave...heave...* It must have had some effect, because we moved forward by a couple of metres, but that wasn't enough to test the police lines.

I was relieved when the heaving stopped, even though it meant that we'd lost the first round. I'd already run out of steam, and now I had time to find my bomber jacket, which had slipped down from my waist and was being stomped into the ground.

Over the revving of anxious engines, I heard one word being spat out again and again.

SCAB...SCAB... SCAB...SCAB...

They made it sound like a scab was the most despicable thing that anybody could ever be.

I stood on tiptoes and clocked one in the flesh. He was a scrawny old geezer with greased-back hair and a roll-up stuck to the side of his mouth, gesturing frantically to be allowed to drive forwards. The scab was flanked by a line of coppers with their arms linked together.

The police had us where they wanted us, hemmed in tightly against the port wall. And not a single picket was allowed out to reason with the drivers.

After another convoy of lorries were loaded up, the chants of *scab* became more half-hearted before dying out completely. I could hear seagulls cawing in the sky above me and cranes moving around in the port. Once the police lines had disintegrated, many of the pickets started to walk away. If I wanted to, I could have escaped and called it a day. It had already been a day that I would never forget, and there were plenty of things on which I wanted to reflect, but I also needed to know what was going to happen next. I followed a group of blokes to see where they went and ended up in a queue for the shop. I bought a can of Top Deck and a pasty and then went to the concrete fence at the back of the grass verge to join the line of miners who were pissing against it.

The ten-box of Bensons had crushed in my front pocket and both fags were snapped at the filter. I turned one around and screwed it back into the butt, but after a crappy couple of puffs, I ran out of luck.

When the next batch of lorries came in, it was like we had a strong wind behind us or were playing on a sloping pitch. The coppers were on the back foot from the off. When their arm-linked fences finally gave way, it reminded me of being in the Shed at Stamford Bridge when a goal went in, getting carried along by the tides of bodies and ending up fifteen feet from your original spot.

*

29

I watched from outside the train station as the heavy mob set about smashing up the sit-down blockade in front of the port gates. I saw bare-chested blokes being frogmarched out with their arms forced up their backs; other were dragged along the ground by their wrists.

I worried what sort of state Tony might be in when I saw him that evening. The beating heat, and my helplessness in the face of their violence made me cough and then retch. I closed my eyes and took some deep breaths, then turned away to go back to the High Street. There was a long row of green police paddy wagons stretching the length of Station Road. As I walked past them, I saw more reinforcements inside. Others were running towards the port with their truncheons swinging at their sides.

If there were so many of them lying in wait, how were the miners able to get in front of the port gates? Did the cops lose on purpose, so they had an excuse to arrest more people, take them out of action and get the courts to ban them from picketing in Essex? Tony had told me this was already happening.

On my walk to the bus stop, along Wivenhoe High Street, the pavements were dark and thick with even more coppers, forcing the rest of us into the road. Someone from our side tugged on my arm as a lorry came speeding towards us on its way to the port. As I backed into the curb, I saw a small piece of coal at my feet. Without really thinking, I bent down to pick it up and zipped it into my jacket pocket. I've still got it, eight years later. It's in an old jam jar on my desk as I write this in London.

The next day, I showed the coal to Verity, like it was proof I was there. But I suppose I could have taken it from the coal bucket in the front room, so I wasn't really proving anything. I tried to squeeze the whole experience into our usual slot, but I got overexcited, and we both clocked that the teas were getting stewed.

'Don't worry about it,' Verity said, 'I like a strong brew.'

'Me too.'

'I don't think I'm cut out to be a picket though, I have to admit. I didn't even have the right kit. I reckon I was the only one there who'd brought a jacket. The bloody thing kept slipping down, and I was sliding around on the ground in my old boxing boots.'

Verity laughed. 'Maybe you should have listened to the weather forecast, Jarrod. And took a flask and some sun cream.'

'Maybe.'

'You were there, mate. That's what matters. I think it's brilliant that you made the effort to go on your own. How many people do you know who'd do that?'

'I can't think of any.'

'I wish I could go, but my dad won't let me.'

I wasn't surprised after what I'd witnessed. 'It's really hard,' I said, 'I don't know how they can keep it up every day.'

'They're *hard*,' she said. 'Wouldn't you be if you had to work down a mine? Can you imagine?'

I couldn't imagine it. Not really. I couldn't even imagine what it was going to be like picking potatoes on Monday.

Chapter Four

Dennis spotted a red dot in the distance and decided it had to be them. He lay down on the dusty ground and sparked a Benson. I trained my eyes on the red dot, which was a tractor, and watched it grow gradually bigger. Colin hawked up a mouthful of phlegm and created a dark patch on the dry cracked soil.

I was frustrated that we were at least twenty minutes late, particularly as it was our first day. Being punctual was one of the few things I'd had going for me in my limited experience of work. Dennis had claimed that his alarm clock hadn't gone off. When he finally arrived to pick me up that morning, he was eating a piece of toast at the wheel. He'd...we'd, bought a beige Cortina Mk4 for sixty quid from a geezer in his street and me and Colin owed him a score each at a tenner a week. It was definitely taxed, cos I'd seen the disc, and apparently it was MOT'd, but Dennis only had a provisional license so we couldn't get insurance. Still, as far as I could tell, he drove well enough that we'd be unlucky to get a pull. The alternative was catching two buses, one to the Cross and another to St Osyth, with a load of hanging about in between. Fuck *that*, Dennis said, and for once I'd agreed.

When he heard the tractor and trailer getting close to us, Dennis dragged himself up from the ground and patted himself down; Colin hadn't been able to stop moving, like he was impatient to get started.

A wiry geezer with straggly hair jumped down from the trailer and came running towards us as if we were trespassers.

'For fuck's sake! What sort of time do you call this?'

Dennis already had an answer prepared. 'All right, Wurz. Sorry mate. It's those bloody miners. We got held up by a roadblock at Thorrington Cross.'

'I ain't got time for excuses, Den. If you're late again, I'll let the old man know and you'll be back down the road.'

He sized up me and Colin and didn't look impressed. 'Which one of you two is Bogie?'

This was the second time I'd been let down by Dennis that day and I hadn't even clocked a potato yet. I nodded, reluctantly.

'What sort of fucking name do you call that?' Wurzel sneered, conveniently forgetting that you don't pick your own nickname. If you did, surely you wouldn't name yourself after a scarecrow on the telly, though I was starting to see the resemblance. It was hard to tell where the dirt on his face finished and the tan began. I reckon you had more chance of getting off with Sam Fox than getting shot of a nickname. Not unless you threatened to deck everyone who said it. But that wasn't feasible, not even for Dennis. Though Dennis was lucky, he was just Dennis. At least as far as I knew.

I looked past Wurzel to the trailer, from where we were being watched by the other pickers and farmhands like we were a road accident. Perhaps we were an accident waiting to happen.

'Come on then,' Wurzel snapped. 'The old man wants six ton done today and we're behind already.'

In terms of the technical skills required, Dennis was right about the job being a piece of piss. Even someone as unpractical and cack-handed as me could claim it was easy, at least during the honeymoon period, which lasted about half an hour. All I was required to do was stand over a conveyor belt, pulling off pieces of dry mud and stones and throwing them backwards into the field to separate the earth from the spuds.

Me and Colin were given the worst places, opposite each other at the mouth of the mud face, where the work was constant, and there were always more clods than we were able to get rid of. Dennis manoeuvred himself into a position opposite Wurzel at the top of the line where there was never much work left to do. And if there was, it gave Wurzel an excuse to shout at us for not working fast enough or throw a spud at our hands. Though the spud-throwing had only happened to me. At the end of the machine were another couple of farmhands, bagging and stacking the spuds. One of them was skinny and had a weathered face, the other ruddy-cheeked and built like a barn door.

After the first few rows, the taste of dust and grit and the stench of rotten spuds were as relentless as the sun on my back. There'd been no mention of breaks on the horizon, just up the field and down again, row after row. And the tractor was so slow that it didn't create much of a breeze. The only respite came when we turned around and I could grab a swig from my bottle of tepid lemon squash. There wasn't even time for a smoke between rows unless you could reduce a JPS to a bum-sucked filter and orange rocket in six puffs like Wurzel. But I couldn't afford to waste my fags like that. Dennis and Wurzel had gone into rounds of flashing each other the ash.

I looked to Colin for some solidarity, but he was immersed in a personal war against the earth, defending his patch of conveyor belt from the brown invaders like it was an arcade game.

I lost count after ten rows: my brain could only process soil and potatoes. My guts told me I was hungry, but I had no sense of the time. I glanced over my shoulder to the hot red metal safety rail where my sandwiches were bouncing around in a carrier bag, which was now coated with grime.

'How come you're not sitting round there with your mate, *Wurz*?' Colin said, emphasising the last word.

I wanted to laugh, cos it was true that Dennis and Wurzel had been acting like old muckers, sharing fags and little jokes that nobody else could hear over the noise of the machine. But I was still too wary of Dennis to take the piss out of him. I knew he could turn in an instant.

I clocked him knock the last shards of his Spar beef and onion crisps into the corner of the packet and coax them into his gob. Then he took a long gulp of cherryade and burped loudly. 'You're just jealous cos I've got it easy.'

I couldn't find a lunch box that morning, so I'd tied my sarnies in a plastic bag, put that bag into a carrier bag and hoped for the best. But it had turned out for the worst: the pieces of cheese, which had turned slimy in the heat, had sunk to the bottom of the bag where they mingled with gritty slices of cucumber, which had begun to evaporate. With nothing to look forward to eating, I slumped back against two sacks of spuds feeling defeated. Then I lit the Benson I'd intended to smoke after lunch.

'It's like being on a bloody chain gang, ain't it?'

'No one's making you stay, are they, Bogie?'

'I'm just thinking about payday,' Colin said. 'How else you going to get this sort of money without robbing someone?' He was sitting on the edge of a pallet with a perfectly symmetrical doorstep sandwich resting on his lap. He had clean hands too, cos he'd even thought to bring gloves.

'The actual work ain't too bad,' I said. 'It's just putting up with that wanker chucking fucking spuds about.' A safer way to have a dig at Dennis was to have a go at his mate. The farmhands and locals were eating their lunch on the other side of the trailer. As far as I was concerned, it was us and them, but Dennis was blurring the lines.

'You shouldn't let him get away with it. It's about time you learned to stick up for yourself, Bogue.'

That hurt, coming from him. I tightened my fist. 'Next time I will.'

'He's just trying to test you out, you plum. I know what the cunt's like, I was here last year, remember. But he don't know you from Adam, do he? You could have a black belt in karate for all he knows.'

I opened my carrier bag to show them my dog's dinner. 'If I did have a black belt in karate, I bet I would have chopped this cheese more evenly.'

Dennis laughed heartily. 'You're a funny fucker, Bogie.' It was as close as he got to a compliment. He picked up a Mothers Pride sandwich, which looked measly in his big hands, and tore it in half with one bite. I couldn't see any filling, so I guessed it was probably meat paste from one of those little jars. Still, if he'd offered me a swap, I'd have bitten his hand off.

I laid a slice of roughly sawn bread across my palm, lined up the least grotty pieces of sweating cheddar and sealed the deal with a second slice of mother's finest stale wholemeal. As I moved in to take a bite, I caught a strong whiff of rotten spud juice ingrained in the pores of my fingers. Above the breadline, I clocked Colin watching me with a mixture of disgust and amusement.

I discovered that smoking a Benson without taking it out of my mouth wasn't as easy as Dennis made it look. Smoke rushed up my nose, irritating my nostrils and making my eyes sting. I shut one eye and managed to soldier on for another puff, but then it got too much, and I was gasping. I rested my smoking hand on the ridge above the conveyor belt and carried on working with my left.

A heavy stone encased in dry soil smashed onto my knuckles and showered the back of my hand with sparks. As I frantically tried to brush them off, I managed to press some into my skin. I could smell singed hairs that I didn't even know I had there.

I clocked Wurzel smirking. 'TWO HANDS,' he yelled over the din of the machine. 'If you can't work and smoke, wait 'til the end of the row!'

My rage made me ten times stronger. If I launched this stone and caught him in the head with a corker, I could knock him flying backwards off the trailer. It would serve him right, the bumpkin bully. To pull off such an accurate shot, I reckoned he must have done it a lot. The shit farmer probably knew which clod to pick, like a skimmer choosing flat pebbles on the beach. I gripped the stone tightly in my throwing hand and gave him a scowl as filthy as his overgrown fingernails.

'Don't try and get snotty with me, Bogie, or you can fuck off now!'

He was right, I could, and before I did, I should kill two birds with one stone: throw this full pelt at Wurzel and wipe the cocky smile from his gob, then walk away from this shitty job and take it as a spur to do something more useful with my life. I looked across to Colin, who was able to carry on working while watching my reaction. If it happened to him, I reckoned that in the moment at least, he'd probably take it on the chin and then he'd plan to slash Wurzel's tyres or something.

I'd hesitated too long, and the moment to be reckless had gone. Afterwards, I gave myself a hard time for a couple of rows, cos I'd been determined to prove Dennis wrong and not put up with any shit. This was my first big test, and I was pissed off that I'd bottled it. But then something Tony had said popped up in my head.

We're here to do a job.

Mum was talking to him about the police bullyboy tactics at

Wivenhoe one dinner time. 'At the end of the day, we're here to do a job.' The way he said it, was like no amount of provocation or injustice was going to deter the miners from their Essex mission. They knew why they were there; it was as simple as that.

Wurzel had acted like one of Maggie's boot boys on the picket line who got a kick out of scraping their size-tens down a miner's shin in the scrum. The old man farmer was like the police inspector, willing to turn a blind eye to the tactics on the ground as long as his lads got the right result. Maybe I was stretching the comparison too far, but it gave me some comfort. Like Tony, I was there to do a job.

According to Dennis, the spudding only lasted for about six weeks. That's how long I might have to keep turning the other cheek. I knew what I wanted to do with the money: go up to Carnaby Street and buy some mod gear you couldn't find around here, treat Tony to a few cans of beer, show Mum I could pay my way. Most importantly, I wanted to be able to take out Verity. That's if she wanted to go out with me.

I'd tried practising asking her out aloud in the bath after work, but I hadn't been able to stop myself cringing.

Will you go out with me?

Did people really still say that? Whatever way *I* said it, it sounded tame and lame and vague. I don't think I'd said those actual words to a girl since junior school. But how else could I move things on with Verity? Would it be better if I suggested somewhere specific? Like, *do you want to come up town one day, just me and you?* Or even more specific, like inviting her to a gig I thought she'd be into? I didn't want to wait though. I was already frustrated with not knowing when I would see her next. If we were going out together, then we'd need to make arrangements, and that meant we were guaranteed to meet up.

I was sure she liked me, otherwise she wouldn't have always come to the kitchen while I made the tea. I made her laugh too, which was a good start. But I wasn't sure how to judge if she liked me in the other way, the fancying way. I'd been tempted to test the waters by asking Dennis to ask Sian if she thought I had a chance. But Verity spoke directly, and I didn't think she'd be impressed with that game. And I'd also have to put up with Dennis egging me on and probably taking the piss, and it would make the act of asking her out seem even more artificial than it already did. Colin had never been that interested in talking about girls. His idea of flirting was to tease them or grab their fags or their bag and make them chase after him. I hadn't seen much evidence that it got him results. I liked to think I was pretty nifty with words, but when it came to chatting up girls, I didn't have the confidence or the knack; my idea of flirting was to maintain eye contact while trying not to come across as a weirdo.

Verity always seemed to look at me expectantly, like I might say something interesting, which had rarely happened to me with a girl before. Or with anyone. But however much I mulled it over or practiced in the bath, I didn't know how to say what I really wanted to say. In the end, I concluded it would be easier with booze. I would find a way to get her on her own when we were both a bit pissed down the prom shelter. And then, like the lager, the words would hopefully flow without me overthinking them.

On pay day, we waited in the farmyard after work while Wurzel went to knock on the old man's back door. When he opened up, the first thing I noticed was his gut. It was like he had a space hopper under his farmer's checked shirt.

He moved slowly along the line, dishing out wage packets, with Wurzel acting as his guide and squire, like a team captain on FA Cup Final day introducing the Duke to the players.

Afterwards, Dennis passed me his holdall when we got to the car.

'Bung that in the boot will you.'

'Bloody hell, that's weighs a ton. What you got in there?'

He rubbed his hands together furiously. 'Chips for tea tonight, Bogue. Chips for tea tonight, mate.'

I strained my grimy ears to tune in when I heard a mention of the strike coming through the speakers on the back shelf of the motor. *Mounted police and officers with riot shields and on horseback have clashed with hundreds of pickets in the most violent confrontation of the dispute so far.* I didn't catch where it had happened, and I was keen to know more, but this was Radio 1 *Newsbeat*, not Radio 4.

Then Dennis whacked up the stereo when 'Two Tribes' came on.

The speakers he'd recently nicked were surprisingly powerful, making the intense rhythm sound like the cavalry arriving as two tribes went to war. Goosebumps came up all prickly on my forearms. I'd guessed the song was about the Cold War, but it also fitted with the strike, which seemed to be hotting up as the weather got hotter. This song was going to be the anthem for the unfolding summer, a summer that was full of possibilities now that I had that little brown packet in the pocket of my jeans. Sixty-two quid: a tenner for the motor, a fiver for petrol and a tenner to Mum for keep - plus a one-off fiver for Dennis's finder's fee - would leave me with thirty-two sheets. That was still seven more than you got on a Youth Training Scheme.

The breeze skimmed the top of my dusty crop through the open window, and I closed my eyes to feel the speed and the beat. I had two days of freedom, but behind my eyelids the conveyor belt was still moving. Spuds, mud and dust; spuds, mud and dust. But nothing would stop me from enjoying my crust.

Chapter Five

I'd bought a Lonsdale cycling shirt and a pair of red, white and blue bowling shoes, which had *as supplied to The Jam* written in gold on the insole. Tonight was going to be the first time I'd worn them out. In some ways it was over the top, cos I was only going to the prom shelter, but now I had them on, I felt like the 'Boy about Town' in the Jam song.

If it weren't for The Jam, I doubt I would have even been a mod; if it wasn't for Weller, I don't reckon I'd have been reading *The Ragged Trousered Philanthropists*. He'd mentioned the novel in an interview when he was asked what had made him a socialist. Tony saw me reading it and confirmed it was a classic. *Without that book, Labour may not have won the '45 election*, Tony had said. Mum was pleased to see me reading literature at all, but she couldn't resist saying that the story didn't show enough of the lives of the women.

I couldn't wait to tell Verity, but of course, she'd already read it, probably back when I was still reading *Roy of the Rovers*. She'd sounded certain she was coming out tonight when I bumped into her at the Community Centre a few days ago.

There was a public meeting about the strike, which Mum had helped to organise, and Tony was one of the speakers. I spotted Verity in the foyer afterwards with her dad and a miner, who was staying at her place. We only had a chance to speak briefly, but she said she would see me at the prom shelter on Thursday. She hadn't come there at the weekend cos she was visiting relatives.

I checked the back pocket of my ice blue Sta-Press for my wage packet before closing the front door. One of these days I would buy myself a wallet, but for the moment I was still enjoying the novelty of being a worker. The packet contained seven pounds fifty, enough to cover all eventualities; the rest of what was left of my wages was stashed in one of the Russian dolls on the mantlepiece.

Colin had come round for me before I was ready. It was well out of his way when we were going to the prom shelter, but he got restless at home on his own. As we started our walk down from the top of the town, I pointed to a faded orange 'NO WHARF' poster in the window of a house on the main road. The wharf had opened a few months earlier and was being used to import scab coal into Brightlingsea.

'Imagine if everyone had a poster up supporting the miners. That'd be more like it.'

Colin told me I was dreaming. People were only against the wharf cos they didn't want lorries steaming past their houses all day, rattling their fucking windows. 'No one in Brightlingsea gives a toss about the miners; apart from people like your mum.'

He had a point about the lack of local support cos there were plenty of empty chairs at the Community Centre. Mum told me the Brightlingsea Miners Support Group had also written a letter, which would be posted through every door in the town, explaining why the miners were there. Tony said it was necessary to counteract the anonymous anti-miner propaganda sheet, which was being left in many of the pubs and pasted to lampposts. At the top, it stated in block capitals: THIS IS OUR TOWN. It went on to say that these militant communists are intimidating our law-abiding citizens and had even been seen fraternising with local women. The miners had heard the people behind it were having secret meetings at the Vic, and it was rumoured the landlord was involved.

On Spring Chase, I finally saw the words Coal Not Dole, standing bold in a front window. The red and yellow poster had the same design as Verity's badge. 'There you go, look.' I was inspired to cup my hands around my mouth and bawl out, 'VICTORY TO THE MINERS'.

When I turned back, I was disappointed not to see that a friendly face had appeared at the window to raise a thumb in solidarity. What I actually got was a chuckle from Colin and a bewildered glare off a snotty yachtie in chinos and deck shoes who was walking his shiny dog on the other side of the road. I stared at him, like I was daring him to take sides and say something snide, but he blinked first and tugged at his mutt. Some people around here cared more about animals than humans, even more so if they thought that those humans had arrived from the North.

I zipped up my parka, cos it suddenly felt like the summer was on holiday; the sky was being taken over by black and grey.

As we passed the Community Centre, I began to hear bleeps and explosions coming out from the open door of the Pizza Parlour on the corner, opposite the new cop shop. I couldn't understand why people called it that, cos I'd never seen anyone in there eating a pizza. Most of the space was packed with arcade games and fruit machines. It was the closest thing we had to an amusements arcade in Brightlingsea and where Colin spent his Saturday afternoons and a chunk of his wages. He was looking over as we crossed the road, lured by the flashing lights of the fruities. They'd been hypnotising him for as long as I could remember.

We walked between rows of caravans on the site off Prom Road and Colin ran a finger along the side of an empty one. I used to hope that caravan girls would be easier to get off with than locals, cos they didn't have to worry about being called a slag and were supposed to be there to have fun. But it didn't work out like that, at least not for us. The only result me and Colin ever got from holidaymakers was when we nicked a top or a flash pair of socks from their washing lines.

A strong wind was blowing in off the sea as we walked alongside the edge of the boating lake. From here, I could see into one side of the shelter, but I didn't clock anybody, never mind Verity. I had to hope that she was around the other side, but I couldn't rule out the possibility that she'd changed her mind. Rather than sit in a cold, windy shelter, she'd decided to curl up on the sofa and watch *Top of the Pops*.

We were halfway up the stony path which ran alongside the concrete-panelled wall of the swimming pool to the shelter, when Colin rapped my arm and said he really needed a favour.

'What?'

'Can you lend us a fiver?'

'That's about all I've got on me.' It was always better to be vague with Colin when talking about money.

'You don't need it tonight though, do you? Come on, you'll be there when I get my wage packet tomorrow. I'm hardly going to try and knock you, am I?'

One of his wage packets. What about the money he was earning from Skully? I handed over my only note and then kicked a stone as hard as I could up the path, forgetting that I was wearing my brand-new shoes. As I polished the toe of my right bowler on the back of my Sta-Press, I clocked a seagull on the pool wall, looking all cocky. I brought my foot down hard to stamp my authority, but the bastard didn't flinch, it just squawked at me. Even the birds could sense I was a soft touch.

Sian and Verity were sat round the side of the shelter that faces the sea. Verity grinned like she was happy to see me, but Sian didn't even say hello; she only wanted to know if we'd seen Dennis. I found out later that his brother had been released from prison that day and Sian was worried that Greg might lead him even further astray.

I sat on the bench in the shelter; Colin stood loitering on the footpath. Sian looked at Verity apologetically and said she was thinking of going to the phone box down the Hard to try and find out where Dennis had got to. But she wasn't totally sure, cos it looked like it could piss down with rain any second.

Verity shrugged, like, *It's up to you.*

I stepped out from the shelter and studied the sky, then told Sian what she wanted to hear, which was also what I wanted her to believe, 'It looks like it's going to clear up soon.'

'Do you reckon?'

Colin said he would come with her cos he needed to pop by Skully's restaurant.

It was hard to take in that we were actually alone. And I didn't even have to put the kettle on.

Verity shuffled closer to me on the bench, leaving a gap of about half a metre between us. She tucked a clump of hair behind her ear. 'I can't help thinking you were trying to get rid of her, Jarrod.'

43

I laughed, perhaps a little too loudly. 'I reckon she would have gone anyway.'

'Probably. I've known her all my life and she's always been chasing after one boy or another.' Verity turned to face me. 'Some girls would be lost without a boyfriend, don't you reckon?'

I reckoned she was searching my face for the answer to another question. Maybe it was: had I realised yet that she wasn't one of those girls?

The short silence between us was as loaded and heavy as the black clouds above Point Clear and Mersea. All I could hear was the blustery wind and the tide rushing over the pebbles on the beach. Surely the weather was too shitty for anybody to disturb us now. I could afford to play the long game. Or was I just putting off what I didn't have the bottle to say?

'I recorded *Top of the Pops* tonight.' Colin had asked me to, as he often did, cos he didn't have a video at home.

'Snap,' she said. 'I thought The Smiths might be on. Ooh, that reminds me, I brought this for you.' She unbuttoned the top pocket of her denim jacket. 'It's a copy of their album. Some of the lyrics are as good as any poet.'

A tingle of electricity shot up my arm as I took the tape box, and my fingers brushed her hand.

As I studied the cover, I was amazed by Verity's immaculate, tiny black writing. I could never do that with a fibre tip, not without smudging. I usually struggled to fit the song titles on one line. I brought the tape case closer to my eyes, but it was impossible to decipher the tracklist in the gloomy grey light.

She narrowed the gap between us even further and looked at the tape box over my shoulder. 'I put some of my brother's dub and punk poetry records on the other side. Maybe you'll get inspired.'

I'd told Verity one lunchtime that I liked to write poems and lyrics and maybe one day I would give her something to read. But the only meaningful words I'd written since school were in the half-price diary I'd bought from Bargain Land, and most of those words were about her.

'I can't wait to give it a listen,' I said, truthfully. 'I'll have to do something for you.'

She softly slapped the inside of my thigh. 'You can start by giving me a fag if you want.'

I reached for my Bensons and handed one over with my box of Swan Vestas. Then I moved nearer, until our legs were touching, and unzipped my parka to create some cover. As she leaned in, I caught a faint whiff of strawberries rising up from her skin.

Her head pressed against my chest, and I remember thinking that I bet she could feel my heart pumping: rain was thumping on the roof of the shelter. I waited for the match to strike; for the stink of Swan Vesta to snuff out the strawberries; for the end of our little moment of closeness.

Instead, I felt her hot breath on my skin, and she began nuzzling my neck and smothering it with tiny kisses like ticklish stings. I heard myself making a weird murmuring noise, like a high-pitched groan. I thought that the top of my head might explode.

Verity's nose brushed across my chin; our mouths clamped together and then we were snogging. Her face pushed hard against mine, taking control; she sucked and bit my lips in a way that was almost aggressive.

I pushed my tongue back against hers to lick it and to slow us down. I could taste a trace of Juicy Fruit, mixed in with the saliva and toothpaste.

It was Verity who pulled away, though I was running out of puff. She pressed one last wet kiss against my bruised lips, then looked around for the matches. As big plops of rain bounced off the prom footpath, I had the feeling we were the only people left in that town.

Chapter Six

Colin was switching between the sink and sideboard singing 'Like a Virgin' as he made us tea and cheese on toast. He was cutting and slicing, washing and wiping, with exaggerated commitment, like he was the star of a cookery programme. Colin's ambition was to run his own caff, and sometimes he acted like he did already, and it was always busy, and he had a dozen hungry punters to serve after me.

I was sat at the light blue Formica table in his kitchen, smoking a Benson and flicking my ash into his wonky art-class ashtray. Behind me was the old twin-tub, which had been gurgling away when I came round for the first time all those years ago; above it a mounted plate with a ring of painted flowers encircling the words, *Home Sweet Home*.

Colin's mum left when he was three. I remembered him telling me there was only a couple of things he could remember about her. One was that she used to take him to the phone box when his old man was on nights and make him wait outside while she spoke to the bloke she ran away with. The other memory, which still made him angry, was that she would dip his thumb into a pot of mustard if she caught him sucking it. He didn't often mention her, but when he did, he always said she was sick in the head. I was never sure if he meant this literally, like she was mentally ill, or she had to be sick to have treated him like that.

His dad still worked nightshifts at the same warehouse and was hardly ever about. But he did provide the basics: teabags, milk, cheese and bread, biscuits.

I caught a strong waft of melting cheddar; I was salivating with anticipation and gasping for a cuppa, but it always took a while cos Colin was a perfectionist, even with tea; if you made him one, he claimed to be able to tell by the colour exactly what it would taste like, and therefore whether he was going to enjoy it or not.

I tried to take my mind off the wait by thinking about Verity.

I'd waited two evenings after our first kiss before calling her, then I made her an offer she couldn't refuse. Did she want to help deliver a batch of the Miners Support Group letters on Sunday morning?

We went to the Manor Estate, a maze of privately-owned modern houses on the other side of the small woods opposite mine. Verity took to the task diligently; she was determined that we didn't miss out anybody. But this wasn't easy, cos many of those Crescents and Closes and Ways all looked the same. And the residents were all doing similar Sunday morning activities: washing their newish motors on their drives; gliding their Flymos over already trim lawns; knocking up family fry-ups. I bet they all had matching three-piece suites in their lounges. If anybody asked me, I told them politely and lightly that the letters were about the strike, like I was talking about something nice, like the Regatta. This was conservative country with a small and probably mostly big C. I was surprised to see even two houses with posters up supporting the miners, though this time I didn't shout out to express my solidarity.

We stopped twice, to get a can of drink from the Mace, and the other time for a fag in a shaded alley, which smelled of freshly cut grass. After our Bensons, we swirled our smoky tongues around in each other's mouths. It was delicious, but it left me hungry for more. Once all the letters were gone, Verity needed to go and practise her mandolin. I didn't have anything pressing, so I offered to walk her home.

We kissed again, next to her front gate, but out of sight of the front room window. Afterwards, she said, 'I'm not going to go out with you, Jarrod.'

What was all that about then?

'It's not you. I don't want to be anybody's *bird*. That's how I am and I ain't going to pretend for anyone.'

'It doesn't have to be like that.'

'Sorry if I've disappointed you.'

I licked the underneath of my top lip. There was a swelling there where she'd bitten me. 'I'd be disappointed if we couldn't do that again.'

She laughed, but it didn't tell me anything.

'I like you, Jarrod. You're interesting and you're funny. And I reckon I can trust you not to get all clingy on me. But…can't we just be mates, like *close* mates, without all that patriarchal crap about boyfriends and girlfriends?'

I didn't even know what *patriarchal* meant. Was it something to do with radical feminism? It sounded pretty radical to me. Mum was a committed feminist, but even she had boyfriends.

Being *close* mates with Verity still sounded exciting though, and full of possibility, but would I still have the problem of not knowing when I'd see her? Bringing that up was bound to sound clingy. Instead, I said, 'I can't think of a better close mate to have than you.'

She pulled me towards her by my jumper and then whispered into my mouth, 'Don't get carried away, Jarrod.'

The next couple of times I phoned her, she wasn't in. I left my number with her mum, but she didn't call me back. The *close* friendship wasn't turning out to be as close as I'd hoped. At least not yet.

I explained my frustration to Colin on our way up to his from the shelter, though I should have stuck with confiding to my diary cos he didn't give me much sympathy. Colin thought Verity was a stuck-up hippy, cos she only came out with us when she felt like it. If you wanted to be close mates with Colin, it had to be all or nothing.

A knocking of knuckles on the kitchen window gave me a start. I turned around and saw Dennis's grinning face at the glass. Instinctively, I muttered, *oh no*, cos I didn't feel like seeing him. That morning he hadn't picked us up for the last day of spudding. And it wasn't the first time he'd let us down with a lift.

Colin dabbed sweat from his forehead with the tea towel he kept folded neatly over his shoulder like a boxer. 'Let him in, will you, Jarrod, he must have smelt the cheese on toast.'

'Do you reckon?'

'Well, he ain't come round to say sorry, has he?'

Dennis was still grinning when I opened the door and breathing out booze fumes as he swung a long green bottle at his side. He bounced past me into the kitchen, looking all hyper and wild-eyed.

'Where the fuck *you* been?' Colin diluted his anger with a splash of sarcasm, but one way or another the question had to be asked.

Dennis smiled like it was a fair cop and shook his head. 'I had to help out fucking Greg. And then it came on top with the motor, so I scrapped it just in case. I owe you both a tenner.'

'We had a little result though.' He held up the bottle, 'Single malt fucking whisky.' Then he tapped the watch pocket of his jeans. 'I've got something for later an' all.'

Colin yanked back the pan on the eye-level grill and carefully spread the melting cheese with a flat knife. 'I don't suppose you'll turn down a slice?'

Of course, Dennis didn't. Nobody in their right mind would.

'I've seen that before, it's crap,' Colin said, after studying a few seconds of a black and white sci-fi film on BBC1. Colin's favourite programme was *Star Trek*, but he'd watch almost anything that showed life on other planets. He swore that he once saw a UFO down the prom, and no amount of piss-taking would ever get him to admit he could be wrong.

He switched to BBC2 and I heard a tantalising mention of Orgreave.

'Leave that on, can you? Just for a minute, please.'

He sniggered at my pleading tone. 'If it's boring, I'm turning it over.'

I had to think quickly how to get them interested, cos the Tory on the telly was rambling. I was like Owen in the *Ragged Trousered Philanthropists*, trying to fit in a lecture about socialism before Crass called the painters back to work. Colin and Dennis were always going on about hating the Old Bill, so I explained how they'd stitched up the miners by allowing them to picket at Orgreave coking plant, and then ran around in riot gear beating them up. 'Six thousand coppers,' I said, 'all looking for blood.'

'I thought you wanted to watch the programme,' Colin said.

'I do. But there's no point in listening to that lying bastard. Did you know that the first thing Thatcher did when she got in was to give the

49

Old Bill a 45 per cent rise? And now look, they're paying her back with interest. Well, they're still getting loads of overtime for it.' I took a sip of my whisky and reached for my Bensons. 'And now she's chucking the weight of the state against the miners: the army, secret services, the lot.'

Dennis took a gulp of whisky without flinching, or even wincing. 'All right, Bogue, there's no need to get all excited.'

'Here we go,' I said, excitedly, when the programme cut from the studio to the fields.

A barricade of crash-helmeted cops, with long plastic shields, stretched across the width of the screen; behind them, pigs on horses rode at a canter between two rows of trees.

Colin snapped a custard cream with his teeth. 'They think they're in a fucking Western, don't they?'

The long shields parted, and the cavalry burst through, sending pickets scattering across the dry field in panic. Then came the ones with short shields, followed by regular nipple-head plods swinging truncheons.

A picket stumbled in no man's land and was grabbed, gripped and coshed. As the nipple-head clubbed him like a seal, two of his cop mates just stood back and watched.

Even Dennis was leant forward on the edge of his chair. *'Fucking hell. He must have nearly killed the geezer.'*

'He'll get away with it as well,' I said. 'That's why they don't wear their numbers, so they can get away with murder.' My hands were trembling with fury, and I spilt half my whisky onto the yellow foam of the ripped settee. Luckily, Colin was too engrossed to notice.

He got up to turn off the telly when the report cut back to the *Newsnight* presenter. 'They've really *fucking* wound me up now. Makes you feel hard, does it? WANKERS.' I could see his reflection in the blank screen as he squared up to it. Above the telly was a framed one-thousand-piece jigsaw his old man had completed, of brightly coloured fish swimming in the ocean.

'The Old Bill have always been cunts,' Dennis said, 'that's their job. If the frigging miners don't like it, why don't they just get back to work, like every other mug has to?'

Dennis didn't have a clue. 'The whole point of the strike is that pretty soon half of them wouldn't have jobs to go back to.'

'*Bollocks*. They're having too much of a jolly ain't they? I saw a few of them down the swimming pool the other day, laughing and joking like they were on fucking holiday.'

'They're just making the most of it. It ain't a holiday going picketing for three quid a day, and risking getting stitched up or battered by the coppers. It's rough mate, I'm telling you. I got a little taste of it at Wivenhoe.'

'Yeah, once. If you feel so strongly about it, how comes you ain't been back?'

'I've done other stuff.' I didn't think I had to justify myself, but Dennis had managed to touch a nerve. There had to be something else I could do.

'I'm going to buy some spray paint tomorrow,' I announced, a few minutes later, 'and put a message on that new pig station.'

Dennis scoffed. 'Yeah, yeah, yeah.'

'YEAH,' I snapped.

Colin sniggered weirdly like the whisky had taken effect. 'There's no need for that.'

'Why not? They fucking deserve it.'

'My old man's got some spray paint in the garage.'

Colin fished a keyring from the pocket of his fawn Farah trousers, then cackled triumphantly as he swished it from side to side like a hyperactive hypnotist. 'I had them cut when me old chap was asleep. I've got ones for his and me brother's bedrooms an' all.'

'Yeah, but I don't want to get you into trouble.'

Trust my big mouth to get *me* into trouble. Still, at least it was going to be for something political. And if I shit out now, I'd be asking for ridicule. Nah, I would show them that I had the bottle to back up my convictions. But I needed to strike while my temper was hot.

'Come on then. Let's go,' I said.

Dennis looked surprised. 'Fucking hell, there's no hurry is there.'

'Whenever you're ready then.'

He reached into his watch pocket and pulled out a small ball of hash.

*

Colin carried the spray can in a carrier bag, swinging it back and forth with two fingers through the handles, like he was ready to launch it at the first sniff of Old Bill. He liked to roam around the town in the early hours; the night was his time of day, though he reckoned the coppers were always stopping him as if being out late meant you were up to no good.

We paused at the corner of the upholstery shop and the High Street to listen out for cars, but the only sign of life was a black cat walking across the low white front wall of the Brewer's Arms. Dennis led the way through the Cut, next to where we'd had catapult fights on the waste ground before they built the new houses. Tonight, the smell of dog shit turned over my guts.

The cop shop lights were off, and the car park was empty. I hopped over the wall and shook the can; the rattle was much louder than I expected. I pressed down hard on the nozzle and heard a satisfying hiss; then the paint flowed as rapidly as my adrenalin across the bricks:

A C A B

I ran over to where Colin was keeping watch at the corner of the Co-op. Dennis was peering through the front windows of the cop shop.

Across the top of the adjacent wall was a large white sign with 'The Co-operative Society' painted in old-fashioned lettering; below it, a huge canvas of virgin bricks. You could fit a whole sentence on there, maybe even a paragraph if you had a stepladder.

I shook the can again. Here's a little reminder, you bastards:

WEAR YOUR NUMBERS!

Colin said, 'It's a bit polite, innit? Here, give us a go.'

I stood on the corner and scanned each direction.

Colin cackled loudly enough to risk waking the neighbours. 'Have a look at this.'

PC COX SUX COX

I cracked up too, but I didn't tell Colin the copper's name was actually spelt *Cocks*. I knew that cos one of the miners had decked him down the wharf and it made the front page of the *Gazette*.

Dennis joined us as we ran across to the pine tree at the back of the Pizza Parlour.

Wear your numbers, I repeated to myself. Now I wanted to spray some more. I had a vision of the wall across the road from the Yachtsmans, where the miners and their supporters all drank.

Fresh black paint on old grey render: VICTORY TO THE MINERS.

But Dennis didn't like my suggestion. 'Fuck that. Why don't we do something useful?'

'Fancy doing the caff down the end again, Col? None of us have got any smokes left, have we?'

Colin lowered his head and released a long string of spit from his gob, like he often did when he was contemplating. He'd never told me anything about them robbing the caff. It seemed like I still had some catching up to do. When the string of saliva eventually landed on the grass, he walked over and chucked the spray can under a caravan.

'Come on then.'

Dennis turned to me. 'You up for it, Bogue?'

I was still elated. The town was now ours for the taking. We could stroll about like it was a giant Monopoly board, and all the other players were stuck in jail.

'Yeah, course.'

We bowled down the middle of Prom Road like we were the ones patrolling; three long shadows with their arms swinging at their sides. It was a still summer's night, but our footsteps sounded as loud as if we were crunching through dry leaves in autumn.

At the back of the wooden beach caff, Colin took out his pocket torch, which I didn't know he'd brought, and shone it onto a panel, which covered the old serving hatch. We yanked it off easily. Then Dennis steadied himself with a hand on each of mine and Colin's shoulders and booted through the piece of plywood which covered the hole. The three of us climbed inside.

The fridges and freezers buzzed like they were alive as Colin gave us a tour of the stock with the light from his torch. It was the same old tat I remembered from when I was little, the sort of things that were of no use to me now: postcards, rubber rings, buckets and spades, crab nets and crappy plastic windmills on sticks.

Dennis went straight for the row of fag boxes on the shelf behind the counter. He passed me and Colin a few packets of Lambert and Butler and stuffed some more into his jacket. Then he ripped one open and flashed the ash.

After three quick puffs, the smoke got caught in my throat and I leaned over and started coughing. There was a poisonous taste in my mouth like the whisky had come back to bite me; my temples warmed to warn me I was close to throwing up. I hadn't realised I was nervous.

Colin said he fancied a Cornetto and slid back the cover from the freezer and shone his torch in. I wasn't hungry, but I took a choc ice cos my throat was burning. Dennis was determined to go one better and he turned on the ice cream machine.

In the corner nearest the front door was a revolving stand of cheap sunglasses. I swivelled it around and picked out a pair that looked the closest to wraparound Ray Bans. 'What do you reckon?'

Colin didn't answer, he was too busy choosing a pair for himself. Dennis was pouring an ice cream.

As I reached into my pocket for my matches, to check out my new look in the mirror, the light in the caff suddenly got brighter, and whiter, despite the fact that I was wearing shades. 'What's going on?'

'You're nicked, that's what.'

I turned around, hoping it was Dennis taking the piss. But it wasn't. A copper was shining his torch on my face through the hatch.

Chapter Seven

I'd hoped that as we'd been caught bang to rights, it would be an open and shut case and we'd be released from the cop shop in the morning. Instead, I didn't even get questioned until the late afternoon. We were kept alone in separate cells and the coppers refused to give me anything to read.

Eddie, Colin's dad, gave us a lift home from Clacton.

After a few minutes of excruciating silence, Colin turned on the car radio, releasing the voice of a Sixties crooner into the void. He'd hardly moved his hand from the knob when Eddie switched it off.

'What a bloody embarrassment.'

'All right, all right,' Colin said, 'don't tell me, you've always been perfect, worked hard all your life, never been in trouble, never had a drink and that's why you're so *boring*.'

I slunk down in the backseat and pulled up my parka. It wasn't really up to me to tell Colin he was out of order. But when his dad did put his foot down, it was only on the accelerator.

Mum had gone away for the weekend and luckily Eddie had agreed to act as the appropriate adult for my police interview. Otherwise, I might have had to ask Adrian, and that didn't seem appropriate to me. Calling him from a cop shop would only have proved to him that I was fulfilling his prophecy.

When we arrived back in Brightlingsea, Eddie pulled up outside the school to drop me off, then I spotted Mum's car parked outside the house and a light on in the hallway. I wasn't expecting her to be back already.

I must have looked a right two and eight.

'I think I'll come round to yours, if that's all right, Dennis.'

Dennis had said that Greg was away with the fair. He wasn't though, he was staring at us from his brown reclining armchair in the corner of the lounge while I held what could have been his breakfast in my parka pocket – the box of eggs Dennis had thrust at me when we'd heard voices from the kitchen. Dennis also slipped a packet of turkey burgers into his jacket like a seasoned shoplifter. After three meals of lukewarm slop at the cop shop, we were planning to go round to Colin's for a slap up.

'The Old Bill have been here wanting to talk to Mum,' Greg said. What the fuck have you done?'

We were stood under an arch on the border between the two halves of the room. Dennis's eyes dropped to the carpet, and he clenched his teeth in frustration at being put on the spot. He looked more pissed off at being caught out by his brother than he was at being caught by the cops. Now he had no choice but to confess. You couldn't get away with saying "No comment" to Greg.

'You brought Mum's house on top over a few boxes of snout?' Greg looked over at his mate, Wayne, then back to Dennis. 'You need to fucking grow up, Snake.'

'First offence though, ain't it? I'm only going to end up with a poxy caution.'

'You only get one caution, Snake, and you've wasted yours on a silly little nicking. What's wrong with you? You can't even get nicked for something decent.'

This time I was certain I'd understood properly. Dennis did have a nickname after all. At least in this house.

'Yeah, yeah. Hark at Mr Big Time over there.' But Dennis was too wounded for his voice to carry any conviction.

Wayne Parkin was sat diagonally across from Greg, sunk into the black leather settee. He was running one hand through his quiff and smoking a Marlboro red with the other. He gave Dennis a sidelong smirk. 'You should take a look in the mirror, old bean, you look like you've been kipping in a bin.'

'Fucking Top Cat,' Greg spat.

I heard myself laughing for the first time that day and Greg shot me a look of suspicion. 'You been locked up an' all, Bogie?'

He'd never spoken to me directly before. I realised how nervous I was when I felt the eggs rattling. I nodded.

'How come you're not on the fair?' Dennis asked, directing the question at Wayne.

'Old Man Wheeler kicked the bucket. They're having a weekend off out of respect.'

Dennis went to get changed in the bedroom he shared with Greg. I stayed hovering on the border, until Wayne told me I could sit down if I wanted. 'Don't worry about Greg, he won't bite you.'

After some of the things Dennis had told me, I wouldn't have put it past him.

I lowered myself carefully onto the settee and stared at the telly, but I couldn't concentrate on the *Deathwish* film, so I stole glances at the fair boys instead. They both had their shirt sleeves turned up to show off freshly needled tattoos; the spoils of their sailors-on-shore-leave lifestyle were spread out around them: slim gold push-button lighters next to boxes of twenty; king-size Rizlas and a big lump of hash; a stack of rented video tapes, and the remains of a Chinese takeaway in cartons on the floor. In the middle of the smoked glass coffee table were two used tumbler glasses and a bottle of the same whisky I'd been drinking the night before.

Obviously, the whisky was stolen, but Dennis never told me the circumstances. Presumably they hadn't risked what Greg would describe as a *silly little nicking*. I had to agree with him that what we'd done was a waste of a caution. I would rather have got nabbed for the graffiti, at least I would have something decent to show for it. Breaking into the beach caff was schoolboy stuff. In fact, it reminded me of climbing through the windows of the kitchens at Oakbridge. At least then we were doing it cos we were hungry.

I considered telling the fair boys about the graffiti. Surely they would approve of my *ACAB*. In the end, I decided to wait to see whether they spoke to me. I studied them again, on the sly, admiring their sharp haircuts and new clobber: Greg had a number two crop and wore shiny

57

brogue boots, but he wasn't a skinhead; Wayne had a quiff, but he didn't dress like a ted. They had their own style. Fair boy style. And they made me look like a clone. I was still trying to copy what Weller was wearing about five years ago.

I turned to the telly and wondered where they'd got it from. It was bigger than the one they used to show films on in the dining hall at school. They had a Sony video recorder an' all. I bet it wasn't rented, like ours.

I was thinking about all this when Wayne paused the film. 'You want a bit of work?'

'What *me*?'

'No,' Greg said. 'Arthur fucking Daley.'

'Doing what?' Why would they ask me?

'Helping put up the Waltzer,' Wayne said.

I didn't hesitate. Not only cos I was skint, but also because I was excited to be invited into their world. The fair world: a world that I'd always been curious about, but until then had been closed off to me. Whatever happened, surely it was bound to result in a good story.

The Green became a tightly packed settlement when the fair was in town, and always seemed to be buzzing with activity. But as I walked between the caravans, trailers, cars and trucks at seven o'clock on Wednesday morning, the only life I could see was a Rottweiler tugging at its chain. And then I found them at the back, where the Waltzer always was; they were already setting up some track.

Wayne nodded, though he didn't introduce me, and I hung around self-consciously waiting to be given a task. After twenty minutes of feeling like a spare spanner, the owner of the ride came out of his caravan to check how we were getting on.

They called him Little Arthur, but he was twice the size of me. Wayne said he was only *Little* cos he was the son of Big Arthur, the one who'd died a couple of weeks earlier. He called me over, by calling me *Jackson*, the name he gave anybody he didn't need to remember. He mumbled what I guessed were instructions, but I was only certain I'd understood the last word. *Boy.*

I clocked a couple of geezers heading towards a flat-bed truck and decided to follow them. The smaller one leapt up onto the back and shoved a wooden panel at me, which looked like a window frame made from four by two. It was heavy, and awkward to lift, but I was glad to finally have something to get on with.

After I'd lugged over quite a few, to where they were being spaced out around the diameter of the ride, I sneaked behind the truck for a quick smoke and then hurried back to work.

Everyone else was rushing around too, and they all seemed to know exactly what to do. Though I'd hardly seen anybody talking. I had been hoping to hear a bit of memorable banter; even better if I could pick up some new slang. But these fair boys were more about actions than words.

Talking too much had always got me into trouble. So, I didn't tell anyone that on the opening night I was determined to hit the punchball and set off the klaxon; to be a man of less words and more action.

Verity was reluctant to come to the fair with me on Saturday, maybe she thought I would act like it was a date. I managed to convince her with the clincher that I could get us free rides on the Waltzer.

Even though I wasn't taking her to the fair in the traditional sense, I still had my eye on trying to win her a prize. Somehow the evening wouldn't be complete if she left the Green empty-handed. But the only thing that was fairly easy to win was a goldfish, and I thought Verity would consider it cruel to keep fish in plastic bags, beings as she was a veggie. And I didn't think she was the sort of girl who'd care for a teddy. Instead, I persuaded her that it wasn't a proper trip to the fair if we didn't have something to eat. She chose a toffee apple, and for some reason I thought it would be a treat to have coconut ice.

On our way past the dodgems, I saw Greg lurking at the back by the paybox. I raised my hand to acknowledge him, but I don't think he noticed me.

The Waltzer always had the loudest sound system, and as we approached, they were playing an old number one which had Syndrums pitched to imitate the thumping heartbeat of the singer in love. Wayne was treading the boards like he was onstage, conscious he was being watched by the small crowd gathered round the steps of the ride. He was wearing a freshly ironed Hawaiian shirt and his quiff had been trimmed for the occasion. Little Arthur was looking through the hatch of the tinted booth.

When the ride started up, Wayne swung our car round as effortlessly and effectively as if he were setting off a spinning top. Verity had one arm looped through mine and the other holding on tightly to the safety bar. I could smell her strawberry perfume, but I couldn't enjoy being pressed against her, cos my guts were doing somersaults. My face was pinned back into a sickly grin; every time I glimpsed Wayne, I dreaded the inevitable spin. And each one seemed to be harder and faster. At the time, I assumed that ironically, he believed he was doing me a favour. Once I'd got to know him better, I wasn't so sure.

When I shut my eyes, I saw bars of pink and white coconut ice speeding past in my mind. Verity was screaming and I wanted to scream too. *STOOOOOPPP!*

We had to stop eventually, and when we did, cold drops of sweat were running down my cheeks. Verity asked me if I was all right and I managed to mutter, 'Not really'. But the music was too loud for her to hear me.

I remembered Wayne saying that they liked to get the punters off quickly, so they could do a sweep of the seats for dropped coins and purses or wallets before letting on the next batch. But was it going to be quick enough for my guts? My head was still spinning long after the car, and when Wayne finally released the safety bar, I clambered out without thanking him or even waiting for Verity. I pushed past the punters on the stairs and rushed to the back of the ride. Hot bile poured from my mouth like vile lava, all over the thick cable from the generator. As I retched to heave the last of it out, the bassline for 'Another One Bites the Dust' started up. Splashes of sick had hit my red, white, and blue bowling shoes and I worried it might rot the leather. My next regret was that I couldn't possibly try to kiss her. At least I found a tissue in the top pocket of my boating blazer, so I could wipe the spew from my mouth and my shoes.

When I emerged, Verity was still waiting, but looking bemused. She'd guessed what had happened, and at arms-length she offered me a Juicy Fruit stick.

'I'm sorry. I didn't want to admit that the rides sometimes make me feel sick.'

'Are you all right now?'

I said 'Yeah', but I meant no. 'Do you still want to go on anything else?'

She chuckled, 'Not with you.'

'I don't blame you.'

'Shall we go?'

'Have you had enough?'

'I reckon you have, Jarrod.'

She turned away and I followed her.

Once we'd left the Green and could hear each other more easily, I said, 'I don't think I'm cut out to be a fair boy.'

'I could have told you that. Like I told you I wasn't a fair sort of girl.'

Early on Monday morning, before the fair left for its next destination, I knocked on Little Arthur's caravan. He didn't answer, so I knocked harder, then took a few steps backwards.

'Can I get my wages?' Arthur didn't tell me to come, but Wayne said it was the only chance I had of getting any money.

'*Wages*,' he mumbled, then chuckled to himself.

Was the free ride I'd had on the Waltzer supposed to be my payment?

Arthur pulled out a fat roll of notes and passed them into his other hand. Then he reached back into his trouser pocket and threw me a couple of pound coins.

'*Something something*, boy. *Something* yourself.'

Chapter Eight

It was the middle of August, and for the first time, Mum had left me alone in the house for longer than a long weekend. She'd gone to Manchester for a fortnight to teach at an Open University summer school. Tony was back in Kent recuperating from his injury. He'd climbed up onto the step of a lorry to try and reason with a driver but was forced to jump off when the scab accelerated, and the back wheel broke three bones in his left foot. It happened at one of the last mass pickets at Wivenhoe, and, as far as I knew, there were now only a few miners left in Essex. Mum told me that even in Kent there were scabs starting to go back, and once Tony had recovered, he would need to picket his own pit.

I missed chatting with Tony about politics and football and getting inside info about the strike. I also missed the better meals Mum cooked when he was around. My only regret was not being able to tell him that I'd finished *The Ragged Trousered Philanthropists*. In just over two months, I'd gone from being proud to be seen with it, to being embarrassed to still be reading it, to giving up completely once Tony had gone. Surely I couldn't be the only one who thought it was too long. Maybe Verity had read a shorter version.

Mum left me some money to buy food, but for as long as possible I would try to survive on Weetabix and fish fingers and spaghetti hoops. And a huge Tupperware of leek and potato soup. I was practising for my upcoming life on the dole.

While I was taking more time to think about what I really wanted to do, the money from the dole would help see me through. It was a guaranteed income that I could top up with bits of cash in hand work. At that time, if you lived far enough from the dole office, like Brightlingsea, you didn't even have to go and sign on every two weeks. All you had to do was post off a coupon confirming that you hadn't done any work in the past fortnight. In some ways they were the glory days, cos you could pretty much work fulltime if you wanted to. I'd already decided I'd be happy to just subsidise my giros now and again, so I could buy a few records and clothes.

I knew there must be untold people dodging their taxes and working cash in hand. This sort of mild criminality was even celebrated in the most popular programmes on the telly. Everybody loved watching Arthur and Terry; Del Boy and Rodney: they never really hurt anybody or got into serious bother. And there was no need for me, or anyone else to feel guilty, cos dole scams were accounted for in the Tory plan. Thatcher knew the price of her policies was mass unemployment, and she thought it was a cost worth paying. If you had a few million on the dole, Tony said, then those in work would feel luckier and more vulnerable, and their bosses could screw them harder, especially when she'd given them the lubrication of anti-union laws.

The two weeks that Mum was away were my summer holiday. And I was free to do whatever I wanted. I didn't even have any mates interfering with my routine. Colin popped by sometimes in the evenings, but he was doing lots of work for Skully – cash in hand, obviously. Sian's mum and dad were in Majorca, so Dennis had moved in round theirs temporarily. Lucy came in and out with her mates as she pleased. I wasn't sure what she was getting up to that Mum wouldn't let her do, but we had an unspoken pact: if you don't tell on me, I won't tell on you.

I would stay up late watching films, or programmes I'd recorded, then rise at ten or eleven and start the day with a pot of strong tea and two boiled eggs and three toast. Then I would sit in the back garden reading novels in peace until lunch time. As it was the school holidays, the only noise I heard from the Colne High was the distant mowing of the playing fields.

I was enjoying reading kitchen sink realism by angry young men like Sillitoe and Storey; and that was just the S's. I hadn't realised that

Mum had such riches on her shelves, until Verity gave me some tips. Those writers knew how to keep it short, if not sweet, and I was able to get through a novel every couple of days. I was still too young to have spent much time in pubs, and it wasn't until later that I experienced for myself the boredom of the factory, but somehow the worlds they created were recognisable to me. And those stories told me more about what to expect from life than anything on the O-level syllabus.

In the afternoons, I worked on my creative project, which was to make a couple of compilation tapes for Verity. She'd gone to stay with her family in Galway for the rest of the summer holidays. Making the tapes helped to ease the ache of missing her and allowed me to have intense bouts of thinking about her, without going through the rigmarole of scrawling illegibly in my diary.

For the first compilation, I chose the theme of unemployment. Once I'd dug deep into my collection, I realised it was a theme which had a fertile seam. There were songs that were angry about the size of the dole queue, like 'Two Million Voices' – which admittedly was out of date, cos we were now over three; ones that highlighted the lack of decent job possibilities like 'To Have and Have Not' and 'Career Opportunities'; tunes about the hardships of dole life, like 'Living with Unemployment'; others that defiantly rejected working in crap jobs and even songs which took the piss out of dole-ites, like 'Let the Country Feed You'.

Most importantly, they had to be great records. And I took great pleasure in rehearsing the sequencing to find the most effective order. I didn't need to worry about buying blank tapes either, cos Mum had a stack in her bedroom. She got them free from the Uni as she needed them to interview old ladies for her PhD, which was about women homeworkers at the start of the century.

I suppose it was ironic that I'd dedicated more time to listening to music about looking for work, than I had done actually looking for work, though I did pause to check the *Yellow Advertiser*, when I heard it pop through the door, to make sure that there was nothing in it for me. It was also an irony that the title of the compilation was *Unemployment Blues*, because I was unemployed, but I wasn't feeling blue. I just liked the sound of it. I reckoned that given an evocative cover and a "pay no more than..." sticker, it would be a good seller. That might sound big-headed, or deluded, but I was confident of my compiling capabilities. I was obsessive about getting them right, and I'd had quite a bit of practise.

At Oakbridge, me and my best mate, Henry, used to work on compilations together in the dorm on weekend evenings when the others had gone to the dining hall to watch films. These were my favourite times of the week. On Sundays, we would take it in turns to hover over the pause button for the Top 40, and, more crucially, during the Annie Nightingale Request Show, and then the following Saturday evening, we would edit together the highlights. When we weren't compiling, we wrote little ditties: Henry would be strumming along on his acoustic guitar and doing most of the singing, and I wrote the words, which were mostly about the teachers, though I did manage a couple of songs for a left-wing mod band that only existed in my imagination.

In the longer holidays, I sometimes stayed over at Henry's in West Mersea, and we spent many hours on his CB radio, talking to truckers and trying to track down girls to *eyeball* with, which didn't come off very often. Henry was fascinated by trucks and truckers, cos his parents ran a transport cafe on the A12 where he sometimes helped out. We would also meet up in Colchester and scour the record shops, and then go to Castle Park to eat battered sausages and chips washed down with Slush Puppies or share pots of tea in the cafe above Martins, depending on the season. And we'd be constantly talking about music, especially songs we thought worthy of including on our compilations, which by the time I was expelled had run to nine volumes.

So, it was a happy coincidence that Henry phoned me one afternoon while I was auditioning songs for the second compilation. This one didn't have a specific theme, or a title as yet, but I was aiming to show Verity that I had broad tastes, and hint that I was keen to deepen our *close* friendship.

Henry told me he was coming to Brightlingsea, cos his friend wanted to look at a boat. He also said he had a surprise for me.

I hoovered the front room in honour of his visit and lined up the first draft of *Unemployment Blues*. I thought it would be useful to try it out on an audience, and I wanted to show off some of my new tunes.

Henry wanted to know if it was cool to roll a doobie.

'You can do what you like, mate. My mum won't be home for another eight days.'

When I came into the front room with three brews, Henry was sat cross-legged on the floor with his back to the coal bucket, preparing a joint on the cover of Mum's *Blood on the Tracks*; his friend, Aaron, was pulling down some of Mum's paperbacks from the shelves above the settee, and had created a stack of those he wanted to explore further. 'Hey, Jarrod,' he said, 'there's some amazing literature here, man. Your mother has very refined taste.'

I couldn't resist it: 'You wouldn't say that if you'd eaten her leek and potato soup.'

Henry beamed, like I told you he was a good laugh. Then he explained that Aaron was starting an English degree at Oxford next month.

'Good for you, mate,' I said, not very friendly. I thought the way he'd bowled in and started mauling Mum's books was a bit of a liberty.

Henry passed the spliff to me and I coughed after a couple of puffs and nodded in appreciation. 'That's a wicked bit of gear.' I didn't have much to compare it with really, but this hash was definitely more pokey than the stuff Dennis had. Aaron explained that Red Leb was good for creativity because it got you high, rather than wrecked. I carried on nodding, but to me they were similar concepts.

Henry asked if I had a job.

'I've been doing a few bits and bobs.' I realise now that I probably sounded as evasive as Colin when I'd asked him the same question a few months earlier. 'I'm waiting to hear about a painting job with my mate, Colin.' Skully had said he would pay us to paint his back wall and clear out his garage.

'What about you, are you still planning on going to college.'

'Yeah,' he said, without enthusiasm, 'as long as I get the right grades.'

'Course you will.'

But he hadn't come here to talk about our prospects. Thank fuck. 'What else you been up to all summer then, Jarrod?'

The way Henry looked for Aaron's approval every time I said anything was making me self-conscious. I decided to tell them about Tony staying and my experiences at Wivenhoe, cos I knew they wouldn't have done anything like that. But if Henry had been on his own, I'd have given him the full rundown about Verity, and the graffiti, and getting ripped off by Little Arthur and everything. Well, everything except the beach caff, cos Henry wasn't into thieving.

Henry was rebellious in ways which didn't get him into trouble. Like me, he was resentful about being sent away; unlike me, Henry never quite understood why his parents had done that to him. He refused to take school sports seriously or get involved in anything he wasn't forced to. His whole five years at Oakbridge had been a long go-slow protest, but I reckon he would have done enough to scrape the required number of O-levels.

When I asked him now what he'd been up to since leaving school, he struggled to come up with much of an answer. Maybe it was cos he was stoned.

'Don't forget the camping trips,' Aaron chipped in, and suddenly they both cracked up laughing.

'What's so funny?'

'When I tell my folks I'm going on another camping trip,' Henry said, 'my mum tells me, *Okay darling, have a lovely time*. Little does she know.'

'Know what?'

'That when we go on a camping trip, Jarrod, we go on a camping *trip*.'

Aaron pinched his beard as he studied me. 'Have you tried LSD, man?'

'Not yet, mate. I ain't had a chance.'

He edged forward on the settee. 'Wow. Then today could be your lucky day.'

'Have you got some. then?'

Henry reached into the front pocket of his Levi's and passed me a small, sealed plastic bag from his wallet. 'I told you I had a little surprise for you.'

There were three of them. They looked like tiny air gun pellets.

'Black microdots,' Aaron said. 'The best LSD around.'

Well, if that posh wanker had done them, and Henry, who'd always been much less reckless than me, then... what was the worst that could happen?

I took one out and put it on my tongue. Before it had even touched my teeth, it had gone.

'Amazing.' Aaron said. He was shaking his head, 'I've never seen anyone take a whole one before.'

'What do you mean?' I snapped. 'You never mentioned anything about that.'

Henry was giggling, 'He's only pulling your pisser, Jarrod. I had a whole one last week and I was on top of the world.'

I passed him back the bag. 'Are you going to take yours, then?'

'Oh no, I can't. I mean, I would...I'd love to... But I promised my dad I'd help him out in the cafe tomorrow.'

'I've got to drive back to the island,' Aaron said, holding up his palms and pulling an exaggerated scared face. 'You don't take the wheel with these little buddies in your system.'

'When I saw three in the bag, I thought it was one each.'

They looked at each other, then back to me.

'It's always best to start out with positive thoughts,' Henry said, 'that way you're more likely to have a good trip.'

'Let down your guard and your mind will follow,' Aaron said. 'Go with the flow and the trip will flow with you.'

Henry nodded in agreement and smiled serenely.

A Russian doll had winked at me from the mantelpiece. I closed my eyes and tried to tune into the "head music" that Aaron fetched from the car; but it sounded like a load of random noises to me. There wasn't any singing, or anything resembling a melody. I wondered if something was being lost on the journey from the speakers to my ears. Then a voice jumped out: *Bony*, it seemed to be saying, *BONY*. Suddenly the voice got louder and clearer: *BOGIE*. I opened my eyes and looked down at Henry and then followed his horrified gaze to the doorway.

At first, I hoped I was hallucinating, but as my eyes focussed, I knew it was true. That presence filling the doorway wasn't an apparition.

It was Greg.

He was beckoning me towards him, like there was a force field around the front room and he couldn't enter. When I got into the kitchen, Wayne was already there, bouncing on the balls of his feet and examining the room like a decorator pricing up. 'Not a bad little abode,' he said, managing to make it sound both mysterious and threatening.

Greg blocked the doorway and examined me like *I* was the one who'd just landed. But surely they were the alien invaders in Mum's kitchen. They were both wearing dark colours: old clothes, work clothes, off-to do-a-job clothes.

'We just need a little favour.' Wayne said. He paused, to let that sink in. 'We need to borrow your old dear's motor.'

My head was roasting under the fluorescent strip light. I tried to speak, but my tongue was too big for my mouth. Maybe it was my body's way of protecting me from saying something stupid.

'What the fuck's up with you?' Wayne said.

The best answer I could muster was to make a V-sign and wave an imaginary joint around in front of my mouth.

'*Yeah*,' he tilted his head back incredulously. 'It must be fucking good gear, then. Sort us out a blim.'

A voice said, 'It's not mine.' It didn't sound like me. Was it me?

'Those fucking hippy cunts bring it did they?' Greg said, like he might have known.

'The hippies know where to get all the best gear,' Wayne said, like the hippies always got the best of everything, not just drugs. 'I'm going to have a word.'

Greg glanced over his shoulder. 'Too late, mate. They've already chipped.' He turned to me. 'We ain't got time to mess about, Bogue. So just give us the keys and we'll-'

'What keys?'

His expression changed for the worse. 'The keys to your old dear's motor, you plum.'

I hesitated. I was distracted by his green and brown teeth.

'I'm warning you. I'm starting to lose my patience here.'

'I don't know where they are, Greg, I promise.' I didn't know anything. I hadn't even noticed Henry leaving. What I really wanted to say was now bursting to come out. I needed to shout: *I'M TRIPPING!* I could hear the words echoing in my head, but instead, I said, 'I'll have a look around but...'

Greg wasn't impressed. 'You don't look like you could find your arsehole at the moment, you useless cunt.'

I stared down at the dirty lino and watched a massive spider run under the fridge.

I was sat in the hallway, with my back to the front door, when the Russian dolls appeared. Their disembodied heads were floating above the stairs; each one encased in what looked like a transparent jellyfish. There were six of them, the same number that were on the mantelpiece in the front room, but these ones were three or four times the size. When I asked myself if I should smoke one of my last roll-ups, they cheered like a football crowd; when I thought about Henry, they booed. I asked them aloud if there was life on other planets. *Cheer.* Did Colin really see a UFO down the Prom? *Cheer.* When I needed to piss, I asked if it was safe to go upstairs. They whispered among themselves before lining up in order of head size and spreading out to fill the space between the stair and hallway wall. They'd made themselves bigger now, and instead of jeering, they were hissing. Then the big mama one, who had bushy black eyebrows and a centre-parting, swooped down to almost within my reach and began gabbling in what I guessed was Russian.

I lashed out at her with the back of my hand, but she didn't move, and the others came in closer to protect her. They all had their mouths agape and were mocking me with silent laughter.

I'm not sure what happened next, but my best guess is that I grabbed the breadknife and legged it out of the back door to the garden. At some point, I became conscious of myself kneeling on the grass and holding on tightly to the ledge as I peered through the window into the living room.

A shadow appeared on the floorboards in the doorway, and I dropped down to the ground and waited with my back against the wall. I tried to listen carefully, but all I could hear was my heavy breathing.

Eventually, I crawled away slowly, sliding along the grass on my stomach like I was impersonating a commando I'd seen in a war film. *One step at a time; get to the hedge and then plan your next move.* The damp ground reminded me I was parched; the inside of my mouth was cracking up, like the potato fields after a week without rain, and my tongue tasted like I'd been licking a battery. I pressed my face down into the grass and sunk my teeth in. For the first few mouthfuls, I wondered why I hadn't eaten grass before when I'd been hungry, but then a clump got stuck in my throat and I gagged as I reached into my gob to pull it out. I'd clearly bitten off more than I could chew.

Colin found me shivering in the porch about two in the morning; I was clutching the breadknife and had a hammer beside me. When I told him about the acid, he turned into my dad; if only I'd had a dad for him to turn into. *Don't ever do anything that I wouldn't do.* He led me through the house, room by room, turning off the lights and checking that nobody was there.

I was angry when Henry phoned me in the evening. Bad vibrations from the trip had been rippling in my brain all day and I pounced at the opportunity to have someone to blame.

'Why didn't you tell me it was so strong?'

Henry gave a nervous chuckle, like *strong* was some sort of compliment. 'Are you all right, Jarrod?'

Had he called to check that I'd actually come back from the trip, so he didn't need to worry? Or was he fishing for a trip report to feed back to his acid guru? 'It's a bit late to be asking that now.'

'Who were those psychos who broke into your house?'

I wasn't going to let him off that easy. 'Why did you just fuck off and leave me?'

'They were scary, Jarrod. How did they get in?'

'Through the back door. You could have told me you were leaving.'

'We freaked out. Aaron thought we were going to get beaten up.'

'They only popped round to ask me a favour.'

'What sort of a favour?' He sounded incredulous.

'It doesn't matter.' I was determined to get an answer to my questions first. 'Why didn't you tell me that stuff was so strong?'

'I didn't think you were going to take it last night.'

'Why did you offer it to me, then?'

'It was supposed to be a present.'

'I still would have had to take it on my own, then.'

'We would have stayed to make sure you were all right. But... who were they, Jarrod? Are they junkies? Is that who you're hanging around with now?'

'No.'

How could I tell him that two fair boys had bowled into my mum's house demanding to borrow her car to do some sort of thievery, when I hadn't even made sense of it myself yet?

The strange thing was, when I did think it over, once the trip had completely worn off, a couple of days later, I didn't find it *that* outrageous. They needed a car in a hurry, and they knew Mum was away (though I didn't know how they knew that, because I couldn't remember telling them). The back door was open and so they'd let themselves in. They weren't to know I was tripping. Maybe if I hadn't been, I could have reasoned with them.

But I couldn't have explained all this to Henry. He may have been my mate, but when push came to shove, he was a nice boy from West Mersea. He would have only seen rough geezers like that on the island when the fair was in town.

As far as I could tell, Mum's car was in the same position. I didn't think they'd succeeded in hotwiring it, but they had managed to bugger the ignition.

'Forty quid it's going to cost me to sort out,' Mum said. 'It's just my bloody luck to get incompetent car thieves, isn't it? At least if they'd actually managed to steal the bloody thing, I could have claimed on the insurance. Where am I supposed to find forty quid out of the blue?'

I didn't want to answer that directly, cos I hadn't given her any keep in ages.

'Maybe it's time to start locking the car, Mum. And the house.'

After the trip, I'd kept the back door locked even when I was at home.

'Why should I have to do that?'

'I bet most people do.'

'The thieves didn't come into the house, did they?'

Perhaps I looked guilty, cos she said, 'Are you sure this hasn't got anything to do with you?'

There were a couple of younger mods on the Manor Estate, who I spoke to when I saw them around. Between them, they were only too happy to buy my boating blazer and Sta-Press; my bowlers and Jam shoes. I even gave up my US Army parka.

I used some of the money to buy two pairs of cheap Italian Army greens and some 14-hole imitation DMs. I also got a grade one crop and bleached my hair with neat peroxide that Sian nicked for me from her Saturday job at the chemists. Then I had my left ear pierced four times, by Dennis. And I got him to tattoo a cross on my hand, like his, with green Indian ink. I reckoned it would help me to look a bit harder. I also thought I knew now who my mates were. Dennis had his faults, but he would never have done a runner on me, like Henry.

Chapter Nine

'Verity asked me to get you these.'

I could feel Sian's breath tickling the inside of my ear. She was leaning against me with an arm around my shoulders. I think she was pretty tipsy already. She slipped me a small box and I looked down at it secretly, although only she could see me. I stared at it until I believed it was true: Durex. Sian smiled playfully as she turned away, leaving me alone with my box of three in the hallway.

I was standing at the crossroads of my party, between the front room and living room, with my back against the staircase. Should I go and find Verity and at least give her a smile or a wink to hint that I knew? Or go and drink a strong rum and black and enjoy the glow of anticipation while I got used to the idea? Half an hour earlier, she was stood on the doorstep clutching a half bottle of vodka already mixed with orange. When she gave me a hug and a smack on the lips, I could smell that she'd already started on the drink; but there was nothing in her actions to suggest the promise that was now in my pocket.

She'd been dressing more punky since she came back from Ireland, and tonight she was wearing a red mohair jumper and a short black PVC skirt with tights underneath; eight-hole Doctor Marten boots on her size five feet. The thought that she'd concocted a plan which meant that it was all going to come off in front of me, and I would finally see, or at least touch, her naked body, was suddenly a prospect that was too much for my guts. I rushed out into the front garden in case I threw up.

I took large gulps of cold air to try and compose myself. It was October, and autumn was firmly settling in; my thin sweatshirt was no match for the loud, gusty wind; even the panes of the windows were shivering.

Dennis had promised to act as a bouncer if it became necessary. And now, ironically, I'd ended up bouncing myself out of my own party.

Lurking in the front garden brought back shards of memories from the night of the trip: staring into the black hole of the porch and being too freaked out to go into the house. Greg and Wayne hadn't returned, so if they thought I'd owed them something, then hopefully we were quits. Mum had stopped complaining about her car once it had been fixed, but she was wary about going away again. She made an exception for the Labour Party conference in Blackpool, and I took this opportunity to celebrate my seventeenth birthday, two weeks early.

I heard people piling into the front room when 'Come on Eileen' came on. It was from the compilation tape I'd made especially for the party. *Come on, Jarrod*, I told myself, you're missing out on the action.

My cheap trick of creating an intimate atmosphere by putting a red lightbulb in the ceiling appeared to be working. At first the party was segregated, along the lines of the school lunch breaks, with mine and Lucy's mates in separate rooms. Now they were all mixed up together, like the concoctions of spirits in Sodastream bottles I'd seen being passed around earlier.

Verity had carved out a space in the corner of the front room, under the wall-mounted rug. We looked at each other for the first time since I'd found out what she'd planned for us.

'Have you been avoiding me, Jarrod?'

I put my glass down and embraced her with both arms. 'Course not.'

Our bodies swayed gently to the music. My compilation tape had been replaced with a recording of the Top 40, and 'Careless Whisper' was now playing. To show we weren't going to be dancing slow, like we were getting all soppy at a Football Club disco, Verity deliberately stood on my toes and then giggled loudly into my ear. I could smell her strawberry perfume, mixed with Bensons and booze. I nuzzled her neck and smothered it with little kisses, like she'd done to me that first time down the shelter.

'Careless Whisper' finished, and we managed to carry on snogging during the 'Theme from Ghostbusters'. Verity's tongue tasted like the party, of alcoholic orange juice and smoke and letting yourself go. And it was slippery and hungry like mine.

'Do you like your birthday present?' She had to shout cos someone had turned up the stereo.

'It's the best one I've ever had.'

She squeezed my hand and grinned. 'Don't you want to try it on, then?'

We took off our boots and lay on my single bed kissing, our hands roaming under each other's tops in the darkness. I stroked her bare back, then reached up to grapple with her bra strap. But she told me there was no need to hurry.

We heard voices on the landing and Verity tensed up and held on to me tightly.

I coughed loudly to stake out our territory.

'What if someone comes in when we're doing it?'

Just to hear her talk about *doing it* made my heart beat ten times faster. 'We can go to the bathroom; it's got a lock.'

Once we were in there, I felt exposed under the bare yellow glare. It was almost like we'd be starting again.

Verity put her bottle of vodka and orange down next to the Head and Shoulders.

'Shall we have a bath?' she said.

I was relieved that she was still willing to take the lead. I wouldn't have been practical or forward enough to have made that suggestion, but there wasn't much else we could do to get in the mood in that tiny, cluttered bathroom.

'Good idea.' I turned on the taps full blast and said I'd be back in a sec.

I peeked out, there was no one about, though I recognised Sian's laugh coming from Mum's bedroom next door. I thought me and Dennis had agreed that nobody was allowed in there.

As I opened the airing cupboard, I heard Colin shouting angrily downstairs. *Fucking little slags*, he yelled as a parting shot, before slamming the front door so hard it made the house shake. In different circumstances, I would have gone after him, but for now I had to block it from my mind. Whatever it was would have to wait. I had an important date with my other close mate. I snatched two towels from the airing cupboard and darted back into the bathroom and slid across the lock. If Verity didn't mention the commotion, then I wouldn't either. At least not until after we'd done it.

Verity had stripped to her matching black underwear; the rest of her clothes were piled up under the sink.

I swilled the water back and forth and chucked in a splash of the posh bubble bath I'd bought Mum for her birthday. When the temperature felt about right, and Verity wasn't looking, I quickly removed my pants like I was in a swimming pool changing rooms and clambered in with my back to the taps. I'd never been naked in front of a girl before.

'Well, isn't this fun?' Verity said. She lowered herself unsteadily into the water, sending a wave sloshing over the edge.

After taking a long swig from her bottle, she passed it to me. I shuddered with how potent she'd made the mix.

She glanced down at her breasts, which were mostly above the water line. 'Do you want to give me a wash?'

I soaped up my hands and shuffled forwards, smearing the lather across her chest. It was the first opportunity I'd been given to caress her bare breasts, but unfortunately it wasn't as exciting as I would have hoped. I seemed to have overdone it with the soap; now I was more like a cack-handed doctor than a sexual explorer.

I scooped palmfuls of water over her tits in a shoddy attempt to rinse them.

Verity manoeuvred a foot between my legs and gently pressed against my balls, then slowly rubbed up and down my erection with the tips of her toes. 'Does that feel nice?'

If she carried on for much longer, it would have been too nice to bear.

We sat on the side of the bath wrapped in towels. The thick Cornetto one, which I'd saved up tokens for the previous summer, was folded over the top of her tits and reached midway down her thighs. I reached up as far as I could as we kissed, my fingertips brushing the damp fur of her pubes.

When we'd stopped kissing, she asked me if I was a virgin.

I'd lied to other people but now I didn't see the point. I was pretty sure it wouldn't make her change her mind. 'Yeah. Are you?'

'No.'

'How come?'

Her laughter broke the tension. I suppose it was a bit of a silly question. '*Well, Jarrod*,' she said, like she was pretending to explain the birds and bees to a little kid; then in her normal voice, 'I met a fella in Ireland, a friend of my cousin Orla's, and I…you know.'

'Oh.' I looked down. I knew I wasn't her boyfriend-boyfriend so maybe I shouldn't have been disappointed. But I was. I could feel the numbness in my bum. Even my erection was faltering.

'I think it's better that way,' she said.

She lifted my chin and turned my face towards her. 'That was then. Now I want you.'

We kissed again and she tugged open the small threadbare orange towel which I'd just about managed to tie around my waist. It usually got left in the cupboard until last, but from now on I would treat it more fondly.

I placed it on the floor in the narrow gap between the bath and the wall to soak up some of the spillage. Verity overlapped it with the Cornetto one and lay down with her head on a ball of our clothes.

I kneeled between her legs, my hands trembling as I ripped the edge from the foil with my teeth. She looked up dreamily as I rolled it on clumsily, then closed her eyes and waited.

If only I could find my way in.

I pushed harder against her; she groaned, but not in the way that I'd hoped.

'Sorry,' I said.

She opened her eyes and looked cross. 'Be careful. That hurts.'

'Maybe you need to open your legs a bit wider.'

78

I tried again, this time she reached down and pressed on my cock to guide me.

I began thrusting tentatively, but once I was confident I was completely inside her, I was sure there was nothing could stop me. *I was doing it...we were doing it. I was really doing it.* I was doing it with such enthusiasm that Verity's head shifted back a few inches and was knocking against the base of the sink.

Then came the crampus interruptus: shooting up into my calf and swiftly stealing my bliss. I didn't even know if I could make it to the finishing line. I gritted my teeth and told myself I had to, otherwise it wouldn't really count. *I've got to... I've got to... I...ahhh!*

I scrambled to my feet as soon as I'd come and frantically wiggled my leg in the restricted space.

'That's not normal,' she said.

'Fucking cramp,' I said, wincing with pain, but I was too embarrassed to face her. I turned my back and pulled off the condom, then grabbed a flannel from the corner of the bath and wrapped it inside.

I rushed to pull on my pants and then leaned with one hand on the door and stretched my leg into the gap. I was flicking my toes towards Verity.

'I'm sorry,' I said. 'It just came on suddenly.'

Verity laughed and shook her head as she fastened the back of her bra. 'It would happen to you, wouldn't it, Jarrod. You're lucky you've got another two chances.'

Chapter Ten

My second chance with Verity would have to wait until she wasn't busy. I wasn't busy enough, and I soon found out the hard way about the devil making work for idle hands.

I hadn't seen Colin for a few days after he stormed out of my party. Lucy had told me that he'd fallen asleep on the settee and a couple of her mates thought it would be funny to put make up on his face. When he woke up and realised what was going on, he went loopy. I decided to go to his house one evening to see if he was okay. I also wanted to make sure he wasn't angry with me. Though I couldn't think of anything I might have done personally to upset him.

The only light in the narrow no-through road which led up to Colin's house was fixed to the front wall of the vicarage. As I walked alongside the front hedge, I heard the vicar's gate creak, then a hooded figure stepped out in front of me.

'What are you up to?'

I could have asked him the same question. It was Dennis.

He glanced back to the house. 'Come here a sec, I want to show you something.'

He beckoned me through the gate, then led me down the front garden path and through a side passage to a patio at the back of the house. He shone his torch on the silver rungs of an extension ladder, which were glinting under the full moon. 'Wayne's up there. We just need a hand carrying the gear down.'

I still don't understand why it didn't occur to me to say no. I didn't say yes either though. I didn't say anything. But I did wonder…

Dennis had a knack of being able to anticipate any doubts about his plans and then deal with them persuasively. 'I don't like heights, do I? Otherwise, I'd go in myself.'

He passed me his square pocket torch and asked me if I had any gloves.

It had been bitter earlier that week and I happened to still have a pair in my jacket.

He said he'd be keeping bogeye down there and would whistle or chuck a stone at the window if it came on top. But there was no need to worry, cos that wasn't going to happen.

I shone the torch around in what I guessed was the vicar's bedroom. It was sparse and old-fashioned looking, with a brown counterpane covering the double bed and a massive dark wooden wardrobe that took up most of one wall. Above the bed was a rectangular painting of a countryside landscape. The room was chilly and smelt of old books.

Wayne appeared in the doorway, and I yelped embarrassingly. This made him snigger for a second, but otherwise he acted like he was less surprised than me. And he wasn't as grateful for the extra pair of hands as I'd hoped he'd be. He told me to have a scout about in here. He was going up in the loft and would give me a shout when he was ready.

I stood at the foot of the vicar's bed and yanked the metal handle of the top drawer of his chest. Inside were neat stacks of his white Y-fronts and vests. I shoved the drawer shut and moved down to the next. This time, I don't know why, I stuck my hand in the drawer and mauled around the socks and hankies. I regretted it immediately. An uncomfortable heat warmed the back of my neck, like there was somebody hovering behind me. I turned around sharply and pointed the torch, but it must have been my mind playing tricks.

When I turned back, I had a moment of clarity: what the fuck was I doing? What the fuck was I doing in a vicar's bedroom, when I should have been round at Colin's?'

Then I heard Wayne calling me.

I went back out to the landing and waited next to the chair below the open loft hatch.

Wayne slid a box across the floorboards above me and angled it down through the hole.

It was long and heavy, and I passed it slowly thorough my fingers until the bottom was resting on the landing. Then I laid the box along the floor and shone my torch on the writing. *Professional Bow and Arrows Set*. What the hell was a pie and liquor doing with a bow and arrow?

After the box of archery, Wayne passed me down a boxed portable telly. And then a brand-new video recorder. Maybe I was in the right place at the right time after all.

I didn't tell anyone about it, but it did weigh on me, so I went round to Colin's to show off and confess. For some reason, I thought he'd be impressed by our haul, but he was full of pent-up contempt. Breaking into people's houses was a dirty crime, he said. But I reckon the vicar must be dodgy to have all that in his loft, I said. That weren't the point, Colin said, and anyway, I was a mug cos Wayne and Dennis were just using me. It would be like the fair all over again, except this time I'd never see a penny.

At first, I thought he was jealous cos he wasn't involved, but once his comments had sunk in, they did really sting. When I hurried away from his place against a cold wind, I took the long route home to avoid walking past the vicarage. I promised myself that I would never break into a house again. In the unlikely event that I ever stumbled into another burglary, I would be ready to find a way to say no.

A few days later, I was being watched by two detectives facing me across the desk of a tiny interrogation room at Clacton Police Station. The younger one wrote down my answers, while the older, fatter, balder one, DS Shearer, asked the questions and pretended he had my best interests at heart. All of us smoked except the young one, and there were no windows. Mum left her Rothmans on the desk and allowed me to tuck in.

Shearer coughed, then asked me to tell him what happened on the night of…

The coppers had come round while I was up town and Mum had agreed to bring me here for what they called a *voluntary interview*. I couldn't get my head around the idea of a "voluntary" police interview, it sounded to me like Catch-22. Though it had meant I didn't get banged up in a cell. We'd spent almost two hours hanging around the cop shop and Mum hadn't exactly been talkative, so I'd had plenty of time to think. I would tell them the basic truth without giving away any names and then get out of there sharpish and move on with my life.

I reeled off the script I'd rehearsed in my head.

'Can you tell us who this person was you just happened to *bump into*, Jarrod?'

'No, I don't want to say.'

Shearer made out he was puzzled. What had this criminal acquaintance done to deserve such loyalty? Did I think he would do that for me?

'It was Dennis Winch, wasn't it?'

I looked on the desk for something to drink, but Mum's polystyrene cup of pissy tea was empty.

He claimed that Dennis had already come clean. It was Dennis who gave them my name.

Bullshit. Then why would he need to hear it from me? I wasn't that green; I'd even seen them playing that blame game in cop shows on the telly.

Burglary was a serious offence, didn't I agree? That meant there needed to be a strong deterrent, wasn't that right? People had to be able to feel safe in their own homes, didn't they?

I kept schtum. I was getting better at spotting the rhetorical questions.

The more I was willing to tell them about that night, Shearer said, the more likely he'd be able to help me later.

I glanced sideways at Mum. She hadn't brought me up to believe that the police were in the business of helping people.

Shearer said he could see I wasn't a bad lad, and I clearly came from a good family… so, if I was willing to tell him the names of these experienced criminals who had led me astray, then perhaps he could have a word with his governor, who was a reasonable and fair chap, and ask that my case be dealt with sympathetically.

'And what if he doesn't tell you their names?'

Shearer dropped the bomb that I should have seen coming. 'Well, *Msss* Goldfinch, refusing to help the police with their enquiries won't go down well with the Magistrates. Especially as he's only very recently been given a caution for his part in another burglary.'

'What *caution*? What burglary? Nobody told *me* anything about that.'

Shearer looked at me like he was enjoying himself. 'Really?'

I stared at the huge tin ashtray on the desk. There were nine butts in there already. We were all slowly suffocating, especially me.

Mum reached for her Rothmans. 'I want to have a word with my son on my own.'

As we walked out into the cop shop corridor, I heard a geezer wailing in the distance that he wanted to see his brief. It was coming from the cellblock where I, and many of the miners, had been locked up that summer.

I told her we'd just tried to nick a few fags from the beach caff. It was nothing really.

'What do you mean, *it was nothing really*?'

'You were away, I didn't want to worry you. Colin's dad sat in on the interview.'

'I can't believe I've been so fucking naïve.'

'What do you mean, Mum?'

'I don't know what dregs of the town you've been hanging around with, but you'd better not be bringing them into my house.'

'I told you, this wasn't people I normally knock about with.'

'Dennis is supposed to be your friend, isn't he?'

'How do you know Dennis was there?'

'You heard them. He's already admitted to it.'

'Oh, come on, Mum, now you are being naïve. That's just one of their little tricks.'

'How else did they know you were there if Dennis didn't tell them?'

'I don't know.'

'Now who's being naïve, Jarrod?'

'I'm not a grass, Mum, and I never will be. It's as simple as that.'

'Listen to yourself, Jarrod, going on about *grasses*. This isn't an episode of bloody *Minder*, you know.'

'You don't understand, Mum. I'd rather go to prison than be a grass. That's just the way it is.'

'Well, that's fine, then, because that's where you're heading if you carry on like this. But I'll tell you one thing...' She narrowed her eyes at me and jutted out her chin, '...I'm not having you living in my house if you're going to waste your time with useless petty criminals. Maybe that's just the way it is too.'

'Maybe I'd have some different friends in Brightlingsea if you hadn't sent me away for five years.'

'Oh, *come* off it. You're doing what you always do, blaming everything on the past. I'm sick to death of hearing it. Anyway, Colin managed to avoid getting dragged into this burglary, didn't he?'

'Colin wasn't there. I was on my way to see him. It was just a stroke of bad luck.'

'It's always bad luck with you, isn't it, Jarrod?'

'Listen, Mum. If I grass, I've got to carry on living in that town with people knowing what I did. What's going to happen to me then?' But it wasn't only that. Not grassing was a matter of principle.

'What about Tony? What would he say? I know he wouldn't agree with what I've done, but I bet he wouldn't dream of grassing on someone. You just don't do it, Mum.'

'What has Tony got to do with it, Jarrod? He's not a petty criminal, is he?'

'I know, but grasses are like scabs, aren't they? Traitors and cowards.'

'Don't be ridiculous. What are you talking about?'

'You can throw me out if you want, Mum, but I'm going back in there to tell them I'm not grassing and there's nothing you can do to stop me.'

Chapter Eleven

I decided I needed to make a fresh start. And the only realistic way this was going to happen, would be if I moved out of Brightlingsea. But to move out, I would need money; to get money I would need a job. To find a job would be even harder with a criminal record.

Mum was right. I'd be naïve to believe that neither Dennis nor Wayne betrayed me. But I had to face it, I was unlikely to ever find out the truth. If I'd told them what the cops had told me, they would have laughed in my face. And if I repeated it, like I took it seriously, Dennis would no doubt have threatened me.

Hooper, my solicitor, told the court that I'd been foolish to allow myself to be taken advantage of by bigger and badder boys. When the magistrates studied me, I attempted to look forlorn, like Oliver Twist, but inside I was embarrassed about being described by Hooper in public as a vulnerable and sensitive young man.

The court showed me mathematically that crime doesn't pay when they gave me a two hundred and fifty quid fine. This was twelve and a half times the score I was eventually bunged for my share of the proceeds.

Dennis and Wayne both reckoned they'd asked for the vicarage to be 'taken into consideration' when they were charged for a different burglary, but I never heard any more details about the case. Having the vicarage as a TIC, meant they couldn't be charged with it later. So now we weren't even all in it together. I ended up in the dock on my own.

The Presiding Justice told me I was lucky not to be sent away for a short sharp shock in a Detention Centre. In mitigation, Hooper explained that I'd been desperate to find work and had now finally managed to secure a position at a local electronics factory. This would give me the opportunity I needed to move on from my mistake. What Hooper and the court didn't know is that I was only able to do the job cos of Dennis and Wayne.

Dennis had heard from his mum's friend, Doreen, who worked at Futurelux as a supervisor, that the company had been awarded a three million quid contract with British Telecom to produce phone sockets and they needed to take on sixty people across two shifts: one week of six to two, the next of two to ten.

The factory was a few miles the wrong side of Colchester, and the only way to get there was by car. Me and Colin and Dennis got a lift with Wayne in his so-called souped-up Escort Mk2.

I saw this job as my chance to turn the tables and use Wayne and Dennis to help me get away from them. The basic take-home wage at the factory was eighty quid a week: a tenner instalment on my fine, a tenner for petrol and another tenner to Mum for keep. That left me with fifty sheets. I planned to use some of that to save up for the first month's rent and deposit on a room in Colchester, which would be a stepping stone to eventually getting where I wanted to be: London. I didn't know yet how much money I would need, but once I'd made some progress with the savings, I would talk about it with Verity, cos one of her brothers lived in a house share up town.

Getting out of bed at a quarter to five felt like the middle of the night, especially in the winter when the house was freezing and it was black outside, but I still preferred the early shifts because it meant I was more likely to see Verity. Sometimes she would pop round mine for an hour after school; or when she was babysitting for her cousins, she'd invite me, and we'd share her plate of crackers and cheese, and kiss and cuddle while watching TV and then usually get carried away and have sex on the settee. We were still close friends, but she was still always busy. It was too cold to hang around outside now, and she only joined us up the youth club occasionally. I also wanted to use the factory money to tempt her into doing more exciting things with me like going up town to the cinema, or to gigs at the Arts Centre and the Uni. Maybe I could even persuade her to come and watch Chelsea.

The worst thing about working earlies was being late. Either Wayne, or more often Dennis, couldn't get up on time, or Wayne's car would let us down. At least three times, when we'd stopped at Thorrington Cross to get petrol, the supposedly super-tuned engine wouldn't fire up again, and we'd have to pile out of the warm motor in a sleepy stupor and bump it down Tenpenny Hill. Me and Colin couldn't understand how when we'd paid a tenner a week each for petrol, the needle on the gauge never seemed to get out of the red.

Whether we clocked in at thirty seconds past six or were twenty-nine minutes late, we still got docked half an hour's pay. The difference was the later we were, the angrier Doreen would be. And then she usually took it out on me. Being late also meant getting behind, and I couldn't afford to be behind cos I was already slow at the job.

Most of us were sat at desks in three long rows, a bit over an arm's length apart, and our work consisted of pushing small components into a sheet of circuit boards, which were set in a shiny metal frame. Each frame contained the circuitry for a dozen sockets, and they all needed to be supplied with the same six components. Therefore, I had to make seventy-two movements. I'd found it was easier and quicker to always insert the components in the same order.

Up first, the one that looked like a decorative staple – if you mixed it in with a box of staples, it would be the queen; then, the boring drawing pin one. If a component was going to slip through my butter fingers, which happened quite a lot, it was most likely to be one of these two. I've always been clumsy, or as Adrian used to call it, *cack-handed*, and was embarrassingly hopeless at all school subjects involving coordination, especially Woodwork and Technical Drawing. Art, I got away with, because we had a radical teacher, Mr Smythe, who was into Funkadelic and The Temptations and always gave me an A for effort. He also refused to tell the truth in my report, which was that my paintings were worse than a toddler's.

My favourite component was the yellow barrel, which looked like a mini explosive. It was the biggest, and therefore the easiest to keep a grip on. Sometimes I amused myself by picking one up gingerly, as if it had 'Handle with Care' written on the side, and imagined flinging it like a Molotov cocktail over the two-metre-high partition that separated us from the old production line. The old production line where they carried on doing whatever they did before the BT bounty, and where you were still allowed to smoke on the job and didn't have to start work until eight.

Most of the people who worked on the old line were women, and I'd noticed that even after we'd been there for a few weeks, some of them still looked at us newcomers suspiciously like the company had been so desperate in its urgency to fill the vacancies that they'd taken on a load of freaks and professional dole-ites. I had to admit, judging by some of the misfits on our shift, including me, it did seem like they were willing to employ almost anybody. But Greg was proof that not everybody was capable of being employed.

He still held the record for the shortest stint, after walking out just nineteen minutes into his first and only shift. I was sitting in the next row at the time, and I'd been clocking him fidgeting in his chair and clock-watching until he finally got up and muttered, *Fuck this for a game of soldiers*. And that was it - I never saw him again.

Soon after the factory, he went to live with his uncle in London, who was into robbing big houses in the country; two years later, he was killed when the police chased him down the A12 and his car skidded into a lorry.

Unless somebody went for an early shit, the first chair I heard being scraped back on each shift was usually Colin on his way up to the Quality Control desk with a completed frame. He'd become one of the top performers since Doreen stopped us from sitting within talking distance of each other.

At the end of our second week, I was made to sit one row back from the front, behind the Quality Controller, Karen Grimm, a skinny black-haired girl with sharp features from Brightlingsea who was a few years older than me. Wayne reckoned that him and Greg used to shag her in their den when they were about twelve. He called her a bike, and said she'd let them do whatever they liked. Each time I looked at her, I found it hard not to think about what he'd told me.

A few feet in front of Karen was the flow solder machine, the huge red and white shining jewel in the crown of the new production line and the symbol of its high-tech futuristic efficiency. On our shift it was operated by Wayne and Dennis. Their job was to collect the stacks of completed frames from Karen's desk and put them through the flow solder process. As far as I could see, this basically meant feeding the frames into one end of the machine and then taking them out of the other. Just as he'd done with the spudding, Dennis had managed to manoeuvre himself into one of the best positions. At least this time it also benefitted me.

I'd been moaning in the car on the way home one Friday that I wasn't able to complete enough frames per shift to get a production bonus. The others all laughed and took the piss and basically said it was my tough shit and then on Monday, Wayne came up with a double-counting scam.

For the scheme to succeed, I needed to be ready to take a finished frame to the QC desk shortly before Karen went for her hourly fag breaks. While she was gone, I would wait for a signal from Dennis or Wayne for me to exchange the new empty frame I was now pretending to work on, for a completed one - done by someone else - that had yet to be soldered.

This meant it was part of my job to observe the flow solder soldiers. Watching Wayne in action at seven in the morning, I noticed he gave off the aura that while his limbs were going through the motions of work, his head had transcended the windowless shed. In other words, he was still wrecked from the hot knife he'd had for breakfast. He swore it was the only way to kick-start the day; a hot knife and a Marlboro, washed down with a can of coke or a cup of coffee, depending on the season.

One day, I was bowling back to my desk with my freebie when I clocked Karen rushing towards me. As she passed, she glanced down and then gave me a look to let me know that she knew. But she never said anything. A few days later we carried on doing it.

Wayne and Dennis surprised me by not asking for anything in return. Maybe it was some acknowledgement that I'd taken the rap for the vicarage. Or could it be that at least one of them had a guilty conscience about grassing me up?

Apart from the money, I'd thought the best thing about working full-time in a factory would be the chance to join a union. Tony was a shop steward with the National Union of Mineworkers and had stressed to me how important it was to have union recognition in the workplace. Without it, the bosses would always find it easy to take liberties, but as far as I could tell, there wasn't any union presence at Futurelux. When I asked around, I was looked at warily like I wanted to cause trouble.

What we did have at the factory was a gantry, high above the shop floor, from where the managing director could look down on us like it was the 19th Century.

I'd noticed that since we'd been working at Futurelux, Colin was more like his old self again, after being moody for a while around the time of my party. When I went back to his house after a late shift and it was just the pair of us, I was reminded of simpler times: playing cards and darts and having a laugh, eating cheese on toast and watching late-night telly. A few weeks before Christmas, his brother, Ryan, had moved in with his girlfriend and taken his record collection; now the only record in the house was Colin's dad's *My Generation*. I couldn't get my head around the idea of only owning one LP, but at least he'd chosen a good 'un.

One night we were playing arrows in Ryan's old bedroom, which Colin had turned into a games room. As well as the dartboard, he'd also brought down the miniature snooker table from the loft and stuck up posters of Madonna and Doctor Spock. On the windowsill was the transistor radio from the kitchen, and we were listening to the pirate station, *Laser 558*, broadcasting sixties hits from out in the North Sea.

'I'm going to start having driving lessons soon,' Colin announced suddenly.

It was turning out to be a particularly slow game of Around the Clock, and for the second go in a row, Colin had failed to hit a four. He yanked the darts out of the board and passed them to me, then went over to peer out of the window as if wondering where he was going to park his motor when he got it. 'We need to sort out our own transport, Jarrod. That fucking shit heap is doing my nut in.'

'I'm surprised it's still going.'

'And them two wankers can't be trusted, can they?' Wayne and

Dennis had dropped us off on Friday afternoon and it was now half one on Tuesday morning and we hadn't heard from them since. Not for the first time, we'd had to take two buses to work and then hitch a lift home. If we'd been on the earlies, we wouldn't have been able to make it in at all.

After I had missed the six with my three arrows, Colin took a swig from his can of lager and limbered up to the oche. He reminded me that he would be seventeen in early January. If he started having lessons straight away, he was confident he could pass his test within a couple of months. Then all he'd need to do was get Skully to lend him the money to buy a motor.

He hadn't mentioned Skully lately, but I knew he still did the odd shift for him. 'Do you reckon he'll be up for that?'

'Course.'

I couldn't understand why he was so sure. But I didn't know then what I found out later.

'I need that job to get some money together, Jarrod. If we keep being late, they ain't going to give us permanent contracts, are they? Don't get me wrong, I don't want to end up in the same poxy factory for twenty years like my old man. I want to be running my own caff one day.'

'I know you do. I reckon it'll be a good one too. I need the job so I can save up to get out of this place.' It was the first time I'd shared my plan with anyone.

'I want to move out as well. But we need to get some money together first, don't we? You can't do anything without money.'

'I know, I'm trying. I've already... I've got nearly a hundred quid.' I was taking a risk, because he would remember it if and when he was skint. But it would also be disloyal to hold back now we were in it together. It was us two and them two all over again, like it used to be with Pilkie and Kevin. And if we were in it together, then maybe my moving out plan was more likely to happen.

'We can get a little house up town, Jarrod. It would be a right laugh. We could do as much overtime at the factory as we wanted an' all if we didn't have to rely on those fuckers for a lift.'

'We wouldn't have to rely on them for anything,' I said.

I found the idea of sharing a place with Colin much more exciting than just renting a room on my own. I knew he would insist that I kept the place tidy, but at least it would solve the problem of me not being able to cook. I had a niggling doubt about the money though. Colin had always been a compulsive spender: capable of spunking all he had on a fruit machine bender. It was hard to believe that he'd really get around to paying for driving lessons and a deposit on a house; but that night he was as determined as I'd ever seen him.

He was pacing around at two in the morning like he still had more energy than could be contained in that room. I can still see him now, running his fingers through his new wedge haircut, a nicked pair of Lyle & Scott socks on his feet. As usual, he was probably the only one still up in his street. I half-expected him to suggest going for one of his night walks round the prom. And if he did then fuck it, I'd join him. We could carry on plotting our exit and planning our future.

Chapter Twelve

My hands and feet were frozen as I knocked on doors with Verity asking for donations of non-perishables for the miners. Verity's dad and his mate, Mick, from the Miners Support Group, were going to drive a van to Kent on Christmas Eve to deliver it.

Verity had a typed list of supporters in the part of the town we'd been allocated, but we were free to chance our arms on any house we wanted. Some residents looked at us like we were worse than Jehovah's Witnesses; others like we were exaggerating. A few people, mostly blokes, wanted to know *Why don't they just go back to work then?* But there were victories, like the old lady who handed over Hobnobs and tinned peaches and processed peas. 'That cow is pure evil,' she said, 'you can see it in her eyes.'

A couple of days later, we went Christmas shopping together in London. Verity would have been satisfied with going to Colchester, but I wanted a red Harrington jacket like the singer from The Redskins, and I already knew they didn't have them in any of the clothes shops up town.

I only really needed to buy presents for Mum and Lucy, but Verity had a long list on a crumpled piece of paper in her coat pocket and she ticked them off as she went along. She told me she definitely didn't want anything from me, but I was determined to get her a present anyway, especially after putting her through the Harrington hunt.

Her parents had given her some Christmas money up front, and while she was looking for new boots on Oxford Street, I told her I was going to find a toilet. Instead, I legged it to the other type of Boots to get her some posh perfume. I tried out some testers on my wrists, but after a few my nose got confused, so I asked an assistant if she could recommend one for a punky feminist. Without speaking, she passed me a black box with gold lettering.

I managed to keep the present a secret until we got on the train, then I dropped it into Verity's lap. She pretended to protest but I could tell she was chuffed cos she put some on straight away. She sprayed me too and told me to think of her while she was in family Christmas hibernation.

On the bus back from Colchester Station, she made me laugh with stories about her massive Irish family on her mum's side who lived in the same village in Galway where she spent most of her school summer holidays. I was jealous when she told me about the traditional music sessions in her granny's garden, which Verity joined in with on her mandolin. She explained that her aunties and uncles were going to Boston for Christmas to stay with another branch of the family; Verity's granny was too old for a long flight, so she was coming to Brightlingsea with Verity's cousin, Orla. 'I'm probably going to have to take her to mass, Jarrod. Imagine that.' I tried to, but I couldn't. The thought of a church reminded me of robbing the vicarage, something I'd never told Verity.

I said at least she didn't have to spend Christmas Day with Adrian. I made her feel sorry for me by telling her about the year he'd thrown the roast potatoes out into the snow, during an argument with Mum about gravy.

Then Verity broke the news that she wouldn't be able to see me until January.

'Surely you can sneak out one night?'

'You don't know my family.'

I didn't, not really. But I still found it hard to believe that where there was a will, there couldn't be a way. But what could I say? My view didn't hold any sway, cos I wasn't her boyfriend, was I? All I could do in protest was to go quiet for a bit. But I realised I was only spiting myself, so I snapped out of it.

On Christmas Eve, the factory laid on a party for our shift. Well, they called it a party; it was more like an extended break in the little canteen, with some free booze and buffet food thrown in.

There were vol-au-vents and triangular sarnies and Yuletide chocolate log; three cases of Kestrel lager and two bottles of egg nog. I steamed into the snowballs until my burps started to taste dangerously pukey.

On Christmas Day, I sat as far away from Adrian at the dining table as I could, which wasn't far, cos there were only five of us.

'Congratulations on your job in the factory.'

When he lived with us, I used to find it impossible to make eye contact with him. Now it was the other way around: as I looked up, he looked down. His voice sounded suspiciously even. If there was a hint of sarcasm, it was very well buried.

Last year, Mum decided it was ridiculous that Adrian should spend Christmas Day on his own. Surely they could behave like adults for Lucy's sake. Well, it certainly wasn't for mine. But after he turned up almost empty-handed and in a foul temper, Mum admitted that it had been a mistake. 'Don't worry,' she reassured me, 'he won't be coming round at Christmas again.' But then suddenly this year was different because he had a girlfriend, and it would be nice for Lucy if we could all be together. Her name was Anita, and she was a fellow so-called philosopher from the Uni, but it didn't take a deep thinker to work out that Lucy didn't even like her. I was determined not to make things any easier either, and I only nodded to give Adrian the bare minimum of an answer.

Folded in my back pocket was his bare minimum of a Christmas present to me. Inside the card would be a small record or book token, a small token of his view that me, his so-called adoptee, was worth at least twenty times less than his flesh and blood, Lucy. He'd bought her a new stack stereo system – though admittedly it was Amstrad – whereas my token was unlikely to stretch to more than a single LP.

'What is it that you do?' asked Anita, dabbing her mouth with one of the red paper napkins Mum had bought especially for the occasion.

'I'm a production operator.'

'It's just for the time being,' Mum chipped in.

'Oh,' said Anita, 'it sounds rather interesting.'

'It's not really,' I said. I was hungover and couldn't be bothered to explain. I also didn't want to give Adrian the thrill of knowing that I pushed components into circuit boards for a living.

Mum raised her glass and changed the subject. 'It's a lovely drop of red.'

I'd noticed it was actually drinkable too. Most of the bottle Adrian brought last year had ended up in a stew. I'd clocked Mum reading the label on this one earlier and then rummaging for the corkscrew. 'Where did you get it from, Adrian?' she asked.

There was a short silence while he took his time to finish a mouthful of food and then Anita answered for him. She told us that she'd recently joined the *Sunday Times* Wine Club, and so far, at least, her expectations had been greatly exceeded.

Lucy kicked me under the table as if to say, *I told you she was a snooty bitch.*

A bit later, Mum said, 'I'm sorry if the turkey's a bit dry. I was trying to do a million things at once.'

I knew from memories of turkeys gone by that it wouldn't be to Adrian's taste, so to wind him up, I said, 'Don't worry, Mum, it's lovely.' It actually wasn't too bad once I'd marinated it in gravy.

'I've always found turkey to be a teensy bit dry,' Anita said.

Lucy burst into a snigger.

'I just mean that…well, in my experience, and perhaps it is only my experience –'

Adrian interrupted her. 'It's fine,' he said. 'The turkey's fine.'

I looked at Mum to check that we'd both detected the old edge in his voice.

Adrian stabbed a sprout with his fork.

Then came the long, dark, in-between days, from Boxing to New Years' Eve: a cycle of ever decreasing leftovers, and hangovers inflicted by whatever booze me and Colin could get our hands on.

During most of this time my mind was as mushy as Mum's bubble and squeak. I didn't read anything apart from the backs of boxes and bottles and the *Radio Times*. I couldn't find the motivation or brainpower to finish the rhymes I'd started about the factory grind. I knew something wasn't right, cos I'd even been waking up in the middle of the night, but I couldn't put any of my cack-handed fingers on exactly what it was that disturbed me.

I really wished I could talk about this honestly with somebody. To be honest, I really wished I could see Verity. Even if it was only for a cup of tea. Or for the time it takes to make one. But she was wrapped up in her close family, until some undisclosed date in January. And she didn't even seem to mind that much.

Chapter Thirteen

The final bell had long since rung, but a few of us stragglers clung on. And then the sound of an alarm bell sent Dennis and Colin rushing out of the Brewers Arms to investigate; I stayed back, I'd been eyeing up the dregs of drinks on the corner table.

First up, a gulp of gin and bitter lemon; then, what was that? Stout? Some flat old man's beer anyway. *Eurrghh, that's got ash in it.* The last one was thick and sweet with an aniseed kick. I shuddered as the Pernod glow warmed my cheeks, then slammed the glass down on the window ledge and stepped outside into Nineteen Eighty-Five.

I was immediately attacked by a bitter wind, but after a gallon of snakebite, I felt like I could cope with anything. I wasn't the only one: I'd never seen so many people on the High Street before, except perhaps during the carnival procession. But that was in daylight; this was after half-past midnight. It was my first experience of going out on New Year's Eve and of pubs being allowed to open until later than eleven. Last year I'd been out for the count before the big countdown, chucking up Mum's home brew all over Colin's garden.

Tonight, there were groups of people scattered all over the High Street and Victoria Place: on the traffic island above the public bogs; next to the war memorial; outside the shops; sitting on the front garden wall of the Brewers. It looked like everybody under forty had stopped on their way home from whichever of the dozen Brightlingsea pubs they'd ended up at. In one ear, I could hear all their shouting and laughing; in the other, the alarm bell from Bargain Land was tringing into my skull.

The biggest gathering was in front of the church on Victoria Place and I could see that this was where Dennis and Colin had got to. I decided to go for a wander instead and see if I could spot Verity.

As I walked slowly past Bargain Land, which was a couple of doors down from the Brewers, I noticed the bottom windows had been kicked through, but nobody had bothered to go in and help themselves to cheap shampoo or dodgy chocolate bars you didn't see anywhere else. Maybe if Bargain Land stocked bargain booze, we could stay out all night long drinking Scotch whisky that was made in Hong Kong.

Over by the war memorial, I clocked a girl I thought could be Verity, so I hurried over. I only wanted to wish her a Happy New Year. Well, it would be lovely to give her a hug while I did so; but I wouldn't try to act like I was her boyfriend. I'd seen her in the Freemasons earlier, as I was on my way through the packed narrow bar to the toilets. She was wedged into a bench seat, below the window, talking to her brothers and a couple of people I didn't recognise. She happened to glance over, and we caught each other's eye. She smiled, but it didn't give off a vibe that she wanted to introduce me, cos she looked away pretty quickly. Later, the hurt stewed to resentment inside me, cos I hadn't felt like telling anybody. Now all I wanted was to make things all right.

But when I got close to the war memorial, the woman I thought could be Verity turned around and I saw she was at least ten years older.

I said, 'Happy New Year,' anyway. That night I'd discovered that the more pissed people got, the more likely they were to say Happy New Year to everybody they bumped into; sometimes it felt like a trap, like if you didn't say it straight back, they had an excuse to call you ignorant and try to start an argument. *Happy New Year*, one of the woman's mates mumbled to me, like she was bored of repeating it already.

Outside the church, by the Christmas tree, I saw Colin and Sian and some older girls who also worked at the factory. They were passing around a litre bottle of vodka, which I assumed had been won in a pub raffle. I didn't know the factory girls well enough to ask them for a swig.

While I was hanging around talking to Colin, a couple walked past the Brewers dressed in what looked like sacks. I guessed they were supposed to be *The Flintstones*.

'Happy New Year,' shouted one of the girls from the factory. The bloke raised his papier mache club in acknowledgement and returned the greeting.

Colin yelled out, 'YABBA DABBA DOO!'

A few minutes later, a patrol car pulled up outside Bargain Land and two coppers, a male and a female, got out to speak with the owner, who was crouched in front of his broken windows.

I moved to the front of the crowd to get a better look. Wayne was talking to a couple of geezers his age, Nutty and his mate Roy Francis. Nutty was massive, and apparently had *cunt* tattooed on the inside of his bottom lip. I'd heard he'd only recently been released from the nick. Wayne broke off the conversation when he recognised PC Cocks. He cupped his hands around his mouth and bawled out: 'WHO'S THAT TWAT IN THE BIG BLACK HAT?'

A chorus of blokes chanted back, *Cocksy, Cocksy...*

...Cocksy is his name, sheep shagging is his game. Who's that twat... The chant trailed off as the two coppers got closer.

The WPC, whose nickname was Bellhead, pushed past me as she moved among the congregation gathered outside the church, spreading the gospel of *Ain't you got homes to go to?*

PC Cocks told the blokes at the front that they'd had their fun. Now it was time for everyone to sling their hooks. Some people were trying to sleep, he said.

Dennis said, 'Well, they shouldn't be such boring wankers, then, should they?'

Cocks had a few inches over Dennis. 'Don't make me show you up again, Winch,' he said, sneering down at him.

I never found out what the copper was referring to.

Sian squeezed next to Dennis and prodded Cocks in the chest. 'Why don't you just leave us alone? We're not breaking any laws, are we?'

Cocks placed a gloved hand on her shoulder and shoved her out of the way. 'Aren't your parents waiting up for you, you silly little girl?'

Sian wobbled on her stilettos and then tumbled backwards onto the pavement. There was outrage that Cocksy had crossed the line of laying his hands on a girl; as he attempted to bundle his way through the crowd, he was followed by a barrage of abuse. Nutty went one further and hawked up a gob full of phlegm, which he flobbed on the back of the copper's jacket.

Dennis sneaked up and caught Cocks with a corker of a punch from behind, then ducked down and slipped away to the edge of the crowd. A space cleared around the copper and a few people cheered, though a fat woman I recognised from the bakery said it was "bang out of order". I thought it was one back for all the pickets he'd picked on down the wharf. Though I knew Dennis wouldn't have seen it that way.

'Let the cunt die,' Wayne called out cynically, like if you knew what he knew you wouldn't show any sympathy.

Somebody was sympathetic enough to haul Cocks to his feet. He was holding his broken glasses and blinking and twitching like he was all confused. Bellhead was already on her radio spreading the news: *Mayday Mayday, slap, crackle and plod. All roads lead to Brightlingsea.* And with the scent of trouble and overtime in their snouts, it didn't take long for reinforcements to swarm into town.

It was below-freezing cold, and if I was honest, I wouldn't have minded being indoors. My snakebite coat was wearing thin, and I was left with only my new Harrington for protection. But there was no way I was going to be the first to leave, and I wasn't prepared to do what the Old Bill told me to.

A distorted PA system blasted out orders from the roof of one of the squad cars: MOVE AWAY FROM THE AREA IMMEDIATELY OR YOU WILL BE ARRESTED.

From where I was standing, next to Colin, I could see about ten coppers in a line across the pavement. They'd even brought a couple of meat wagons. I could hear their dogs yapping too, but I hadn't yet seen one in the flesh.

It reminded me of being at the picket in Wivenhoe, the way they'd turned up mob-handed, no expense spared. But they couldn't nick us all, could they? Not if we all stuck together.

I tried to start off the miners' chant: *Here we go, here we go, here we go…* Unfortunately, it didn't go anywhere.

Colin ducked down and shouted out: 'WAN-*KERS*.'

My turn: 'KILL THE BILL!'

People around me were laughing, but when I looked over, the coppers didn't appear to have taken any notice. I bobbed down again and shouted as loudly and clearly as I could. 'KILL THE FUCKING BILL!'

This time I clocked a copper looking in my direction. Well, my general direction, cos he couldn't have known for sure who it was. *It weren't me, officer,* I said, in my head. *Anyway, don't worry, it's only a slogan. It's not like I'm giving orders, is it? Otherwise, one of you would be getting killed by now.*

The copper started talking to his mate, then another two joined the huddle. *Are you going to kill us instead, are you? It wouldn't be the first time, would it? How many hundreds of people have died in your cells? And not one copper has ever got done. No wonder everybody fucking hates you. Scum.*

I shouted, 'SCUM.'

'Shit,' Colin said, 'here they come.'

We were backed against the church wall and there was nowhere to run.

I was snatched by the scruff of my Harrington, swung around and dragged out with my right arm up my back, and pinned to the bonnet of a squad car; my left arm was then pushed so far up my back that I felt it crack. Handcuffs were hooked on, snapped shut, and tightened to a sadistic notch. And then they dragged me over to another cop car and shoved me onto the backseat.

Colin's face pressed against my window like a pissed paparazzi. I heard his fist pounding on the roof of the squad car. 'Let my mate go, you fucking pricks. He ain't done nothing!'

Soon after that, he was nicked too.

Chapter Fourteen

On the second of January, Colchester Magistrates reconvened for a special hearing just for us: the Brightlingsea Fifteen. After leaving the court, I went to buy some fags from a newsagents on the High Street. That's when I saw the headline on the front page of the *Evening Gazette*: RIOT IN B'SEA. All our names and ages and the roads where we lived were printed underneath.

Seeing my name in the paper gave me a perverse thrill, like it was proof that I'd had the bottle to stick up to the Old Bill. Over the next few days, I also enjoyed the minor notoriety, especially at the factory where there was plenty of interest from people who weren't from our town. We'd put Brightlingsea on the public disorder map, and on BBC radio headlines during the middle of the night. When a mate of Nutty's heard about it at 4am in the nick, he smashed up his cell cos the news made him so excited and homesick. Apparently, we even made it into some of the national papers, under an umbrella story about New Year's Eve disturbances in small towns around the country. The trouble was blamed on *lager louts*, a new moral panic to describe young men without a political or social agenda, who got over-lairy after a too-many-pints bender. But I didn't think that description fitted me. I told myself I'd been having a go at the enemy – though admittedly, I could have done it more articulately. But the trouble with the trouble was that it could be whatever it suited anybody to be, including the authorities.

The *Gazette* may have sold more copies by calling it a riot, but we were actually charged with affray. Hooper, mine and Colin's solicitor, told us *affray* meant causing the public to fear for their safety. Making out we were a danger to normal people enabled the prosecution to insist that our bail conditions needed to be strict. The magistrates agreed: we were ordered not to leave our homes between 7pm and 7am, except to go to work. We were also banned from every pub in Brightlingsea and Thorrington. I thought Thorrington was a pointless add-on, cos it only had one pub and I'd heard it was rotten.

The case was adjourned for four weeks, and then another four weeks, and then again and again until June. During all that time, we were on bail with a curfew.

Two things surprised me in a good way about having to stay in: I hardly ever got bored, and, on the whole, I was less dissatisfied than I'd been before. Having my options restricted made my life simpler. For example, there was no point in thinking about leaving home until this was over. I doubted the court would even have agreed to bail me to a different residence where there were no adults to keep an eye on me. I also had something certain to look forward to: getting the court case out of my way.

I was more constructive during the curfew too. I started reading regularly again, including more kitchen sink classics. I also read some of the texts Verity was studying for English Lit, so we could talk about them together; not that she needed my help. I'd already studied *An Inspector Calls* at school, and I'd enjoyed it – it made a family of rich gits look like hypocrites – and I remembered Mr Griffiths telling me that Priestley was a socialist.

But I couldn't understand why Verity was so keen on *Jane Eyre*. When I said I wasn't sure if I agreed that Jane was a feminist pioneer, she accused me of not reading it carefully. Which was true, cos I started skimming about halfway through.

Reading also inspired me to finish my rhymes about factory life, and to start something new about curfew.

Mum was much less pissed off with me than I thought she'd be. It was partly cos she didn't trust the police and was therefore willing to believe they were exaggerating. 'And anyway,' she said, 'doesn't everybody shout at them?' She also knew that while I was in every evening, I was unlikely to be getting into more trouble. And she liked to see me getting stuck into a novel.

Mum was sceptical when I told her I was going to learn to cook, but within a fortnight, I'd knocked up a reasonable cauliflower cheese and a cracking Lancashire hotpot. After these delicious successes, I didn't want to stop. I got into making big stews, so that even when I was working the afternoon shift, Mum and Lucy could still eat it, and I'd have something to look forward to when I got home. Mum had made an effort when Tony was around, but she'd never been a good cook. I suppose, as a feminist, she'd always rather have been doing something more interesting, on principle, like transcribing the interviews she'd done with old ladies for her PhD.

I started to see why Colin enjoyed cooking; it took your mind off your worries for a while, and there was always a reward at the end. And I took comfort from the fact that one day, when I did manage to escape, at least I'd be able to feed myself properly.

Another bonus was that when I cooked, Mum would wash up. After dinner, we'd watch *Channel 4 News*, which happened to start at the same time as my curfew. Every day we heard: *According to figures from the National Coal Board...* and we braced ourselves to hear their version of how many miners had returned to work. Mondays were always the worst.

A scoreboard would appear on the screen, with figures for the day, the week, and the year so far. And then they showed a map with arrows pointing to the areas where there were pits open. But they made out a mine was working even if only one scab had gone back. Tony had told Mum that. She'd spoken to him on the phone over Christmas to thank him for his card. It was still sat on top of the gas fire now, at the start of February, the only one she hadn't chucked out, and the last trace of festivities to be found in our house. Tony had told Mum that he'd already decided he would never work down a pit again and was thinking of going back to college once the strike was over. He was lucky he wasn't as badly off as many miners, cos his wife still had her job at Tesco.

One evening, when the news had moved from South Yorkshire to South Africa, we heard a knock at the back door. It was Colin.

I could tell by the hurt in his eyes that he was on a downer, but he still managed to smirk when he clocked I was wearing pyjamas and a dressing gown at seven-thirty. He appeared to be kitted out head to foot in new clobber. All dressed up and nowhere to go.

Mum closed the living room door to keep the heat in. She said he was always welcome here whenever he wanted, but she pleaded with him to be careful. 'If the police catch you out, you could end up in prison.'

This gave Colin a chance to release some of his bottled-up anger. He didn't give a shit if he was caught; it was already like being locked up, being forced to stay in on his own every night.

Mum rubbed his shoulder and said she'd bet he wouldn't say no to a cup of tea. She'd always had a soft spot for Colin, cos he didn't have his own mum, and cos sometimes she came home from work, and he'd cleaned our house for something to do.

When she'd gone to the kitchen to put the kettle on, he told me he'd been feeling like his brain was going to explode. 'Normally when I get too many thoughts, I can go out for a walk, and it sorts my head out. This curfew is like fucking torture.'

'I know what you mean,' I said. But I didn't, not really. Mum was around most evenings, and even if Lucy only came out of her bedroom to make toast, at least I knew she was there. Also, when I had too many nagging worries cluttering my head, I could write some of them down in my diary. But Colin didn't know I kept a diary, and I wasn't going to give him advice I knew he wouldn't take.

At the start of March, the day after the miners went back to work, I received a hefty envelope in the post. It was a book of statements made by all the coppers, defendants, and witnesses in the New Year's Eve case. I rushed to see what the Old Bill had said about me, then read the whole thing from cover to cover, like it was an addictive piece of trash fiction. Well, it wasn't literature, and some bits were definitely made up. They accused me of lashing out and violently resisting arrest. I may have been pie-eyed that night, but I knew this was lies. They'd clearly been up to their old tricks, of collaborating and corroborating in the cop shop canteen, conspiring to ensure that their fabrications and exaggerations matched up.

And it wasn't only the cops who'd been telling tall stories. QC Karen Grimm from the factory, and her husband, Terry, had both claimed they saw Dennis knock Bellhead onto the pavement, while Wayne was chanting *KILL THE BILL*.

'That weren't even me, that was you,' Wayne said, turning round to glare at me in the back seat of the car on the way to work. I was tempted to suggest for a joke that I could go to the station and clarify the situation, but Wayne wasn't in the mood for jokes; he wanted revenge on the grasses.

When we got to the factory, we found out that Karen had asked to be moved to the opposite shift. I read through her statement more slowly that evening, and it struck me that some of it sounded like a copper speaking. There was no way Karen would have referred to Wayne as "the youth, Parkin". The "youth Parkin" who used to seduce her in his den. Karen and Terry also claimed to have witnessed a hell of a lot for people who were only passing by on their way home. I tried to get a second opinion from Mum, but she said she had more stimulating things to read about than the drunken behaviour of teenagers. Though another time she did tell me she'd overheard a posh woman in the lounge bar of the Cherry Tree saying that her neighbour's bin was set on fire during the *riot*. Mum couldn't resist asking her where she lived – which turned out to be nowhere near the High Street. I guessed people had their reasons to exaggerate the trouble, or play it down, but everyone in the town seemed keen to have a story to tell about it, even if most of them were bullshit. The only indisputable fact was that fifteen geezers had been nicked and charged.

'Such a charming and precocious girl,' Mum said, the day after Verity came to try my part-veggie shepherd's pie. 'If only you had more friends like that, Jarrod.' She kept encouraging me to invite her more often, but Verity usually only came round on Thursdays. Most of the time Mum went out for those evenings and told us she wanted to give us some privacy. I guessed we all knew what she really meant by *privacy*, but I did have to look up *precocious* in the dictionary.

Verity didn't seem to have any inhibitions about sex and her openness helped me to become more confident too. I wasn't embarrassed to buy condoms from the chemists, and I developed the boldness to ask her for a blow job, the same way she would tell me when she wanted me to go down on her. The difference was she could make me come, but despite all the practice I never managed to give her an orgasm that way. When she showed me how to make her climax with my fingers, rather than just sticking them inside her, I felt like she'd taught me one of the most important skills of my life. After that, I wanted to do it every time as part of our foreplay.

One evening, at the end of March, we were recovering from sex in our usual positions: I was sat with my knees up and my back against the headboard; Verity liked to lay side-on with her legs stretched out, dragging her toes back and forth across the yellow-painted woodchip. She'd done it many times since my party, and if you looked closely, you could see the grubby marks.

'I've got my plane ticket to America.'

I knew she had family in Boston, and she'd mentioned a couple of times that she'd like to visit them one day, but it still came as a shock.

I didn't say anything straight away. I could hear the old fan heater I'd dragged in from Mum's room and the crackle at the end of my Bob Marley LP.

'How long are you going for?'

'End of June 'til the third of September.'

'Oh.'

She slapped the inside of my naked thigh. 'What do you mean, *oh*, Jarrod? You should be excited for me.'

'I am. Of course, I am.'

'You don't sound it.'

'It's just that…' I almost said something lame, like, *What about us?* 'I'm going to really miss you, that's all.'

She grinned and reached between my legs and gently tugged my balls. 'You'll live.' Then she swung her legs down from the wall and stood up to get dressed.

I stared longingly at her freckly narrow back and her plump white bum and had an urge to grab her hand and pull her back on top of me. I also hoped for reassurance that this wasn't the beginning of the end of our close friendship.

'I've got to go. I promised my mum and dad I'd be back by nine.'

I sat on the edge of the bed and reached down to the carpet for my boxer shorts. 'I'll come with you.'

'You're not allowed to.' She reminded me about the curfew. As if I didn't remember.

'I don't give a fuck,' I snapped. It was one of the few times I really resented not being allowed out.

We were only a few doors down from mine when I reached out to hold her hand. She laughed at me, because we never held hands, but she didn't pull away. She told me once that couples over fourteen and under sixty looked ridiculous holding hands. I guessed I was feeling vulnerable, not least cos I was new to this curfew-breaking business.

It was a surprisingly mild night, and as I unzipped my bomber jacket, I wondered if winter was finally over. Neither of us spoke for what seemed like ages and then Verity said, 'What plans do you have for the summer then, Jarrod?'

I said I didn't know, I needed to get the court case out of my way first. But the way I said it sounded grumpy and defensive, like I thought she was trying to catch me out or rub it in about her plans. But what was the point in taking the risk of breaking the curfew if I was going to be like that? I wanted her to think I had ambitions and I needed to come up with something quickly. 'I've been thinking,' I said, 'after the contract has finished at the factory, I'd like to go to college.' I was exaggerating a little bit, cos I'd only been vaguely considering looking into the possibility of an English evening class at the Adult Education Centre.

She gripped my hand. '*Really?*'

'Yeah. All that talking about books with you has made me feel like studying Literature again, maybe eventually even writing a story.'

'Good for you, Jarrod. I reckon you're wasted in that factory.'

We were close to the bottom of Seaview Road, when car headlights appeared around the corner. I instinctively let go of Verity's hand and looked for somewhere to run to in case it was the coppers.

When she realised what was going on, Verity walked off like she was in a hurry.

The car drove slowly past me; it was only a kid I knew at junior school who'd passed his test already.

I ran to catch her up. 'Don't be like that.'

'I told you not to come out, didn't I, Jarrod?'

'But I wanted to walk you home.'

'Yeah, and I don't want anything to do with you getting in more trouble.'

From that night until she went, I saw less of Verity. She told me she'd promised her parents she would study really hard for her O-levels if they let her go to America. When I did see her, even sex was never quite the same. It took me longer to make her climax, and at first I thought I'd lost the knack. Was I exerting too much or not enough pressure with my clumsy fingers? When she opened her eyes and told me to stop, it was me who felt under pressure, but she said it was cos she couldn't concentrate. It had gone from being natural and magical, to feeling mechanical, like I was doing it to her, not something we were experiencing together.

At the end of April, after the curfew was relaxed to 10pm, me, Colin and Dennis would sometimes spend the evening down at Wayne's bedsit getting stoned.

One Sunday night, after we'd all had a hot knife, Wayne broke the news that his car was fucked. Truly fucked, beyond repair.

How are we going to get to work tomorrow, then?' I asked.

'You tell me.'

'I don't know.'

'Roy Francis is selling his Transit,' Wayne said. He left it hanging in the air for me or Colin to pick up on. But neither of us chose to take the hint.

He reminded us that he'd been giving us a lift to work for five months and hadn't asked for anything towards the tax and insurance. Now it was only fair that we all chipped in for another motor.

I looked at Colin, who was sat next to me on the grubby single mattress on the floor, then back to Wayne. 'You mean we'd be like co-owners, so we can drive it as well?'

Colin kicked my foot. 'You can't fucking drive.'

Trouble was, nor could he. Well, not legally. He'd had a few lessons with his dad until they'd fallen out over it, and a few more with an instructor, but as far I knew he still hadn't put in for his test.

'I'll teach you to drive, Bogue,' Dennis said.

'How much is the van?'

'A two-er,' Wayne said, 'fifty nicker each.' He reckoned it was a good deal though, cos it had plenty of tax left and six months on the MOT.

Colin was chewing his lips. He was usually quicker at detecting danger than me. I knew he'd be angry with himself that our plan to stop relying on Wayne and Dennis hadn't come off. And now we'd been put right on the spot.

Maybe it was cos I was looking at the situation after doing a hot knife, that I thought part-ownership in a van could be an asset in my life: a chance to learn to drive; the possibilities of new adventures; being able to get to work tomorrow morning.

'What about you, Colin?' Wayne asked. 'You ain't said much.'

Colin looked down at the mattress and blew out a spit bubble while he thought about it. But what choice did he have? What choice did we have? Once he'd sucked the bubble back in, he reluctantly nodded to go along with it.

'The only other thing,' Wayne said, 'is the insurance.'

Dennis looked at me, 'What about your old dear, Jal? She must have a clean license.'

'Yeah, probably. I don't think she's going to want to buy a van though.'

Dennis grinned at Wayne. 'She don't have to pay for the van, you plum. She can just put the insurance in her name and have Wayne down as a named driver. And any of us if we pass our test. Otherwise, it's going to cost us fortune'

'I can try,' I said. 'She might be up for it if she thinks I'm going to learn to drive.' I thought it was unlikely that Mum would agree. But I didn't want to be the one to put a spanner in the works.

Chapter Fifteen

One Thursday afternoon in June, we were lurking around the waiting area of the Magistrates Court in Colchester when our various solicitors came to tell us the news. The prosecution had offered a plea bargain: if we all pleaded guilty to the much less serious charge of 'obstructing a police officer in the execution of their duty', then they would drop the 'affray', and the case would be over that day. Most of us were given eighty quid fines, though Nutty and Roy Francis were sentenced to twenty-eight days suspended because they had previous as long as Nutty's arms.

Colin reckoned that now the curfew was over he was going to make sure he was never home before 10pm as a matter of principle; Dennis suggested we did a crawl of every pub in Brightlingsea to celebrate being allowed back in, even if it took us the whole weekend. The full crawl never happened, but on Friday we did go to a few.

On Saturday me and Colin got the train to London. He'd never been to the West End before and I was looking forward to showing him the bits I knew.

Colin was so full of plans it was like he'd been reborn. He'd been practicing his driving manoeuvres in the van and the following week was booked in for his test. If he passed, he would get a bank loan to buy a car of his own. He'd now given up working for Skully completely, so it was no longer feasible to ask him to front the money. We talked about going camping in Wales and to a music festival in Cornwall I'd read about in the NME. We both wanted to spend as much of the summer as possible away from Brightlingsea. After the summer, we would get a house up town; after the summer I would do an evening class at college; after the summer, I would find another job. But first, after six months on curfew, we were going to celebrate our freedom.

Oakbridge was close to the last stop on the Essex side of the Central Line, and I'd sneaked out a few times and taken the twenty-something stops up to Oxford Circus to join the gathering of mods on Carnaby Street. I took Colin there first because I knew from my trip with Verity at Christmas that a few shops had now opened selling the gear he was into: Lois, Pringle, Kappa, and Tacchini. After a couple of hours in and out of changing rooms, we'd both spent most of our money. I didn't know how much cash he had stashed in the front pockets of his Farahs, but I reckoned it was at least a hundred and fifty. He told me that Skully had owed him some wages. He must have been feeling flush cos he treated me to fish and chips and mushy peas in an Art Deco café in Soho where I knew that Paul Weller had once done an interview.

I wanted to look around all the record shops on Berwick Street, but Colin got itchy feet pretty quickly and said he'd come back in half an hour to find me. When he turned up about fifty minutes later his pockets were weighed down with 10ps. He was buzzing about an arcade he'd discovered which had a fruit machine he hadn't seen before called *Winsprint*. He told me the whole story about how it worked with the *holds* and the *nudges* and how he'd managed to win four jackpots on two different fruities. He'd also spotted a black geezer wearing a Kangol bucket hat like LL Cool J's on *Top of the Pops*, and now Colin was determined to get one. After trying about eight shops, he finally hit the jackpot again and bought a bright red hat which he wore straight away; I didn't see him take it off for the rest of the day. He even walked differently with it on, like he was trying to make himself taller.

By mid-afternoon we were completely spent out. We finished our day trip in a packed Soho Square, sitting on the grass near a footpath and watching a million different characters walk past. Colin realised what I already knew, that in the West End you could properly clock what people were wearing without being asked what you were staring at. We bought four cans of Red Stripe from an offie, and once we'd drunk them, Colin lay on his side and stared contentedly at the new Adidas Lendl Court trainers on his feet; eventually he fell asleep with his new hat pulled over his eyes to shield them from the sun shining down on us from a cloudless sky.

One of my favourite things about being in London was listening in to snippets of conversations and trying to pick up on new slang words and expressions. There were a couple of blokes with their tops off on the bench closest to us, smoking weed, and I overheard them talking about a geezer they knew who'd got hold of a load of *moody* perfume. At first, I assumed that *moody* meant nicked, until one of them said that the perfume bottles looked so *pukka* that nobody would be able to tell it was moody. That made me think that *moody* probably meant fake, but I decided I'd better wait until I was sure before starting to use it myself.

The best expression I heard came from an old cockney geezer we asked the way to Covent Garden. He said it was a *fair old trot*. After that, it became mine and Colin's catchphrase for the rest of the day.

On the tube back to Liverpool Street, I asked Colin what he liked most about London. He said there was so much going on that he didn't have time to think. He'd had enough of thinking when we were made to stay in. Colin didn't need to ask me that question, cos I'd been going on to him about London all day.

Whenever I was up there, I felt at home. And eventually I wanted to make it my home. I thought I knew how to behave, how to study people on the tube without them noticing, cos they were all in their own worlds too. London had never done me any harm. Nobody had ever started trouble with me, or cheated me, or tried to rope me into a burglary.

That evening we went to the Railway Tavern in Brightlingsea. Wayne and Dennis and a few others had got to know the new landlord after he'd turned a blind eye to them drinking in the public bar during the curfew.

We had a couple of games of doubles at pool – me and Colin against Wayne and Dennis. Afterwards, Wayne said he was bored and wanted to go to Colchester for a decent night out. It was true that the pub was dead, and Brightlingsea was a comedown after the buzz of London, but all the excitement had also left me knackered. It was our first weekend of freedom though, so I thought I should make the effort. For some reason Dennis was being moody – in the original sense of the word – and reckoned he didn't care if we went up town or not. Colin was keen to go. I reckon he was desperate to show off his new clobber to a wider audience. His bright red hat had shone in London, but in the back room of the Tavern, it stood out like a lantern.

On the way out of Brightlingsea in the van we saw PC Cocks driving towards us.

Dennis leaned across Colin to open the passenger window and shouted, *Who's that twat in the big black hat?* We all called back: *Cocksy, Cocksy…*

Then Wayne came up with a variation: *Who's that bitch who's a dirty snitch… Karen, Karen…*

We'd just finished laughing about that one when Dennis went, *Who's that twat in the crap red hat… Colin, Colin…* Wayne sniggered briefly, but none of us joined in the chanting.

Who's that twat in the crap red hat? This time Dennis tried to grab the Kangol from Colin's head.

Colin managed to slap him away. 'Fuck off, Snake. Don't touch what you can't afford.'

I'd only heard Greg use that nickname before.

Dennis grabbed Colin by the neck and held him against the passenger door. 'You can't take a joke you weirdo, that's your problem.' As he let Colin go, he scoffed, 'Well, *one* of your problems.'

'And you're fucking sound,' Colin said. 'You can always rely on Dennis.'

'Always rely on Dennis to let you down,' Wayne said, though he said it in a jokey way, like he was trying to lighten the mood.

'Where did you get the money for all that new gear anyway?' Dennis said. 'Don't tell me, from your fat nonce-case mate, Skully.'

Colin turned to stare out of the window. A couple of seconds later, he said, 'You think you know everything, don't you?'

'You two better fucking sort it out before we get up town,' Wayne said. Neither of them answered and he put on some music.

Once we'd been served our first pint in The Castle, Dennis asked Colin to come outside for a word. A few minutes later they came back laughing so I guessed it was all sorted. Later on, Dennis even admitted that he wouldn't mind having a hat like Colin's. Trouble was, he said, if he bought one and they wore them at the same time, they'd look like a right pair of wankers.

After the pubs had shut, we queued to get into a swanky nightclub called L'Aristos, but we weren't dressed smartly enough for the bow-tied bouncers.

We ended up at the kebab shop where at least they weren't fussy about who they let in. While we were queuing, Nutty and Roy turned up, and Wayne offered them a lift back to Brightlingsea.

A few minutes later, they'd all left with their doners, but I had to wait for my large shish to cook. I'd reasoned that as it was my first taste of post-curfew freedom, I may as well treat myself to the best thing on the menu.

A bloke behind me was ordering his doner; ordering being the right word. I don't know if it was all the lager, or having to hand over money to a foreigner, or some kind of kebab shop etiquette, like wiping your greasy hands on the wrapping paper instead of a serviette, but I didn't think there was any excuse not to say please and thank you. I wouldn't have dared tell him that though, cos he looked like he'd enjoy knocking someone's teeth out. I wouldn't have much use for a shish then.

I clocked myself in the mirrored tiles on the wall and got an urge to grin. I thought I'd better not though, cos you never knew who was watching; especially as another hungry pissed-up crew had just walked in. I took the chance of having another sneaky glance: I looked smart in the glass; freshly shorn crop, my best jeans and a brand-new Fred Perry top. I thought back to when we were in the Hole in the Wall a couple of hours earlier and a mod girl next to me at the bar said, *nice top, mate.* We got talking about music and London and were getting on blinding until one of her mates came over and said they were leaving. In just over a week's time, Verity would be flying to America; perhaps I should have asked Alison for her number. I was mulling this over when a sharp tug on my arm pulled me back to reality. It was Colin: 'Quick, Jarrod. We've got to get going.'

'I can't. My kebab will be ready in a sec.'

'*Come on*,' he hissed. You don't want to get left behind, do you?' And then he turned and steamed out of the shop without waiting for an answer.

I lingered by the door on the way out, hoping they'd notice me and call me back. Just the bread and meat would do, or even a bag of chips as a consolation.

I had to run down the road to catch up with Colin. 'I wish I'd ordered a doner now.'

'Serves you right for trying to be different.'

Said the man with the bright red hat. 'What's the big hurry for, anyway?'

He checked over his shoulder and then whispered, 'Nutty's stamped on some geezer's head and he ain't moving.'

We arrived at the car park before I'd had the chance to ask him what had happened. Dennis was waiting by the back doors to shut us in; Wayne was already revving the engine.

Once I'd clambered into the back of the van, I had to sit on a dirty blanket on the floor. Nutty had nicked my spot on the settee and Roy had plotted up in the front of his old van. Colin was next to me, perched on a wheel arch; opposite us was a stack of bricks we'd nicked on the way back from court. Wayne said they were Suffolk Reds and he knew someone who'd pay 60p each for them.

Up the front they were laughing about what had happened: Wayne joked that even if the geezer didn't drink, he was going to have a rotten headache in the morning; Nutty thought it served the *Paki cunt* right: he wouldn't be fucking mouthing off like that again, would he?

Not if he ain't moving. Though hopefully Colin was exaggerating, and they'd just given the poor bastard a bit of a kicking. I looked across at Colin now and noticed his foot was tapping really fast on the floor of the van like he didn't have any control over it.

Wayne whacked up the music and we pulled away. It was The Doors, 'Riders on the Storm'.

Colin got up a couple of times to look out of the back windows, but whoever was behind us, it wasn't the coppers, cos he didn't say anything when he sat down again. It seemed to be taking ages to get home and

118

my arse was getting cold and numb. It was all right for that lot up there, enjoying the luxury; Roy and Nutty were where me and Colin should be. It was only right, we were shareholders in the van, weren't we?

Nutty was kneeling on the settee, leaning into the gap in the front seats between Roy and Wayne, but I couldn't hear what they were talking about over the sound of 'Roadhouse Blues'. I liked the tune, and in my head, I was singing along, but I couldn't get the attack out of my mind. I gave Colin a nudge: 'What was the fight over then?'

'It wasn't a fucking fight,' he said. Then he hissed through gritted teeth that Nutty had shouted abuse at a couple of blokes on the other side of the street. When one of them said something back, Nutty and the others ran over and laid into them.

'What about you?'

'I ain't a cunt, Jarrod. I don't go around starting on people over nothing.' As he leaned forward and gobbed on the floor, he was shaking his head. 'There was no need to jump on him like that.'

I looked at the back of Nutty, who took up most of the settee. I reckoned he must have been at least eighteen stone. I said I hoped the bloke was all right. Colin didn't reply.

Eventually the van stopped, and Dennis came round to open the back doors. Roy was stood next to him, then Nutty clambered past me and Colin to join them. They each took a brick from the stack.

'We'll be back in a sec,' Dennis said.

Colin got up and jumped down from the van. As he looked back in the direction of where the others had gone, we heard the echoes of breaking glass, crashing into the stillness of the warm summer's night.

Chapter Sixteen

I didn't think to plan an alibi, beings as I hadn't done anything wrong. But after the six of us were nicked at dawn on Monday morning, I managed to snatch a word with Colin in the Clacton cop shop reception before we were banged up in separate cells. 'Tell them we were staying in at mine' I said, 'watching telly with my mum.' It didn't occur to me that they would go and see her to check out our story. I guess I wasn't thinking straight after my very rude awakening.

You only get one shot at an alibi, and after blowing mine in the first interview, with a badly thought-out lie, the only remaining way I could feasibly deny was not to tell them anything at all.

Halfway through the second interview, they started lying too. They were now claiming that the Grimms had been looking after a friend's baby on the night their windows were smashed. Shards of glass had landed in the baby's cot, they said. *What do you think of that?* I thought it was bullshit. Cos if it was true, they would have at least mentioned it during the first interview. I thought they were making stuff up and trying to call my bluff, to tempt me to stray from my mission of answering *No comment* to every one of their questions.

Afterwards, when they returned me to my cell, there was no longer any daylight coming through the small square of glass bricks above the bench at the back.

I lay down on the mattress, which was covered in blue thick shiny plastic, and stared up at the dirty dimmed light in the ceiling. It was ironic, cos after all those *No comments*, I'd never felt more like I needed to talk. It struck me that I would have done anything to get out of there except for the one thing that could have worked, which was to go on the record to tell them everything I knew. Aka, grassing.

It was now about 10pm, and they'd already had me in their custody for sixteen hours. During this time, I wasn't allowed a book or magazine to read, but they couldn't stop me from reading the graffiti scratched into the walls. Among the names I saw was Pat Magree, a nutter a couple of years above me at Oakbridge.

I guessed the coppers wanted me to stew about what I'd done. Or in my case, what I hadn't done. They told me the poor bloke Nutty jumped on was in a coma. *What do you think of that?* I was shocked. But I also thought that the one stroke of luck I'd had was not to have been there to witness it.

As I tried to get comfortable on the clammy mattress, I remembered what they'd said about the bullshit baby. It made me retch. You could get four years for this, the Detective Sergeant said.

By plotting with the Grimms and their friends to pretend there was a baby in the house, the cops weren't only trying to drop us in worse shit, they wanted to make out these were comparable crimes rather than one just being an attack on property. They weren't called *the law* for nothing; they were a law unto themselves. You only had to watch a few episodes of *Rough Justice* to realise that. As I lay there shivering, I even wished for a moment that I was one of those people who had faith in the police, like I occasionally wished I believed in God.

My experience with the New Year's Eve case had already shown me that the police weren't interested in telling or finding out the truth; that was the job of the courts if you were lucky. The cops' job was to 'solve' the case by any means necessary.

Instinctively, I stood up when I heard voices in the corridor. A pissed geezer was giving them grief as they locked him into a neighbouring cell. The bloke didn't give up shouting though and was making a racket by booting the door. I heard more coppers gathering in the corridor, then a few minutes later some muffled noises and then silence. I was pleased to have peace, but I wondered what they'd done to suddenly shut him up. Was it a quiet word, or a quiet kicking? I looked down at my mattress on the floor. That's what I'd heard they do, cover you with a mattress and then jump on you so the bruises don't show. I assumed, or hoped, that they wouldn't do it over nothing, but then hadn't I called them *scum* on New Year's Eve?

I didn't hear any movement or noises for what seemed like ages, and I lay back down and covered myself as much as the itchy grey blanket would allow. I was still dressed in all my clothes. It was like a desert in that cell, or what I'd read that a desert was like: sweltering in daylight and uncomfortably cold at night. I wondered if this was just the design, or was it a sign that they were manipulating the temperature as a form of mild torture? The smell in the cell was different at night too, like mildewy old shoes, or damp clothes, or the inside of a wet tent. By the afternoon it whiffed of unwashed bodies, particularly feet, but that was probably me.

Eventually my thoughts stopped going round and round and I was nearly ready for sleep. I decided they weren't going to come and beat me up. Why would they when they could fit me up instead? Now there was a comforting thought to put me to bed.

I slept for a while, at least I think I did, until I was woken by what sounded like an aeroplane going over my head. When it came by again, I was sure it touched my hair. I lashed out in the dim light, into thin air. It went silent, and then when I heard it again it was slightly quieter. I sat up and scanned the cell; the noise seemed to be coming from over by the steel toilet in the corner. Was it a fly? No. I worked out that it was the sound of a mosquito. How did it get in there when there were no openable windows? Eventually I slipped back into sleep, until it came again. Looking for blood. Just like the coppers.

Apart from passing paper plates with lukewarm food through the hatch of my cell, and a couple of plastic mugs of weak tea, for most of the next day, the Old Bill ignored me. And then, thirty-five hours after they'd first turned the key, Colin was moved into my cell. I didn't understand why, but I was grateful for the company.

An hour or two later, we received a visit from one of Hooper's assistants. His name was Marshall, and he came bearing cigarettes and hope. The fags were even more important than the hope, at least at first, cos we were roasting to the point of temporary insanity. The custody coppers had banned us all from smoking on the first night after Dennis burned his initials into his pillow. As he fed us Bensons and pretended to be our friend, Marshall persuaded me and Colin to tell him what really happened, though he didn't expect us to reveal any names. He said if he were going to be able to help us, we would need to be straight with him. Which we were, except Colin didn't admit that he'd witnessed the attack near the kebab shop. Marshall then convinced us that if we told the Old Bill we were in the van but didn't throw any bricks, then we couldn't get done for it. Simple as that, he reckoned: Marshall Law. He left soon afterwards, but promised he'd pop back later with some McDonalds. Which he never did, the slippery bastard. Colin persisted in shouting in vain through the cell hatch, *Marshall, Marshall, where's my fucking Big Mac?* Until a custody copper told him forcefully to shut his trap. I'd been most looking forward to the banana thick shake, cos my throat was raw from smoking so many Bensons in such a short time.

We didn't see Marshall again. When I thought about him a few weeks later, I couldn't even picture him. It reminded me of Inspector Goole in *An Inspector Calls*. Did he even exist? Well, I knew he wasn't a ghost or a ghoul, but was he even who he said he was? Or perhaps he'd never actually said he was from Hooper's firm at all, and we'd just assumed it.

Maybe it was like what happens at the end of the play, and if I'd phoned the solicitors' office once I'd been released, they would have said they'd never had a Marshall working there.

Could he have been a rogue duty solicitor who'd been put up by the Old Bill to trick us? And we'd been so blinded by the dazzle from the gold box he'd been flashing that we'd failed to listen carefully to what he was actually saying. I remember Mum telling me that one of the reasons why Chamberlain ended up appeasing Hitler, was because he was desperate to get out of the room for a fag and the Fuhrer hated smoking. I don't know if that's true, but it's scary to think what people might be persuaded to go along with when they're roasting. We went along with the Marshall Plan.

The next morning, which was Wednesday, me and Colin were

separated again, and I was taken to an interrogation room for my third and final interview. This time I applied Marshall Law and stuck to my truth. *I don't know what happened, I was waiting for my kebab. I was in the back of the van, but I didn't throw any bricks. I'm not prepared to tell you who I was with.*

Surprisingly, they didn't try too hard to get me to grass or go on that much about the geezer in a coma. They seemed almost satisfied to have got me for something. That evening I was charged with *criminal damage with intent to endanger life*. I didn't know if that *life* referred to the baby's; maybe not, because if none of us could have known it was there, how could *endangering* it have been the intention? Or was it Karen and Terry's lives? Or all three? It didn't seem appropriate to ask the cops though, cos the criminal damage had fuck all to do with me.

I didn't see Colin until Thursday when we were transferred by sweatbox to Colchester Magistrates Court and put in another cell together. We'd only been apart for twenty-eight hours, but he'd definitely gone downhill in that time. He had scabs all around his mouth, and his wedge haircut, which was usually immaculate, had finally gone haywire without access to hairspray. I reckoned he could have done with that red Kangol hat to hide his barnet. I also clocked there were cuts on his knuckles from where he'd been biting them. Or maybe he'd been punching the walls.

We sat a few feet away from each other on the bench at the back of the cell. He leaned forward to gob on the floor. 'We could go down for years, Jarrod.'

'What for? We're not guilty, aren't we?'

Colin made a noise he often did, like a cross between a scoff and a sneer. I call it a *sceer*. 'They don't give a shit about that, do they? We were there. That's all that matters to them.'

He turned to look at me. 'Anyway, whatever happens, I'm going to end up with a longer sentence than you.'

That sounded paranoid, even for him. 'What do you mean?'

'I've been charged with theft as well.'

'What *theft*?'

'Nicking money off of Skully.'

So that's how comes he had all that dough in London. 'How much?'

124

He shrugged. 'Fuck him. He deserves it.'

'Why?'

Colin opened his mouth, then changed his mind about answering me. He stood up and kicked a metal food tray instead, sending crinkle cut chips jumping into the air as it hit the wall with a clank. 'Fucking… SCUM.'

We heard a jangling of keys and were expecting to be told off. But when the door opened, Hooper walked in.

'How are you bearing up, chaps?'

Hooper was as tall as the door, and bald except for some bushy tufts at the sides. He sat down between us on the bench at the back of the cell and pinched the trousers of his pinstriped suit to lift them above his size-teen brogues, then gave a posh little cough to clear his throat.

'I've just been to see how the land lies on the other side,' he said, 'and unfortunately, they were adamant that you should both be remanded in custody. However,' he paused to unpeel the seal on a packet of SuperKings and offer us a fag, 'I've managed to persuade the prosecution to agree to one of you going to a bail hostel. That will be you, Jarrod, as you've got the extra charge, Colin.'

'What's a bail hostel?' I said.

'How long am I going to be on remand for?' Colin asked.

'Well, the current waiting time for Crown Court is six months, but really it rather depends on you, Colin. The theft charge is not the only sticking point, I'm afraid. The police are convinced you witnessed more than you have let on so far and are immovable from their position that unless you help them to secure a conviction, they will keep opposing any attempts to get you bail.'

'You mean if I don't grass, then I'm fucked?'

'Your words, not mine,' Hooper said, as he stood up to leave. 'But if you give them what they want, I should be able to secure you the same deal as Jarrod.' He splashed the ash again and told us he would come back and see us in a while.

I thought I had some idea of what it would be like to do bird, after all the stories I'd heard. But nobody had ever mentioned a bail hostel.

I guessed it was some sort of halfway house. Would I be halfway in, or halfway out? Hopefully, it meant that I'd be leaving the court by the front door, rather than being cuffed to a copper and shoved back into a sweatbox. I supposed that had to be progress. After eighty hours without fresh air, the prospect of being up there in the sunshine made my head throb. Then I had a coughing attack, which turned into a retch. Chain-smoking SuperKings on a nervous stomach probably wasn't a great idea; but I knew I couldn't rely on those bastards to give me a light.

'You're not going to throw up, are you? I know what you're like with your dodgy guts.'

'I just feel a bit rough.'

'You look fucking rough.'

Said the geezer with a load of cop shop slop stains on his top and scabs all over his gob.

He stopped pacing the cell for a moment and stared at me. 'There's no way I'm getting banged up on remand for six months cos of a nasty cunt like Nutty. Do you reckon any of those wankers would go down for us?'

'I don't know, I doubt it, but…Aren't you worried that Nutty could come after you?'

Colin sceered. 'Nutty ain't getting out for fucking donkey's years.'

'Or other people? Maybe you wouldn't be able to go back to Brightlingsea if you…'

'If I what? Spit it out, Jarrod. If I *grass,* you mean.'

'I didn't say that.'

'That's what you meant.'

Yes, that's what I meant.

'I'd be happy if I never saw Brightlingsea again. So, I'll be doing myself a favour, won't I? I can go to college in some town where nobody knows me and do a catering course. Then one day I'll have my own caff.'

'Yeah, but it's the principle as well though ain't it?'

He sceered again. 'Look where your fucking principles have got you.'

I shrugged. Principles were important, whatever and wherever they got you.

'You've always been a lucky bastard,' he said, surprising me with this change of attack.

I shrugged again, and this time I pulled a face. 'I don't feel very lucky, mate.'

'You know what I mean. You just *happened* to order a shish.'

And he just *happened* to stop me from getting it so he could drag me off towards trouble.

'I just fancied a change. Well, I ain't fucking psychic, am I?'

'How can you call it *grassing* when he's put the geezer in a coma over nothing?'

He was trying to put words in my mouth now, like the coppers would put words in his.

'Yeah, but...say you did tell them what they wanted to hear. How can you trust the Old Bill to let you get bail?'

'I don't trust them, you knob. I'm not a fucking idiot. But I trust Hooper... sort of. Anyway, what have I got to lose?'

He'd be losing a bit of respect from me for starters.

'You'd better not be thinking I'm a grass.'

'I didn't say anything.'

'You'd better fucking not.'

I didn't. And I still regret it. But I couldn't bring myself to say what he needed to hear: that I would have done the same thing if I was him. It was impossible to be certain what I would have done, but it wouldn't have hurt me to show my best mate some solidarity.

Part Two

Part Two.

Chapter Seventeen

There was a shrivelled old geezer lying on his back in the other bed. He was slowly sucking up all the clean air in the small room as he snored. Every few minutes, he made a squawking, retching noise which sounded like it came from deep in his gut; then he snorted and trembled like he was struggling to catch his breath and his snore missed a couple of beats.

As I undressed, the old man farted; a rippling raspberry that could have been funny in different circumstances, like if I was walking past him in the park – not sitting six feet away from his arse. I sniffed the air, hoping it would stink so I could make myself even more miserable and resentful. But the loud ones rarely do.

'You'll be sharing with Ted for the time being,' the hostel warden had said. I wondered now if *for the time being* meant until Ted snuffed it, because he sounded very unhealthy to me.

I was still awake when daylight began to seep through the flimsy curtains, and, for about the fifth time that night, I went to the bathroom for some cooler air and to drink from the basin tap. While I was sat on the toilet seat, slumped forward with my head in my hands, I coughed loudly, then coughed again. I could hear my dry nervous cough echoing off the bare walls. I drank more water and chucked some in my face. While looking at myself in the mirror, I had an anxious thought: people were identifiable by their cough. What if I'd disturbed some nutter, like Nutty, and I'd already made an enemy before they'd even met me?

*

Oliver, the duty warden who'd let me in last night, was manning the eye-level grill in the kitchen, turning the toast and controlling its distribution.

'Sleep well?'

I pressed my fist against my gob to stifle a cough, then forced a smile cos I couldn't ignore him.

'One slice or two?'

'Two.' Another stupid question.

There was a large container of cornflakes on the counter, but cereal often made me throw up in the mornings. It was different at night though; a big bowl of Frosties went down a treat with the munchies.

I clocked a padlock hanging open on the fridge door. Another freedom gone. I wouldn't be helping myself anymore.

As I carried my plate of toast through to the dining room, I noticed that everyone there was at least twenty years older than me. Ted was sat in the back row of small tables pushed together, with his arms folded, while a fat man with a blotchy face poured him a cup of tea. I turned away quickly, before Ted could spot me, and headed for a table in the opposite corner by the window. Outside in the small garden a younger bloke with cropped ginger hair was straining as he did curls with a gallon squash bottle filled with sand. Two pigeons were also watching him, from the top of the high wooden fence at the back.

I poured myself a cuppa from the pot on the table and wolfed down my first slice of toast and marmite. Mum was right about Mothers Pride; it doesn't really fill you up, especially the thin sliced. I thought about the last time I saw her, when the police were carting me away, very early on what looked like it was going to be a beautiful summer's day. She was stood in the porch in her dressing gown. She didn't look proud of me then.

There was nobody else sat in my row, so I tuned into a tasty conversation going on behind me: two of the residents were discussing an armed robber who'd recently published his autobiography.

I stole a glance backwards to check out the speaker. He wore a white vest, which showed off his furry back and impressively wide shoulders. He had long frizzy hair, like a mane.

'I'm telling you for a fact. Bobby Sparks was a *grass*.'

'Leave it out,' said the other bloke, as if the idea were preposterous.

'Listen. I shared a peter with one of his Co-ds in Wandsworth. Must have been about, what, '77...'

'Before my time,' said his tablemate, then took a loud slurp from his tea.

For a few seconds it seemed like he'd had the last word, then:

'Wandsworth was worse than Colditz in them days. You used to *pray* you never got sent there.'

'Oh, *come* on, Trev. Don't exaggerate.'

'What do you know, boy? You ain't even done any birdlime.'

A chair was scraped back, the sound made me wince, then the fat geezer who'd poured Ted's tea stood up.

'Will you *please* STOP talking about prisons.'

The room went quiet, and all eyes were on the fat man, including mine.

Trevor stood up and bared his palms in defence. 'I'm only telling a fucking story, Len.'

'YES. But why does it always have to be *those* sorts of stories?'

At nine o'clock, when the other residents had left, Oliver took me into the office and gave me a rundown of the bail hostel rules. We had to be out between nine and five thirty on weekdays unless we were ill; nobody from the outside world was allowed in; no smoking in the bedrooms; no alcohol on the premises or in the vicinity; no drunkenness. Most importantly of all: if for any, *any*, reason I arrived back after the 11pm curfew, the Old Bill would be called, and I'd be locked up in the cells for breach of bail.

As he was talking, I clocked a whiteboard on the wall behind him, which showed a list of all the hostel residents and the date of their next court appearance. There were fourteen of us, and my name was at the bottom. I was due back in front of the magistrates in four weeks for my case to be committed for trial at Crown Court.

Oliver sent me on my way with a photocopied piece of paper, which had a map showing the addresses of the dole office and the doctors. He told me I should register with both of them that day. And that was that: I was out on my ear, though at least I had something to do.

I took my Income Support form to the library to fill in. Once I'd finished, I had a look around at the books, and in particular the True Crime section, which was tucked away in a dark corner. I picked out one about the first Mafioso to turn informant. But the librarian told me I couldn't be a member unless I had proof of where I lived. I showed her my name and new address on the freshly completed dole form. It wasn't good enough. 'Why would I write that if I didn't live there?' She gave me a suspicious look down her nose like I was a criminal as well as a dole-ite. Maybe she'd recognised the address of the bail hostel.

The sky spat rain at me as I left the library, so I hurried to the new indoor shopping centre, with its gleaming escalators and yards of glass; it also had automatic doors, a fountain and security guards. I felt exposed under the bright lights as an outsider with no money to spend. I walked quickly around both floors without entering any shops; I couldn't wait to be out on the street again.

I scanned the faces of geezers walking through the precinct, looking for any I recognised from breakfast that morning. Where had they all gone? How would they be filling the four and three-quarter hours until they let us back in? Hanging around the town when you're young was one thing; but what if you were fifty-odd, like Len? What do you do then? Try and make a half last an hour and a half? Sit in the park until it rains? Hang around the station playing spot the train?

Hooper said he would try and get me bailed back home in four weeks' time. Until then, I would just have to find ways to get through it. Like searching out which was the best caff in Drewich.

They didn't make us go out at weekends. But on Saturday morning, after checking the rota and completing my allocated chore of sloppily mopping the kitchen and dining room floors, I decided to treat myself to a spliff. I still hadn't met anyone I could offer to share one with. I walked along the main road to the shopping parade to buy baccy, then sat on a nearby bench in the shade of the only tree around and rolled a single skinner.

Once the first couple of puffs had kicked in, I stared at the empty red phone box a few feet away and thought how easy it would be to give Verity a ring. I was supposed to meet her last week to say goodbye. She'd be flying to America tomorrow.

But what if one of her parents picked up the phone? They would have heard what had happened, or even read about it in the paper. When we were on the front of the *Gazette* after New Year's Eve, I'd kept the cutting; now I would be gutted and ashamed to be named on the same page as Nutty.

After a couple more puffs, another inner voice chipped in. *Maybe she doesn't want to hear from you. Maybe she's not interested in what you call the truth.* Maybe Colin was right, and the only truth that mattered was we were there.

It had been a week since I'd had a smoke and my tolerance for dope was low. By the time I'd finished the joint, I was too stoned to speak on the phone or even to know whether or not it was a good idea.

A group of geezers around my age walked past. They were eyeing me up suspiciously, cos they didn't recognise me. Who was this, sat on their patch in the best spot around? When they'd gone, I decided I didn't want to take any chances, so I got away from there sharpish. I found a shady bank in the park, smoked another joint and fell asleep on the grass.

Later, I went back to the hostel and sat in the lounge next to Len and flicked through his *Daily Mirror* until *Football Focus* came on. At one o'clock, Doug, the duty warden, let us into the kitchen in groups of three and supervised us making ourselves a cheese or corned beef sarnie. Only the wardens were allowed to chop the cheese: one slice each off a big catering block, and that's your lot; back in the fridge and back on with the padlock.

In the afternoon, there was an argument over whether the TV should be tuned to *Grandstand* or *World of Sport*. Len stomped off when one of his horses fell at the last hurdle.

Next to the lounge was the games room, which had a bar billiards table with missing pieces and a broken cue. Two blokes were playing chess across the coffee table, and I asked if they minded if I watched.

Playing chess had been something me and Adrian were able to do together cos you didn't need to talk or make eye contact. He even ran the chess club at junior school for a while and I played number one board for the team. It didn't earn me anything like the respect from the other kids that I'd have got if I was the best at football, or fighting, but it was something which proved I wasn't totally useless. I also practised hard cos I was determined to be better than Adrian. When I was twelve, I beat him for the first time, a few months before Mum and me moved out. After that I still played occasionally, but without the incentive of having somebody I really wanted to beat, I was never as focussed or hungry.

I could tell the blokes at the hostel were serious players, cos despite the distractions of the telly blaring from the lounge and other residents constantly passing through, they kept their eyes on the board and took their time with their moves. After they'd finished, I played the winner, an old geezer with a ponytail called Eric who'd studied the game in the nick.

I was rusty, and he beat me fairly quickly, but not too embarrassingly. More importantly, I'd enjoyed the challenge and the chance to escape from my worries. That night, I decided to make it a mission to get good at chess again during my residency at the bail hostel.

Chapter Eighteen

The Drewich branch of the National Association for the Care and Resettlement of Offenders (NACRO) was located on the fourth floor of an office block next to a roundabout on the edge of the town centre. I'd overhead Len saying they had cookery lessons on Thursday mornings, so I asked him for directions and headed straight there after we'd been kicked out. Hopefully this would be one day of the week that I wouldn't have to worry about lunch.

I was let in by a friendly Scottish woman called Linda and invited to help myself to a cup of tea. She also suggested I had a look around, but there wasn't a lot to see. I went over to read the whiteboard, which was on a stand in one corner of the open-plan room. It had a diagram showing different pathways that could be taken after being released from custody. I turned around quickly and went to make a cuppa, but they'd run out of teabags, and I had to make do with a mug of Happy Shopper chicory coffee and a couple of soft digestives.

Twenty minutes later, Len showed up. He was dabbing sweat from his brow with a piece of cheap bog roll and complaining about the lift being broken. When he clocked there was no sign of activity in the kitchen area yet, he said he was going to fetch the Monopoly set.

As he was slowly unpacking the box, I watched Paul, the ginger geezer with the squash bottle weights, sneak up and make him jump. Len didn't find it at all funny, but I suddenly felt more like my own age again. My spirits were lifted by the thought that I might not have to hang around on my own, or with old men, like Len. Paul had brought some energy into the room and now I wanted to be his friend.

'Fancy a game of Monopoly?'

After that day, I hung around with Paul until he left a few weeks later. He'd only recently been released from Feltham, so unlike me, he was halfway out rather than halfway in. I guessed that's why he was usually smiling.

One morning, we were walking through the market when I heard Paul mutter, 'Look out.' Trevor was sat at a picnic table outside the Robin Hood pub. He'd spotted us first and was waving us over.

'How's it going, boys? Fancy a bevy?'

Paul didn't hesitate. 'I can't Trev, I'm boracic.'

'Same here,' I said.

'Get us one back when you can afford it, chaps. I've had a little tickle as it happens.'

'Nice one, Trev, but I was just on me way to get some chips. I'm Hank Marvin.'

'I thought you just said you were skint, Paul.'

'Well, I ain't got enough for a beer, Trev, you know what it's like.'

If he did know what it was like, he'd forgotten. 'Siddown and stop whinging,' he ordered, 'and I'll get you some nuts.' Trevor looked at me and raised his eyebrows, then nodded at Paul. 'He's gone soft, ain't he? Turning down a sherbert.'

He came back from the bar with his hands around three pints, and two bags of salted KP between his teeth. The peanuts dropped onto the table like they'd been released from a vending machine. 'Get them down your neck.'

I guessed he meant the lager, but I ripped open a packet of peanuts first and tipped a pile into my palm.

Trevor wiped Guinness froth from his moustache. 'What's been happening back at the ranch then, boys?'

Paul shrugged. 'Not much, Trev, you know the apple.'

'Yeah. Fucking depressing. You're all right though, Paul, I don't hear you complaining... much. Jarrod don't say a lot but...what's up, Jarrod? You spotted some decent fanny, mate, or what?'

I'd been distracted by a waft of fried onions drifting over from the hot dog stall on the market. My guts were grumbling, despite the nuts, and there was still nearly five hours until dinner. I was going to have to shoplift something to tide me over. The wait for my first dole cheque was dragging on, and all the money I'd brought from home had now gone.

I picked up my once half an ounce of Golden Virginia and peeled back the foil. By the evening, I'd be down to dust. Perhaps I'd have more luck if I sniffed it like snuff. I rolled a fag, but my GV was so dry it burned down halfway after just one drag. Meanwhile, Trevor was delivering a lecture on personal finance and responsibility.

One of the many things that pissed him off was people moaning about being skint; there was plenty of money about, you just needed to use your initiative. Though if anybody was *really* struggling and he thought they were all right, then he'd be happy to help them out. I nodded along. Afterwards, he turned to me and said, 'If you ever need to borrow a few quid, Jarrod, Paul knows I'm always good for it.'

The committal proceedings were over in less than twenty minutes. Hooper applied for a variation to our bail conditions, which would have allowed us to live at home until the trial, but the prosecution convinced the magistrates there was a strong risk we'd try to interfere with witnesses. They couldn't resist going on about the glass that had supposedly got into a baby's cot and also reckoned the Grimms were living in fear of further attacks to their property. After hearing the prosecution laying it on thick with this vindictive bullshit, I was gutted and angry to be sent back to Drewich, but I wasn't exactly surprised. Colin was in a better position to take this in his stride. He'd been relieved to find out that the others were being dealt with separately; even more relieved when Hooper also told us that Nutty had changed his pleas to guilty.

After we left the court, Colin wanted to go to the new McDonalds on the other side of the High Street. It suited his tidy and impatient tendencies that the place was spotless, and the food was handed over almost immediately. We sat upstairs, and for the first time in my life I was blasted with chilly air from the ceiling while I was eating. It wasn't only the restaurant and thick shakes that were cold; I thought Colin would be celebrating now he didn't have to give evidence against Nutty in court, but when I brought it up, he froze, with a thin chip between his lips, then glared at me like I was shit-stirring. It was the same look he'd given me when he accused me of calling him a grass.

We finished our grub in silence, and afterwards I asked him about the regime at his bail hostel in Peterborough. He told me he was allowed to go to bed when he wanted, and he'd been staying up late watching sci-fi films and a series set in an Australian women's prison. We didn't speak about the prospect of us going to prison; the trial was still ages away. And anyway, Colin didn't want to talk about the case, or the others, or the past. He preferred to tell me about a warden he was friendly with at the hostel, who'd helped him to get a job as a trainee gardener with the council. I was jealous, I don't know why, cos the thought of trying to find a job in Drewich when I hadn't done anything to deserve to be sent there in the first place would have seemed like a double punishment to me. I suppose I was envious of Colin's sense of purpose and the fact that he had a few quid in his pocket. More than anything, it was cos he had a bedroom to himself.

He knew I was skint, and he paid for the meal, though he didn't offer to lend me any money. Eventually, I asked him for two quid, so I could at least buy a half ounce of baccy.

I had hoped we could hang around Colchester together for a few more hours, like old times, but Colin wanted to get back soon cos his hostel had arranged a five-a-side football match for that afternoon. I didn't have anything to look forward to.

We walked to the train station together and then separated to wait on opposite platforms. I paced up and down my side in the shade smoking a skinny rollie; Colin was sat on a bench with the sun on his face, blowing out smoke rings from a Benson. Until then, in all our years of friendship, it had always been him who couldn't stop moving. Maybe he was finally learning to relax; or was he conserving his energy for the football match? I was psyching myself up to bunk the train back and for another confrontation at the dole office.

*

I spent the next weekend going back and forth to the phone box with the same 10p coin. I wanted to persuade Mum to bail me out with a tenner until I got my giro. I finally got hold of her on Monday evening, but it was still bad timing. The coppers had just been round to hassle her about the van again. How had she managed to get herself dragged into this? How could she have been so fucking naïve as to let Dennis convince her to put the insurance in her name?

I had been hoping she could cheer me up, not the other way around. 'We didn't know what was going to happen though did we, Mum? I honestly thought I was going to learn to drive.'

'But you didn't, did you?'

'Yeah, but that's not the point.'

'Well, what is the point, then?'

'It's cos you always try to see the best in people, Mum. When you're like that, it's bound to lead to a bit of what you call *naivety*. But surely that's better than going around being suspicious of everybody?'

I didn't give her a chance to answer, cos I needed to get to the point of the call. 'Where have you been anyway? I've been trying to get hold of you.'

Her tone sounded a lot more upbeat, as she told me that she'd had a lovely weekend in Brighton with her new boyfriend, Bill. He was a Sociology lecturer, she said, but added that he also liked football and ska. Mum thought the two of us would get on really well.

It sounded promising, but when she gave me the chance to speak, I explained the situation: I had been doing everything I could to get my dole money sorted, but it had all been in vain, cos now they were claiming that my claim had been mislaid.

Mum listened without interrupting, but when she spoke again, she was more guarded. 'How much do you need to tide you over?'

'Twenty quid?' I bid, with the lack of confidence of a novice haggler.

I was surprised that she agreed straight away to send me a score *this time*, but she reminded me she was also struggling to get by. She asked me what support was available at the hostel. Couldn't the wardens help me to find a job? Or at least a course, or some training?

I didn't want to muddy the waters by telling her about NACRO, or the fact that a couple of the geezers at the hostel had jobs. 'You're joking, Mum. They chuck us out on the streets all day and that's it.'

'So how do they expect you to fill your time?'

It was a good question. But I didn't have the answer.

'Well, surely if you're going to be there for months on end, you may as well try to do *something* constructive.'

By Friday, the money still hadn't turned up. I went back to the phone box another five times, until I finally caught Mum in at nine in the evening.

'Are you *sure* it hasn't arrived?'

'Course I'm sure. I wouldn't lie about it.' Though she obviously thought that was a possibility. Otherwise, she wouldn't have asked me.

'I sent it First Class on Tuesday morning. It should have got there on Wednesday.'

'But it didn't though, Mum. Did you send it by registered post?'

The line went quiet for a second, then, 'When do you suppose I've got time to go to the post office?'

I was startled by a banging on the phone box door. One of the junkies I'd seen hanging around earlier had returned to call his dealer. I raised my hand like I'd be out in the minute, then turned my back on him.

'Is there any way you could send another tenner? If the other letter turns up, I promise I'll give it back.'

'I don't think I've got a spare ten pounds to give you, Jarrod.'

As she reeled off a list of her financial commitments, I was distracted by a second junkie, peering in the phone box through one of the dirty windows.

I reckoned I'd had a little insight into what it would be like to be one of them; a desperado who would come up with any old crap to try and con his mum out of cash. Worse than that, I couldn't detect anything in her voice which made me think she'd relent.

She was still lecturing me when the pips went. 'I've got to go, Mum. I've run out of coins.'

The following day, I went to the Robin Hood to find Trevor. He was sat at the same picnic table which he'd joked was his office. This time he was in a hurry and stuck to the facts: he could lend me a score for thirty back. If it took me more than seven days, then he'd add on a tenner a week after that. He also wanted my Walkman as surety.

Chapter Nineteen

Despite not having created or written anything for ages, when I found out NACRO were going to hold Creative Writing classes, I didn't hesitate. I also hoped there were going to be biscuits.

The teacher was a geezer in his late twenties who wore a Fred Perry polo and a gold sleeper earring. When Carl told us that writing had helped him to turn his life around, I wondered if this was code for having spent time in the nick. Or maybe he meant that writing had saved him from that. He didn't let slip many personal details, but he did reveal that he'd studied for a master's degree in Creative Writing and had a novel about to be published.

At the start of the first class, he said that we all had stories to tell, and any of us could learn to tell them well. It was the significant details that made them convincing, he said. Specificity was the key, even if it wasn't easy to pronounce it properly.

Over the next four weekly sessions, Carl would teach us about the basic elements of storytelling, and we would try out a few of the exercises he'd found useful. On the fourth and final week, anybody who felt comfortable to could read out their work. It didn't have to be fiction: it could be an anecdote or a memory, or even a poem.

At break time, I knew for sure that Carl was one of us when he brought out the McVitie's Chocolate Digestives and Jaffa Cakes and Tetley Tea that he'd bought with his own money. I reckoned he must have known what it was like to be hungry. Maybe he was also aware that his course had replaced the cookery classes after the government cut NACRO's funding by 40 per cent. I'd been playing Monopoly with Len when Linda told us the news; he smashed his fist down on the table, scattering hotels and houses all over the carpet. 'But it's *always* been cooking on Thursdays!'

There were only five of us in the Creative Writing classes: Len, me, an ex-heroin addict called Mickey, Karen, who claimed to have had a story published in *Woman's Own*, and Martin, a new geezer from the hostel who spent most of the time doodling. Though he wasn't shy when it came to helping himself to biscuits.

I needed something to write about. Maybe I could find a way to explore my truth. I was stuck in Drewich for something I didn't do. But I'd learned from being collared at the hostel by blokes who were desperate to tell someone about their cases that I wasn't the only one who thought I was innocent. And I didn't want to write something that could sound whiny and depressing.

Carl helped me to realise that although I hadn't written down any stories since leaving school, I'd still been enjoying telling anecdotes. I also remembered how much I used to love spinning out jokes. I wasn't really bothered if they didn't end up being that funny, as long as there was potential in the build-up. All I needed was the punchline, then I could work backwards to give the joke an extended remix and make it my own. I relished the anticipation in people's faces as they waited for the payoff, even if I knew they probably wouldn't find it worth waiting for, and they would moan and groan if it turned out I'd given a radical overhaul to one they'd heard before. I wasn't intending to write a shaggy dog story though, but I did want to try and make people laugh, even if the subject was serious.

Inspiration struck while I was stuck in the DHSS, attempting yet again to chase up my claim. As I listened to my guts gurgling and grumbling, it occurred to me that I was literally hungry for my jam roll money, and this gave me the title which started me off. Mislaid/delayed/ not been paid/we've lost your form I'm afraid/ provided the rhymes for the first few lines I came up with. And then I borrowed a pen from a geezer who was doing a crossword and scribbled them down in the front of the library book I'd brought with me. I added to and honed the poem in my head when I was in bed, or on my solo walks into town.

After the break on our final week, when we had the opportunity to read out our work, my stomach was stuffed with biscuits and fluttering with nerves. But I didn't have any fear - in fact, I was the first one to volunteer. I hadn't told anybody what I was writing about, but now the words were bursting to come out. I'd been fucked around so much by the dole, I'd begun to think that my claim had been cursed. But by transforming that torment and frustration into verse, I could reclaim and retain some pride. Even though I knew in my guts that poetry couldn't save me from going hungry, never mind save me from Trevor.

Hungry for my Jam Roll

I made a decision to launch a new mission
And go and take the fight to the opposition.
Again.
Last time they claimed that my claim was mislaid;
Therefore, my jam roll would be unfortunately delayed.
That was three weeks ago.
And still no sign of the jolly green giro.
This time I brought a book, I wasn't a fool.
You need a distraction when you're in for the long haul.
I heard the indication system click and looked up,
Number eight, I wish you luck.
I was still on page six when my number clicked,
It was me reading slowly, *they* hadn't got quick.
I put the book back into my carrier bag and bowled up to the booth.
Phew, at least it wasn't the robot from last time who'd said I was rude.
This one looked quite friendly, like she wasn't already riled,
If I'd have made the first move, she might even have smiled.
In the booth was a fixed plastic stool for me to park my arse.
I explained my situation through the toughened plate glass:
Bail hostel resident, almost two months without cash.
Claims, counters, and counterclaims.
Please help me, I'm desperate. But I'm not looking for someone to blame.

She stood up purposefully when she didn't want to know any more,
My story was only a variation of what she'd heard many times before.
All she really needed from me was my name.
She already had a face she could put to the claim.

Was it a good sign she was taking her time?
Probably not.
But whatever happened, I knew that I mustn't kick off.
I was escorted out by the bouncers the other week.
For having the audacity not to turn the other cheek.

She came back with news that I found hard to believe.
I'm afraid that your claim has not been received.
I dropped onto the counter in shock,
Like I'd been shot.
Luckily, my forehead was cushioned by my wrist,
And I resisted the temptation to lash out with my fists.
I lifted my head a few inches and bellowed out, *NOOO.*
That made me feel a tiny bit better, so I had another go.
NOOO.
Then I shut my eyes and waited for the bouncers to run and have
their fun.
But the tug of the thug didn't come.

A fellow dole boy called out, *Come on then, mate.*
As if I should just roll over and accept my fate:
Walk away empty-handed after a three-hour wait.
I looked up slowly. Hang on, was she smirking?
Surely that ain't allowed when you're supposed to be working.
You're going to have to make a new claim I'm afraid.
I don't know why it's them who are always afraid.
It was me who owed money to a loan shark and hadn't been paid.
A bouncer was watching on, arms folded, but eager to pounce.
I told myself not to give him any reasons to bounce.
If I took these new forms and re-joined the queue,

She would try her best to see what she could do.

But she couldn't promise anything.

If everything was in order, I should receive a payment very soon.

Maybe even as soon as this afternoon.

But she couldn't promise anything.

There were a couple of seconds of silence once I'd finished, and then they all clapped. Len even leant over and slapped me on the back. He'd written about what he would do if he could take his kids out for the day, though I never knew why he wasn't allowed to see them in the first place.

I hung around afterwards to speak to Carl and we walked together to the train station. He told me I'd reminded him of his signing on days, and my style and delivery was like some of the ranting poets he'd seen performing at punk gigs. I knew the type of poets he meant, cos I'd seen some too, Verity had introduced me to others from her brother's record collection. I said to Carl that I reckoned a rant was an appropriate medium for the scenario I was describing. Though I doubt I used the word medium. It was only a short walk to the station, and I hadn't planned to use it to talk about my predicament. I wanted to thank Carl for the course and to let him know that although I'd always liked rhyming, he'd inspired me to write something down for the first time in a while.

He mumbled some encouraging noises, but he didn't say much, so I carried on thinking aloud. I was surprised to hear myself confess that writing, the actual physical act of pressing the words onto paper, was hard for me. Now and again, I'd tried to keep a diary, but my hand couldn't keep up with my thoughts. Even *I* found my handwriting a job to decipher, and that was why I'd stumbled on a couple of lines earlier.

Carl listened, and that would have been enough. But then he asked me if I'd been given any help at school.

I laughed bitterly. 'At school, they just thought I was clumsy and cack-handed.' Though admittedly, it was only Adrian who used to actually call me *cack-handed*.

'I've got a mate who's a teacher,' Carl said, 'and he told me about a pupil of his with a similar problem. He's been diagnosed with something called dyspraxia.'

148

'I've heard of dyslexia.'

'This is more to do with co-ordination, I think. Difficulties with handwriting is apparently one of the main signs.'

'*Dyspraxia.*' I tried out the word aloud. The idea that I might have something; an explanation for how I was, was a revelation to me. 'Do you know how the kid found out that he had it?'

Carl wasn't sure of the details, but he promised to speak to his mate and then phone me at the hostel to let me know.

We were almost at the station. 'Keep writing, Jarrod,' he told me. 'If you build up a few poems, who knows what might happen?'

I told him I would try. Then we shook hands and said goodbye.

As I walked away, back towards the town centre, my head felt giddy, and I was light on my feet. I craved the comfort of something hot to eat. A sausage roll, or a pie. Instead, I sat on a park bench and got by on the high of reading the poem aloud a couple more times.

That evening, I phoned Mum and told her about Carl and the classes and the poem; more than anything, I wanted to say something to her about dyspraxia. She hadn't heard of it either and offered to do some research, though she claimed to have always known I had something. At junior school, they thought I might have 'clumsy child syndrome', she said, but I was never diagnosed officially. *Clumsy child syndrome* slipped off her tongue easily, like it was a disorder that everybody had heard of. It was a new one on me. But she did spark off a memory of being tested for something at junior school, though they probably didn't tell me what it was called. I had to cut along straight lines with scissors, which I still struggle to do, and to copy odd shapes and colour them in.

I told this to Mum on the phone. 'But I don't remember anything about handwriting.'

'You always found it difficult. Adrian wanted to force you to write right-handed, but I said no.'

I wished she'd said no to him more often.

She tried to be more positive by reminding me I'd also had my IQ tested at junior school. 'It was *really* high, Jarrod. You were such a bright boy. Wasn't it 143?'

'I don't know, Mum,' I said, though I was pretty sure that was the figure she'd always told me. I'd found out the hard way that telling people at junior school, or any school, you had a high IQ was asking for abuse and ridicule. Cos it wasn't like they gave you a certificate to prove it; and it didn't get you anywhere, not like passing the 11-plus.

Mum told me she'd love to hear the poem one day. I still had it in my pocket, but it was getting dark, and there were a couple of noisy girls waiting impatiently outside the phone box.

That night I had trouble sleeping, cos my mind was buzzing with what I'd heard. I went to put some music on my Walkman, so I didn't have to listen to Ted; then I remembered I'd needed to give it to Trevor. I pressed the covers hard against my ear instead and tried to travel back in my head as far as I could. When did I first realise I was a clumsy child? It was probably from tripping over my shoelaces. But then, surely that was only cos I couldn't tie them properly in the first place.

Another memory came back to me, from when we were still living in Tollesbury. A woman came to take me out of school one morning and we went to Colchester Castle. I would have been six. She was friendly and asked me lots of questions and bought me my first Twix. But I couldn't recall seeing her again.

Chapter Twenty

I was five metres from the exit when I felt a strong hold on my left arm. I swung around sharply and clocked a stocky geezer who was only a couple of years older than me; he was wearing a garish brown and gold uniform like he'd stepped out of American TV. He attempted to capitalise on his element of surprise by trying to swiftly drag me back inside. As I pulled my arm the other way, we eyeballed each other. His face was set in a determined scowl, like he wanted to show me he was tough, but I also detected a pleading in his eyes, like he was asking me to *please* just accept my lot; go with him calmly back into the shop, and admit that *okay* it had been a fair cop.

I needed to get away more than he needed his job; if necessary, I would prove it, by punching him in the gob.

I wrenched aggressively to release my arm from his grip. This time I heard a loud rip. The arm of my long sleeve tee shirt had torn away from the seam, and now he was holding my sleeve and not me. My reaction to this was quicker than his. I dropped the carrier bag and chipped. I sprinted through the precinct, weaving between old ladies with trollies, fists clenched ready to lash out at vigilantes. I ran past the sorting office on the corner and across the main road to the little park. When I glanced back for the first time, there was no sign of the guard.

I sat on a bench and recovered my breath, then realised I must look conspicuous, if not ridiculous, with only one arm on my tee shirt. I took it off and ripped the other arm away from the seam with my teeth. Then a thought struck me: if my tee shirt had been of better quality, I would probably be trapped in some dingy office at Londis, while the security watched over me like he'd caught a prize fish. By tomorrow night I'd most likely be in HMP Norwich, doing porridge; on remand until the trial for two pasties and a poxy scotch egg. I looked down at my left leg and watched it trembling. I had to stop it: not just the trembling, but the thieving.

Londis had been perfect up until now, because it didn't have any signs warning of operating store detectives, like Sainsbury's or Tesco but it was big enough not to feel guilty. They called it a *convenience* store, and conveniently there was a blind spot behind the rack with the boxes of crisps where I'd disappear to conceal my scotch eggs or sausage rolls, or those ham-and-cheese pastry slices which weren't as nice cold, but... they did slip under your armpit, or into a carrier bag, a treat. I'd never seen a security guard at Londis before, and I'd been regularly nicking lunch from their convenient store for weeks. I'd not even clocked the vacancies advertised in the Job Centre. But then, I hadn't been looking very hard.

A cold breeze forced me to fold my arms across my chest. Soon I was shivering in my self-inflicted vest. My guts were complaining more than usual, cos they were convinced I had lunch in the bag. The stress of the chase had left me gasping for a smoke. For the first time, I considered lowering myself to pick up butts from the park; rolling a rollie so rough it would make my throat bark. But I didn't even have any Rizlas.

The only option I could think of was to go back to the shark. I got up from the bench and strode across the grass, then followed the main road, which encircled the town centre, until I eventually reached the Robin Hood.

Trevor wasn't interested in hearing about when my giro might finally turn up; he didn't even ask what had happened to my top, but he did agree to lend me another tenner for fifteen back. He reminded me, though I didn't need to be told, that my debt to him was now ninety-five quid. This was roughly two-thirds of the jam roll I was owed. It would be the last time though, Trevor warned. If I didn't pay him back soon, he would have to think of other ways I could settle the debt.

*

I was fretting about this threat on Sunday night while pretending to watch the film Oliver had let us stay up to see. I did try a few times to follow the plot, but when I came back from throwing up with anxiety, the actress I fancied had been fatally shot. After that, I could only think about my money worries.

What had Trevor meant by *other ways* I could pay? After ten weeks of relentless incompetence, how could I trust that the dole would give me my jam roll anytime soon? It was tormenting me that however hard I tried to solve the situation, it was ultimately out of my hands. I was stuck between Trevor and the DHSS; caught in a rut between a thug and a sad place.

I was snapped out of my misery when the bell above the lounge door vibrated loudly. All eyes turned from the telly to the clock. Its thick hands were splayed in a V-sign, either side of the hour, as the second hand steadily climbed the face. In less than ten seconds, it would be five past eleven.

Suddenly the movie was no longer the priority. Someone was on the way to the cells.

An argument flared up about which resident hadn't come back yet, so Eric, my chess mate, went to peek into the office to settle it.

When he came back his face was alive, like this was the most exciting thing that had happened in a long time. 'Trevor's doing his bleeding *nut*! He'll be looking at a murder charge soon. Never mind breach of bail.'

Richard, the longest-serving resident, said that Trevor would go in front of the beak in the morning, and if the hostel didn't want him back, then he'd be remanded in custody until his trial.

Len said, 'But it's *only five minutes...*'

'Don't matter if its two minutes,' Eric said, smiling, 'if it's after eleven, then they've got ya.'

The lounge door swung open violently, and Trevor loomed over the room. I hoped he wouldn't look at me, but he didn't look at anybody, he headed straight for the back door. When he'd yanked it open and stepped outside, a light came on automatically and illuminated the yard.

Ted managed to lift himself out of his favourite armchair to get a better view. Everyone else was now standing too. From behind, I watched Trevor put his best foot forward and lick the middle fingers of each hand in turn.

Oliver came into the lounge as Trevor's feet disappeared over the fence. The warden's face froze for a second in shock, like he'd popped into a shop and come out to find that his car had been nicked. Then he turned and bolted back to the office.

I think it was Eric who started the cheering, but I was quick to join in. There were clearly a few of us who owed money to Trevor, though I'd never heard anybody say anything. To me it would have felt like a form of grassing; in no version of my poem had I ever mentioned him by name.

I placed one foot on the coffee table and was about to step up the celebrations by banging on the ceiling when I remembered that Trevor was holding my Walkman.

I slipped out of the lounge and legged it upstairs to his room. Smelling his heavy black leather jacket hanging in the wardrobe gave me a shiver, like Trevor being Trevor, he'd find a way to reappear. I paused to listen for footsteps on the landing, then went through the drawers of his locker. In the bottom one, I clocked two Sony Walkmans, an electric razor and a smart-looking watch. I grabbed my red Walkman and ran to my room, then stuffed it under my mattress.

I don't know why. I was only reclaiming what was mine.

Chapter Twenty-One

Once my giro eventually arrived, I was able to concentrate on other things. Like trying to find out more about dyspraxia. I started by asking at the library, but they didn't have any books on the subject. All I could find was a definition in a medical dictionary which mentioned *motor learning difficulties*. I didn't know what that meant, but it was true that whenever I'd attempted to drive the van, I'd had problems even getting it started.

I went to see the GP, but he didn't want to know. He looked at me like I'd come to the wrong place, like why was I bothering *him* with *this* on a Monday morning?

It took Carl a few weeks to phone, but he'd spoken to his teacher mate who said I would need to see an educational psychologist if I wanted to get tested for dyspraxia. To get an appointment with an educational psychologist, I would need to be in education. And there was no chance of that for the moment. I was stuck, cos I couldn't make plans. My future was out of my hands.

The next day, after I'd come back from town, Oliver handed me a letter. Somehow, I knew it was from Colin, without recognising his writing. Well, I'd have struggled to recognise his writing cos I don't think I'd ever seen him write anything, definitely not a letter. I'd written to him from Oakbridge a few times, but he'd never replied.

I took his letter to the bog to open cos it made me nervous. What could possibly have motivated Colin to put pen to paper?

How's it going? he said, then got straight to the point. He had something top secret to tell me. The world was going to end in November 1993. He'd found out from doing the Ouija. He didn't tell me who he'd been communicating with – as if it really mattered – but he knew that only a few small islands were going to survive. Luckily, he also knew where they were. I'd better not tell anybody, but as his best mate, he thought it was only right that he should tell me.

Better save up, he said. Save up with what? Anyway, 1993 was still eight years away. Surely it would have been more timely if he'd checked with the Ouija if we were going to get a *guilty*.

The more I thought about it though, the more I hoped it was supposed to be a joke. But then, I'd never known Colin to joke about ghosts or Ouija or UFOs, or anything else that was out of this world. In the end I decided not to reply. I didn't want to have to acknowledge his prediction by either taking the piss or taking it seriously, and it wasn't like he'd had much else to say.

After receiving Carl's call and Colin's letter, I was a bit down for a couple of days, but I perked up when I worked out that Ted's case had finally come up at Crown. He'd arrived for breakfast all spruced and wearing his best worsted suit; then a couple of days later he didn't arrive back in the evening. I never found out what he was accused of, or even whether he'd been convicted.

My next roommate was Mick. He was twenty-one, and like Trevor, he spent as little time as possible at the hostel. Unlike Trevor, he didn't speak much. Sometimes he made me feel like an annoying little brother, like when I asked him what he was going to do that day or where he'd been, and he never gave a straight answer. Though he did reveal to me that he'd grown up in Drewich before moving to Billericay, so he didn't have to worry about walking the streets and going hungry; he had places to go and people to see, and two nans to feed him whenever he needed.

One morning, I was setting off for yet another three-mile trudge into town on my own when Mick surprised me by calling me back. He was on his way to get some hash. I could come along for a smoke if I wanted.

He took me to a flat on the Bluebells Estate, a maze of narrow covered walkways and low-rise blocks which seemed designed to put strangers off. I followed closely behind Mick as he bowled along with his head held high and his left arm swinging at his side, proud that this was his old manor, and nobody round here would touch him. It was a freakishly hot day for late September, and the sun felt like it was going to singe my hair whenever we broke cover from the maze.

The geezer who opened the door was only about the same age as Mick, but he already had his own council flat. I didn't even know that was possible.

'He's safe,' Mick said, as I was given a suspicious onceover.

His mate peeked out to check if there was anybody about, then dropped one of his pumped-up arms from the door frame to let us in. Mick nodded for me to go through to the lounge while they talked out of my range in the kitchen.

I sat on the shiny two-seater settee and looked around the small room, which smelt faintly of emulsion. After a minute or so, I shifted my arse to the edge of the cushion cos I couldn't relax. It didn't feel natural to be in a home again after spending almost three months in the bail hostel. It wasn't like I knew the geezer; I was only there cos of Mick. A twinge of yearning ached in my chest when I clocked the hi-fi with a record on the turntable and thought about my stack of LPs. How long would it be before I could enjoy the simple pleasure of choosing a record to play? My own home seemed like a long way away.

To distract myself from gloom, I tried to see the room differently; as Carl might, as a writer. What sort of character would have a framed picture of Bruce Lee above the telly? And a weights bench and a bar that looked way too heavy for me? Who would have a large wooden chest on the floor by the door, with a keyhole below the lid?

By the time the other two came back into the room, I was gawping at the fish tank, which somehow made me think about food. Mick passed me a mug of instant coffee, then rolled a strong joint with sticky black hash, which caught in my throat before I'd even been offered a puff.

'What's it like living in the nonce-house, then?'

'Bunch of plums and whinging old cunts most of them,' Mick said. 'A couple of the wardens could do with getting their snotters twatted an' all.'

His mate said it would do his head in to have to live in a gaff where there were nonce cases and not know who was and who wasn't. At least in the jailhouse, the beasts were kept separate.

Mick had already told me, though I wished he hadn't, that the locals thought the hostel was crawling with rapists and child molesters. Since then, I'd become more wary about being seen coming and going and had kept an eye out for potential vigilantes. I used to feel reassured that the hostel looked inconspicuous from the outside. There weren't any signs: it was just two ordinary semis on the end of a new town estate that had been knocked into one and extended.

Mick and his mate didn't say much else in front of me. The way they communicated, with looks and gestures, reminded me of how Wayne and Dennis used to make me feel left out of their business.

'Come on then,' Mick said, once he'd stubbed out another strong joint and we'd finished our coffee. I didn't really want to leave. Although our host hadn't exactly been friendly to me, I'd began to get cosy sunk into his settee.

They exchanged a glance I couldn't read, then Mick said, 'Have a butcher's at this.'

His mate squatted to unlock the chest. When he'd lifted the lid, I stood up and peered in. I saw nunchucks and knuckledusters and coshes and crowbars and baseball bats and other weapons I hadn't seen before, all piled on top of each other.

I don't know if it was shock or cos I was really stoned, but I had what I guessed was an out of body experience. It was me, watching me, gazing at the weapons like I was a character in a short story, and this was the twist at the end.

I didn't know what to say, and I couldn't face looking at Mick straight away, so I carried on staring at the armoury until his mate closed the chest. It seemed to take him ages.

I was still in a daze on the way back through the maze, when it occurred to me that I only had a very rough idea of where I'd been. I didn't even know the bloke's name.

We walked in silence, until I asked, 'What's he got all that for?'

'He's holding it for the ICF.' Mick glanced at me to check that I was clued up about who they were.

I hesitated, then, 'I support Chelsea,' I said, to prove that I knew this was hooligan related. 'Though I've never been... I've never been involved in all that.'

Mick never invited me to go anywhere again. It still puzzles me why they showed me the contents of the chest. Had Mick wanted me to get the message that I wasn't like them, so then maybe I'd stop bugging him? Or perhaps they both needed to show off. What was the meaning or moral of this story? Maybe it wasn't necessary to have one.

Chapter Twenty-Two

We had our first monthly residents meeting in October. It was an innovation from the new hostel manager, Mary.

Were there any improvements that we'd like to see?

Somebody mentioned a new telly. The old one had started distorting whenever the volume was adjusted.

Mary made a note, but I didn't hold out much hope. As far as I could tell, nothing had been replaced in that place for years.

I thought that if she really wanted to listen, then a long-standing resident, like me, should be the one to tell her some hostel truths. Maybe then she could try to put herself in our shoes. Our shoes that were worn down from trudging the streets all day. I'd had to use my first giro to buy some new trainers, cos the old ones were letting in rain.

'It's hard,' I said, 'having to leave here every weekday still feeling hungry. Especially when you don't have any money for lunch. It's counter-productive too, cos when your guts are grumbling, it's difficult to think about anything else.'

Mary swallowed, and I clocked her Adam's apple bob. I'd gone straight to the meat and potatoes of our plight and her job. She mumbled something about a very tight budget, but said she was open to suggestions.

'How about a boiled egg for breakfast?' The previous afternoon I'd seen a character eating one on *EastEnders* and it made me hungry and homesick.

Mary glanced at Oliver, who looked sour, but remained tight-lipped. He knew it was the wardens who'd be lumbered with boiling and distributing the eggs. Mary suggested the option of one each, twice a week.

It sounded like a result to me. But where was the harm in trying to push it to three? To my surprise, she agreed, at least in principle.

'What about better bread?' Len said.

Oliver narrowed his eyes at him, like this was getting ridiculous, like, where did we think we were staying, the Ritz? 'What's wrong with the bread, Len? It's a popular brand, Mothers Pride.'

Len started to answer, but was getting flustered, so I chipped in to help him out. 'It doesn't fill you up,' I said, looking from Oliver to Mary, 'why do we have to have the thin sliced?'

Mary looked to Oliver for an explanation, but for all his faults, I doubt it had been his decision. 'Well, we do provide cereal as well,' he said.

'Some people can't drink milk,' I said. Oliver and I both knew there was a resident a couple of months ago who'd claimed to have that allergy. It didn't get him an extra slice of toast though.

'What do you suggest?' Mary asked.

'Well, if we could have the medium, or even the thick sliced, it would make life much more bearable for us when we have to skip lunch.'

'Thick sliced,' said Eric, gruffly. Other people leaned forward and made supportive noises. I'm sure I also heard someone's stomach rumbling.

'Okay,' Mary said, 'let me look into this and I will see what I can do.'

The next day, she gave the green light to green and white packets of Mothers Pride thick sliced.

That night, I told Mum, cos I knew she'd be proud of me. She hated the idea that we should have to go hungry. 'Giving you thin sliced bread is so mean and petty.'

I thought of Tony too, cos I knew he would have approved. He'd told me that people like us had always had to fight to get a decent crust.

After the meeting, I was approached by a new resident, Geoff, who'd arrived the previous evening. He congratulated me on the victory and made me laugh by calling me *comrade*. He seemed all right, so I offered to show him the score with the dole and the doctors. I noticed he spoke clearly and without any identifiable accent. His clothes were smart, but a bit grubby, and his leather deck shoes looked worse for too much wear and were definitely in need of a polish.

In the afternoon, he bought me a couple of pints. We'd been getting on well, talking about music and football and even a bit of politics. The first personal question he'd asked me was which team I supported. Once we were settled in the pub, it wasn't long before he found a way to bring up his case. He'd already told me he was a Spurs fan, and now he was saying he'd been charged with affray, for fighting with Real Madrid hooligans after the home game of their UEFA cup tie last season. Drips of lager ran down his chin as he described the ruck, which he said took place on the stairs and southbound platform of White Hart Lane station. I thought back to what Carl had said about it being the details that made a story convincing, but Geoff's story was stuffed with detail, even about how the Spanish fans were dressed; he told it well but somehow I weren't convinced. It wasn't only that he was well-spoken and clever and claimed to be left wing; I just had a strong hunch that the things he was describing hadn't happened to him. But I seemed to encourage him, cos I was nodding a lot and looking him in the eye.

By the middle of Geoff's second week, we were both skint again and could only raise enough shrapnel between us for a 6p cup of tea each at the Unemployed Workers Centre after we'd walked into town. As we were talking about what to do next, a builder in his thirties came over and asked us if we wanted a couple of days work. Instinctively I didn't, but before I could think of an excuse, Geoff had agreed on behalf of us both. His only concern was if he could borrow a top, cos he didn't want to mess up his Lacoste-a-lot jumper.

Geoff was taller and older than me, and probably came across like he had more confidence and common sense, so Dean, the roofer, got him up on the roof to help strip off the front face. My job was to carry down the busted slates and ripped up old felt and wrenched-off battens with nails sticking out and chuck it all on the back of the truck. I hadn't been up a ladder since robbing the vicarage, but I soon got into the swing of it. It was a fresh and bright early autumn day, and I had to admit it felt good to be doing something different even if that *different* meant putting in a shift.

Going up and down the ladder was thirsty work, and after an hour or so I began to fantasise that the owner of the house would soon pop out with a tray of teas and a decent selection of biscuits. But the only signs of life in that posh cul-de-sac, which was in a village about twenty minutes' drive from Drewich, were a ginger cat sleeping in next door's bay window and some lively magpies rattling in a tree across the road.

Dean said that we would stop for lunch once the front of the roof had been completely stripped off. By the time he finally came back from the bakers it was gone half two, but at least he didn't scrimp: he'd brought us hot meat pies and crusty rolls and crisps and cold drinks. It was the best weekday lunch I'd had in months.

We only stopped for long enough to wolf down the lot, then Dean and Geoff cracked on with refelting and battening, and I was charged with lugging the new slates up the ladder and stacking them in rows on the platform of scaffold boards.

A sudden blast of cold air made the hairs on my arms stand on end. Three seconds later, large plops of rain were running down the dirty dried sweat on my forehead. I ducked into the porch, until I heard Dean shouting, then the rattle of metal as he pegged it down the ladder.

'I said, "Get the fucking tarp off the truck".'

I didn't have a Danny La Rue what he was on about, and he glared at me like I was a simpleton. I followed him over to the truck, and while he leant in the back to grab the plastic sheet, I looked up and saw a huge dark cloud looming directly above us. The sky had sucked all the colour from the street, and I had the impression we were in a black and white film, though I wasn't optimistic it would have a happy ending.

Dean led the way up the ladder, dragging one end of the plastic sheet over his shoulder. I was a few rungs behind, holding up the bottom as it splattered with rain. At the top, he and Geoff crawled slowly up the rafters with their end of the sheet while I squatted in front of the guttering at the edge of the roof, trying to keep my end down as the rain blew into my face.

It didn't take long in that position before cramp started attacking the back of my thighs. I lifted the plastic sheet slightly as I straightened my legs and a powerful gust of wind sneaked underneath and blew it up into a tent. For a couple of seconds, it blocked my view of the other two, but I could hear Dean yelling curses over the frantic flapping of plastic. I tried in a panic to yank the sheet back down with all my strength, but as I was doing so, my left trainer skidded across a piece of wet slate, and I landed hard on my side on the scaffold boards.

'YOU USELESS WANKER. WHAT THE FUCK'S WRONG WITH YOU?'

I scrambled to my knees, still gripping the sheet, and through clenched teeth I hissed that I'd slipped, and it wasn't my fault.

'It's your fucking job to keep the deck clean!'

I was tempted to let go of the sheet and cut my losses. But I didn't really know where I was, or if there were any buses. I also wanted what he owed me. Instead, I pulled the plastic down so tightly that I saw my fingers turn white. It helped that I was pretending Dean was underneath and he was suffocating.

He dropped us off on the main road by our estate and said he'd pick us up there the next day at nine.

At 9.30 we were still waiting as the traffic sped past us.

'Something must have happened,' I said.

'Yeah. He's ripped us off.'

Geoff pulled out the scrap of paper Dean had given him, and we rushed to the phone box.

He came out shaking his head. It was a fake number.

I half-expected Geoff to explode into a temper and show me a sign of the hoolie he'd claimed to be. Instead, he said, 'At least I hung on to his jumper.'

All I had to show for the day's graft was a four-inch nail in my pocket. I swore that I was going to stick it under the front wheel of Dean's truck if I ever saw it parked up. I even kept the nail in my jacket for a while, but those pick-up trucks all looked the same to me.

Geoff did belatedly try to expand on my theme, and said he'd love to get his hands on Dean. But as far as I was concerned, he'd already shown me his true colours. He may have been to some Spurs matches, but I was now convinced that he'd never been into fighting for kicks.

When he left the hostel a couple of weeks later, Geoff gave me Dean's jumper. I only wore it when all my other tops were in the wash. Obviously, I didn't like to be reminded of being cheated, but there was also a black stain on the back that wouldn't come off. It was a work jumper, and I didn't intend to do a day's graft in Drewich again.

Chapter Twenty-Three

There weren't any fireworks at the hostel, but on Bonfire Night I was promoted to one of the three single rooms on the top floor. Soon afterwards, I caught a cold, and decided I would take the opportunity to spend a few days in my new bed. I also wanted to get stuck into reading *Papillon*.

I'd worked out from hearing the experiences of other residents that I would need to exaggerate my cold to 'flu', otherwise the wardens would find me light chores to do to make me earn my thick slice of Mothers Pride and can of Heinz soup.

I thought I'd earned a rest. I'd been traipsing the streets every weekday for four months. I was now literally sick of the sight of them. My cold had come at a good time too, cos the forecast said there were storms on the way. I didn't even own a coat that could cope.

Since I'd been allowed to be a member of the library, I'd mostly chosen to read the autobiographies of criminals and gangsters. I took comfort from reading about people who'd been in worse shit than me, and I particularly enjoyed the escapades of escapees: McVicar, Jimmy Boyle and now Pappi; geezers who'd managed to get one over the system, at least for a while.

During this period, when I didn't have any mates in the hostel, the best part of the day was playing chess against Oliver in the evenings when he was on duty. Since finally getting the better of Eric, who'd now left, it had become my mission to beat Oliver. On the last afternoon of my 'flu', we were playing in the lounge, and I clocked his beady eyes darting from side to side as his brain went into overdrive. It was five past five, and he was calculating the quickest way to finish me off before the other residents started to arrive at half-past. I'd come to detest losing to him, but this time I preferred that he killed me quickly, because it wouldn't look good if I was clocked playing chess with a warden in the warm when the others came back cold and hungry and drenched by the storm.

I moved my knight backwards to protect my rook, but Oliver was at least one move ahead of me. He snatched one of my pawns from the board triumphantly and gripped it in his fist before sliding his bishop onto the empty square. In my book, that made him a bad sport. Even Adrian had better chess manners than him. I'd been taught that the civilised way to take, was to remove an opponent's piece only as you are replacing it with yours.

Oliver was staring at me impatiently, waiting for me to make my next move, when at quarter past five, the bell in the lounge vibrated and he had to go through and answer the door.

As I assessed the board and my losing position, I was distracted by the scent of toad in the hole, floating in from the kitchen. It was a weekly highlight of hostel life, and I reckon I'd had it about eighteen times, since I'd taken up my abode in that hole.

A few minutes later, Oliver led him in. 'This is Patrick, our new resident.'

As I looked over, the geezer was looking me over; then he came closer and shook my shoulder.

'It is you, ain't it?' he said. '*BROOKY*, you wanker. What the fuck are you doing here?'

'Ahem,' Oliver coughed to assert his authority. He glared at Pat, then at me. 'Let's save the reunions for later, shall we?'

'Hang on, mate. I ain't seen this fucking geezer in years.'

'Don't ever call me *mate*. I'm not your *mate*.'

I bet he'd prefer *mate* to Socio-Ollie-bollocks, which is the nickname Trevor gave him.

When the warden turned to continue the tour, Pat made an exaggerated wanking gesture behind his back. 'Laters, Brooky,' he said, all pleased with himself, then walked away giggling, leaving me stunned in the wake of his whirlwind.

I looked back at the chess board, but the game was now history. My first thought was: what a pity I couldn't tell Henry. I hadn't had any contact with him since the trip. And even if I did, it would only make sense if I could tell him the whole story. But what a great punchline it would be: you'll never guess who walked in...*fucking Pat Magree.*

I hadn't seen Pat since Pat left our school, though I'd read his name carved into a cell wall in Clacton cop shop. PAT MAGREE – CHELSEA FC. He was always a handful at school, and I knew he was bound to be an unusual suspect in the hostel... but still, the place could do with livening up a bit. And at least now I had somebody to knock about with.

On the way to town the next morning, I offered to show Pat the ropes. But when I mentioned going to the doctors, he cracked up in disbelief, like I was making a joke.

'Leave it out, there's nothing wrong with me, mush.'

'You've only got to register, Pat, it don't take long.'

But what I'd said hadn't registered with him.

'Remember the sickbay, eh? I used to heat my forehead up on the radiator and go down there for a little holiday.' He put on a sickly voice, *'Matron, Matron, I think I'm coming down with the lurgy...*I used to love it, mush: dossing in bed all day watching telly and having a sneaky J Arthur.' He sniggered like a dalek, then shoved me with both hands.

'Do you miss school, Pat?'

'Piss off,' he mocked, but I'd clocked that he'd hesitated. 'I bet you do, don't ya, Brooky?'

'I wanted to leave so bad I got expelled.'

That got him going. 'You naughty fucker, what for?'

I'd been looking forward to telling him this. Even Pat Magree had made it to the end of his CSEs. But I also wanted to make sure I had his attention - if that was possible. 'I'll tell you another time, it's a long story.'

'Might as well tell me now, mush. I fancy stopping for a snout anyway.'

We sat on the wall outside a low-rise block on the Winsmead Estate and Pat lit his last JPS.

'Remember the village near the school?'

168

'Course I do...Ryford.'

'Bryford,' I said. 'Ryford was that English teacher who was really into CND, weren't he?' Mr Ryford had taken a minibus of seniors to see The Jam at the Rainbow, but I was too young to go. When Pat went on the ponce for a pair of mod shoes, the trail inevitably led to me. Pat always stuck up for me after that. And we both supported Chelsea.

'We used to go wandering around down the village in the middle of the night, then one time we found a full barrel of beer and –'

'Shh,' Pat said. 'Listen.'

A phone was ringing in one of the flats behind us. Pat cocked his head and tuned in intently. When it rang off, he took a last pull on his fag and passed it to me. By the time I'd stood up and turned around, he already had his hands inside the bathroom window and was hauling himself up onto the sill. He pushed his head inside, then wriggled the rest of his body through; the last I saw of him was the soles of his trainers, sliding down the obscured glass. 'Fucking nutter,' I muttered, but I couldn't help being in awe of his guts.

I checked up and down the street to see if anybody was coming; maybe they'd only popped out to the corner shop. Then I looked over to the flats opposite: perhaps one of the neighbours had seen us and was watching me now; what if someone had called the Old Bill already? How was I supposed to warn him, without bringing it on top for myself?

I couldn't see anyone around, and the only sound I could hear was my breathing and a builder banging in the distance. My heart was pounding like a hammer in my chest. 'For fuck's sake,' I hissed, 'I could do without this.' I decided to count slowly to twenty; if Pat wasn't back after that, I'd be off.

When I'd got to fourteen, I heard a soft click as the front door closed and Pat bowled out like he lived there. As he passed me, he stepped up his pace.

I followed a few metres behind him, trying to act normal.

At the end of the road, he ran off and I got lost. I'd only ever cut through the middle of the Winsmead before; it weren't really a place anyone would want to explore. When I finally caught up with Pat, he was doubled-over in front of a row of lock-up garages, laughing and panting.

'Fucking hell. You could have warned me!'

He tapped his head. 'You've got to be on the ball in this game, Brooky.'

'What d'you get, then?'

'That's for me to know, ain't it?'

I clenched my teeth with indignation. After dragging me into this unawares, it was only fair that he gave me a share. 'I was keeping bogeye, weren't I?'

He laughed, then took up a boxer's stance and punched my arm. 'You don't think I'd hold out on you, Brooky, me old mate?'

I grinned. 'Don't call me *mate*. I'm not your *mate*.'

He sniggered at my joke, then dipped into the pockets of his jumbo cords. 'Here-yah, look,' he said, as he shielded his right hand with his left.

In his palm were at least three gold rings and a tangle of necklaces or bracelets.

That night in bed I thought about what had happened. I knew it was out of order to steal from people's houses, unless they were rich, but I was still fascinated by what he did and how he really didn't seem to give a fuck about the consequences. He was like one of the criminals I'd been reading about; in the early chapters, when they were just starting out.

Maybe *I* didn't give enough of a fuck about the consequences either. And that's why I was willing to repeat the mistake of the vicarage; except this time, if I was caught, I'd definitely be going to nick. I told myself that like Dennis, Pat had sprung the burglary on me, and if he'd bothered to ask me, I would have said no. I'd also promised myself that I was going to stay out of trouble after Londis, but then, perhaps it was normal to have a little blip. I would tell him tomorrow that I wasn't up for anymore. He didn't need to prove to me that he was up for anything.

A couple of days later we were walking past the sorting office, when Pat said he needed to check if his parcel had arrived.

It was the first time he'd mentioned it. 'What parcel?'

I followed him inside and there was no one in sight. Then Pat jumped the counter. In five seconds flat, he was back with a mail sack, and we ran across the main road to the same little park where I'd legged it from Londis.

Pat tipped the contents of the bag on the grass.

'Right, Brooky, let's do this properly. The thing to look out for is cards.'

He was already on his knees, between the back of a park bench and some trees.

I checked nobody was watching and I joined him. 'What, birthday cards?'

He pulled a face like I had to be kidding.

'You get money in birthday cards, don't you?'

'I don't.'

'I do. Well, I used to.'

'All right, birthday boy. You look for your cards and I'll look for mine.'

Pat sorted through letters like a postie on speed, but it was me who scored the cash to buy us a feed.

Have a wonderful birthday, Dearest George.

All Our Love,

Nana and Granddad Blyth

I folded the crisp fiver and stuffed it in my jeans.

'I told you, didn't I, Pat?'

But Pat wasn't listening. He'd just struck gold too. 'YES! American Express. That'll do nicely, Brooky. I know a geezer who'll give me fifty quid for that.'

'Fifty quid?'

'You heard, mush. Let's chip.'

He'd better share some of that fifty with me. Well, by rights he should give me a pony. 'What about this lot?'

'They can deliver 'em when they find 'em, can't they?'

'What about our fingerprints though?'

'*Leave it out.* The Old Bill can't be bothered with that, mush. Anyway, they're supposed to be looking after the letters, ain't they? That's why they make us buy stamps.'

'I heard that nicking mail was like nicking off the Queen.'

'Bollocks. You fucking worry too much.'

Well, Pat didn't worry about anything, so that balanced things out a bit. Though as long as we didn't get caught, I didn't think I really gave a shit.

And then, I don't know what came over me; I picked up George's *'I AM 10'* badge and chucked it under a tree.

I knew it wasn't right. It had happened to me. But when my score went missing, I'd assumed it was a bent postie.

The next day, Pat went to Clacton to sell the tom. When he came back, he gave me a tenner and a silver bracelet and said he hadn't been able to find the geezer who bought credit cards. I wasn't sure whether I believed him, but I knew that if I asked him to prove it, he would act all offended and then refuse to show me the card even if he still had it. *You don't think I'd hold out on you, Brooky?* Well, I wouldn't put it past you... One of the things I'd learned from my dealings with Dennis and Wayne was that those who took the initiative also knew how to take advantage. Like when they told me they couldn't get anything for the vicar's bow and arrow and all I could do was accept it.

Now he had some cash, Pat wanted us to go and see Chelsea vs West Ham on Saturday. I was nervous about what chaos he could cause in the capital and reluctant to blow a massive hole in my fortnightly jam roll, but I couldn't resist the lure of the Blues and a day out in London.

A packed tube train released us at Fulham Broadway and hundreds of Chelsea boys piled onto the platform: *ChelSEA* doof, doof doof... *ChelSEA*...doof, doof doof. *ChelSEA*...

The Met provided a welcoming committee outside to funnel us towards the ground. We were hemmed in by horses; the smell of their fresh shit battling with stale fat from stacked-up burgers. I clocked a line of meat wagons across the road; cop-dogs getting excited; the whiff of hot dogs and ketchup was enticing but definitely too pricey.

'Wear yer colours,' an old boy called, as we reached a row of stalls: pendants, badges, scarfs, tee-shirts, bobble hats, ski hats ... Pat didn't want me to stop, but I wanted a pin-badge like he'd got, displaying the lion and staff of the club crest. As I handed over a quid, a chant started behind us: *We are the famous, the famous Chelsea. We are the famous, the famous Chelsea.* I stuffed the badge and change into my pocket and raised my hands above my head to clap along with the rhythm.

A tout popped up outside the chip shop: 'Tickets for the game. I'll buy any spare.'

'How much?' Pat asked.

'Fifteens.'

'Where?'

'Shed.'

'I'll give you a score for two.'

'Don't waste my time, chief.'

'Come on, it ain't long 'til kick-off.'

'I know, so fuck off and stop wasting my time.'

Pat dismissed the tout with the back of his hand, and we walked away. 'They'll be plenty more up by the Shed,' he said. 'We might even bump into someone I know.'

We didn't though. We didn't even get as far as the Shed. The coppers were blocking the road up ahead. Typical Old Bill, deliberately ruining the fun for everyone as usual.

And then we heard:

ICF...ICF...ICF...ICF...

'It's the Ice Cream Firm,' Pat said. 'They must have all got off at Earls Court.'

'What are we going to do?'

He looked at me like it was obvious. 'Come on, Brooky. Let's go and have it.'

'Have what?' I asked, but he'd already gone.

While Pat was pushing to try and steam in, I was trying my hardest to squeeze out. As the weight of untold bodies pressed against me, I had a flashback to the chest in Mick's mate's flat: knuckle dusters, nunchucks and baseball bats.

I spotted an open gateway that led to one of the stands. I didn't know what I would do when I got there, but at least I'd be out of the crush. I managed to slip out of the crowd and was leant against the wall behind the West Stand gates when a roar went up inside the stadium. It was loud enough to briefly drown out the commotion on the street.

Someone shouted: 'Who needs a ticket?'

'YEP.' My hand shot up automatically and he was standing right in front of me.

'Come on then, mate.'

'How much?' I started to rummage in my jeans' pockets, though I knew I had about sixteen quid.

The bloke tugged my arm. 'Quick, come on. We'll sort that out later, son.'

We bustled our way through to the turnstiles: a geezer in his forties whose mate hadn't turned up, and me, whose so-called mate had fucked off to get stuck into a ruck. I couldn't believe my luck.

Sunday was one of our boiled egg days, and I took mine with my toast and a pot of tea for the table and sat by the window looking out into the yard. A robin was bobbing about on the concrete with a morsel hanging out of its mouth.

It was now mid-November, but I could feel some warmth from the sun reflecting through the large windows, and I noticed the way it glinted and twinkled on the Formica tables. It was the first time I could remember being on my own in the dining room and a rare moment of silence in the hostel. I enjoyed the sound of the clean smack as I whacked the top of my egg with the back of my spoon. My mood lifted further as I removed the shell lid and saw a gooey yellow yolk that was perfect for dipping. I couldn't have timed it better myself. I cut my first slice of toast into soldiers, something I would have been self-conscious about doing in front of the others, then dunked a squaddie headfirst into the yolk.

A few minutes later, I was scraping out the last of the white onto my final soldier when I heard muffled voices, then footsteps upstairs in the corridor. I wondered if one of them was Pat. My shoulders stiffened, as I imagined him bounding in and grabbing me round the neck, or roughing up my hair, his rattling laugh like a magpie. *BROOKY! What the fuck happened to you?*

What happened to me? Chelsea didn't, but I had a fantastic result.

We were losing three-nil with ten minutes to go, and my new mate stood up and said he'd *had enough of watching this shit.* I asked him how much he wanted for the ticket. He paused for half a second, then told me not to worry about it, son. Afterwards, I got away with bunking the train back too, so the only things I had to pay out for were the tube and some food. I'd been looking forward to telling Pat about my luck, but now it occurred to me that he'd see it as his luck. And he'd quickly think of ways to spend the rest of my giro.

Pat had sprung three major surprises on me: his arrival, the burglary and the sorting office. By getting up and out early, I could finally be one step ahead of him. And I was determined to keep it like that. You needed to be on the ball in this game.

On my way through the office, my eyes were drawn to the whiteboard. I scanned down the list of names for Patrick Magree, but I couldn't spot him. I looked more slowly as my heart beat faster; there was a smudgy gap where his name had been wiped out. *What the fuck had happened to him?* With a bit more luck, I'd never know the answer.

Chapter Twenty-Four

I walked up and down the bays at the bus station as I waited. I knew which bus she was coming on, but I was too nervous and excited to stay still. And if I did, my feet would soon be frozen stiff like bricks. I hadn't had any visitors, except Mum, during the almost half a year I'd been in Drewich and then, a week before Christmas, Verity called me out of the blue. It was the first time I'd spoken to her since June. She told me she was visiting her great aunty, who only lived a bus ride away. She could come over the next day if I wanted. Of course I wanted. I wanted it even more than beating Oliver at chess. But once the prospect had sunk in that evening, I began to have mixed feelings. I'd got used to not hearing any news from my hometown and I was stubbornly proud that I hadn't tried to find any out. How could I be jealous of things I didn't know about?

When the bus pulled in and I clocked her walking down the aisle, I noticed that her hair was in a completely different style, and she was wearing tight red and black stripy trousers that would have stood out anywhere, never mind in Drewich on a Monday morning.

We hugged each tightly, but briefly; then she released me. Afterwards I noticed that hugging her hadn't provoked any strong emotions, like longing. I don't remember feeling anything. Was I frozen on the inside as well as the out?

An icy wind followed us through the town centre. I needed to warm up before attempting a proper conversation, so I pointed to the raised pool in the square, and said the sculpture was donated to the new town by a famous artist whose name I'd forgotten. That building over there is the DHSS. I carried on pointing out places until she said she didn't need to know where the sorting office was. If only she knew why I did.

'How about a good spot to have lunch?'

The caff I'd gone to when I first came to the town had shut down. The only other places I'd eaten out were the Unemployed Workers Centre and the Wimpy when Mum came to buy me a coat.

Verity clocked a pizza restaurant, and we chose a table by the large windows that looked out onto the precinct.

'I love pizza. I pretty much lived on it in Boston.'

'How was it?' I knew I had to ask.

'Oh, Jarrod, it was amazing. Everyone was so friendly, and the music scene was incredible. I reckon you'd have loved it out there.'

She said there were more Irish people in Boston than Galway. In South Boston, where she was staying, you could join in a music session in a different Irish bar every night. 'It nearly turned me into an alcoholic, but…I've learned loads more tunes on the mandolin.'

She wasn't boasting; she was just being enthusiastic. And it made a change from stories about court cases and prisons and people complaining. But I was also struggling to take it all in. I tried to shift the conversation subtly. 'Are you still playing a lot of mandolin?'

'Well, I'm keeping my hand in. But I'm not playing as much. Cos now I've got a mean black bass guitar and a new amp.' Her smile sparkled in her eyes. 'As you can imagine, my parents are absolutely delighted about it.'

The way she said *delighted* sounded different. A hint of an Irish accent, or was it American? Maybe a mixture of both.

After we'd ordered our pizzas and bottles of beer, I told Verity I liked her haircut. It was shaggy and uneven and confidently messy.

She leaned forward and shook her head and said it was her Throwing Muses look. I guessed, correctly, she was talking about a band, but I had to admit to her that I was out of touch with new music. They were fronted by two women, she said. She'd seen them live twice in Boston and they were so *intense*.

'I can imagine you playing bass in a band.'

She glanced down and turned her bottle of beer on the table. 'Maybe one day. Nothing is allowed to get in the way of me and my A-level grades. At least according to my dad.'

She raised her glass to knock it against mine. 'What about you? What do you do all day in this place?'

'I've been trying to make the best of it,' I said. 'And stay out of trouble.' On the long walk to town, I'd been thinking of how to give her the impression that I hadn't been wasting my time, but her directness had taken me by surprise.

'Do you get homesick?'

'A bit.' I tried out a smile, a different one to any I'd given for six months. 'Certain things spark it off.' A few swigs of beer had gone to my head.

Our pizzas arrived. After she'd scoffed down her first slice, I detected a hint of mischief in her eyes, and I felt the flicker of a glow inside. Then she said, 'What do you reckon about the big news from Brightlingsea?'

'What big news?'

Verity wiped her lips. 'About Sian being pregnant. Unless you know something bigger.'

'No *way*!'

'Yes way. I'm serious. It's due in May.'

She was serious, though only Verity would wait that long to reveal something so juicy. 'Do you know if it's Dennis's?'

'Of course it is. Unfortunately.'

'But he's supposed to be in nick, on remand.'

'Well, now he's living with his aunty near Cambridge. Sian goes up there almost every weekend. Stupid cow got engaged the other week too.'

I felt a surge of rage at the thought of Dennis spending his days lounging around at his aunty's and shagging Sian at weekends. How could it be right that he had it cushier than me, when he was the one who was actually guilty? 'It's not right,' I said.

Verity shook her head. 'It's not right at all. But she can't say I didn't warn her.'

I hadn't needed warning about Dennis, I already knew. And now I'd ended up getting punished worse than him for something he did.

A bit like with the vicarage. But I couldn't mention that cos Verity didn't know about it.

Instead, I apologised for not having the guts to call her to say goodbye. I wanted her to know that I hadn't done anything wrong though. I was inside the kebab shop when the bloke got attacked. And I was in the van when the windows got smashed.

'They didn't even warn me and Colin they were going to do it. I'm not trying to get you to feel sorry for me. It's just so you know the truth.'

'I believe you, Jarrod. But isn't it inevitable that if you hang around with those sorts of people, then you're going to end up in trouble? It's like if you're a girl and you're not careful, you can end up with…little Dennises.'

'That really would be a big sentence.'

'Do you think they're going to put you away?'

'I'm going to plead not guilty, cos I am not guilty, and hopefully I'll get found not guilty. But I know it's not as simple as that.'

She wanted to know if I'd heard from Colin, and I told her what I knew without mentioning Armageddon. I thought it would be disloyal to him, especially if we ended up laughing.

When Verity asked about the bail hostel regime, I ran down some of the highlights, like the chores and the curfew and getting kicked out. 'It's got a bit more bearable since I helped to negotiate us a boiled egg for breakfast.'

Finally, I made her crack up. 'I can remember you always going on about boiled eggs.'

'Did I ever make them for you?' I said it like I had a special recipe.

'I remember the part-veggie shepherd's pie with the walls of mash.'

I embellished the story to make out there was more resistance to the eggs from Mary.

'Maybe you could try to be a shop steward one day, Jarrod. I reckon it would suit you.'

'I'd love to. At least it would give me some time off from doing a shitty job.'

'Sometimes *it is* the job though. My dad's mate works for the Royal Mail in Chelmsford and all he does is union stuff. He's even got his own

179

little office. The bosses hate him apparently.'

I laughed. 'I reckon I could cope with that.'

As if to further demonstrate my credentials for the role, I explained how I'd helped other residents to fill in their claim forms and chase up their dole. 'Some people who come into the hostel can't even read and write.'

'That's really nice of you, Jarrod.'

Nice, but it wasn't exciting. Not like Boston and the Throwing Muses. 'I'm probably not the best person to be filling in their forms though, not with my handwriting.' That reminded me. 'Oh yeah, I found out I might be dyspraxic.'

Verity had never heard of it either. I told her all about the writing classes and Carl and how I'd admitted to him what I'd never told anyone, that my hand couldn't keep up with me when I tried to write quickly.

'You could have told me. It's not as if I didn't notice you had an *original* handwriting style. Don't they call it the Jarrod Brook font?'

I didn't drop any hints to Verity that I was almost skint, but she still insisted on paying for lunch. Afterwards, I took her to The Hummingbird where the punks and goths and other misfits hung out, and where maybe they'd appreciate her rock and roll trousers.

There were posters on the walls saying that DJ Radical would be playing Alternative Music on Friday nights, but on this Monday lunchtime it was dead. I ordered myself a pint of snakebite and black; Verity opted for Guinness.

We took our drinks over to the jukebox and I bought us seven tunes for starters. As we peered through the glass screen at the titles, I found myself pressing against her. I could smell her perfume, and though I knew it wasn't the strawberries or the posh stuff I'd bought her last Christmas, I had a sensation of déjà vu - but I still didn't feel any lust. My first tune was The Smiths cos it reminded me of us. She picked The Waterboys cos it reminded her of the U.S.

There was a battered low leather sofa at the back of the pub, and I told Verity it was really comfy. I was acting like a local, but I'd only been there once before. And my arse had never made contact with that sofa.

Verity and me both sat side-on with one hand on the back; our fingertips and feet were a small stretch away from touching. I noticed the dangle and jangle of her silver bangles and I thought they would go well with the bracelet in my pocket.

I asked her about the Sixth Form College and the books she was reading for A-level English, then halfway through my pint I had to go for a piss. Standing in the empty toilets, I started muttering to myself, which was always a sign that the snakebite had bitten. I looked in the mirror and rubbed at the blackcurrant stain above my top lip. I felt in my coat pocket for the bracelet Pat gave me, then watched my reflection as I practiced handing it over to Verity. *I've got something for you... No, it didn't cost me anything. I found it in the park.*

'Eton Rifles' was playing on the jukebox when I came back from the bogs. 'Do you remember that time we went to London?'

'Is this song reminding you of all those mod shops you dragged me to in Carnaby Street?'

I laughed awkwardly. 'Nah, I was thinking of that little pub behind Oxford Street with the ancient jukebox. It feels a bit like that here. Being in a place where nobody knows us.'

'I was still at the Colne High then,' she said, like it was donkey's years ago. It must have been almost exactly twelve months, cos we were up there doing our Christmas shopping.

'We had a great time,' I said. I tried to weigh my words in a way that sounded like I didn't just mean that day. Then it hit me that I was getting pissed pretty quickly. Had I moved on from the being happy stage to melancholy already?

Another of my choices came on the jukebox: 'Walls Come Tumbling Down'.

'I'm not a Paul Weller obsessive like you. But I like this one. It's political and it's got a bit of balls.'

'You could say the same about 'Eton Rifles'. And loads of his songs, like...'

'It's okay, Jarrod. I don't need a list.'

She told me about Red Wedge. How a group of musicians, including Paul Weller and Billy Bragg, were working with the Labour Party to get more young people engaged in politics. 'I don't need the encouragement of famous men,' Verity said, 'but I've been thinking of joining the Labour Party Young Socialists.'

'Why wouldn't you?'

'Because I'm not sure if I can forgive them for not properly backing the miners. Imagine if they had done? We might have won.'

I knew what she meant. That's why people like her dad thought they weren't worth voting for. But how else were we realistically going to get rid of the Tories unless we had a Labour government? 'I reckon you should get involved. People listen to you.'

She lowered her eyebrows. 'Like Sian you mean. I think you may be overestimating my persuasive powers, Jarrod.'

I smiled and held her gaze. Maybe now would be a good time to hand it over.

'Anyway,' she slapped my hand. 'What are *you* going to do for the cause?'

'I don't know yet. It's a bit hard for me to make any plans at the moment. I'd like to find out more about Red Wedge.'

She giggled at a memory that tickled her. 'Have you sprayed any more political graffiti?'

'I told you, I'm trying to stay out of trouble.'

'It's still there. A bit faded, but the message remains clear. '*Wear Your Numbers*,' she repeated slowly. 'It makes me chuckle whenever I see it.'

'At least I left a legacy when they expelled me from Brightlingsea.'

The bell for last orders at twenty to three brought me back to the reality of a Monday afternoon. 'I'll get us a swift one for the road?'

Verity checked her watch. 'I don't know. My bus is at quarter past.'

'Get the next one, then.'

'Nah, they're only every two hours and I promised my aunty I'd be back for tea. We've got time for a short, I reckon. It's my round though.'

While she ordered two Jamesons, I put a couple of final tunes on the jukebox. It felt right that we should listen to The Pogues. I chose my favourite, 'Sally MacLennane'; then hers, 'Dirty Old Town'.

'Still the best gig I've been to,' Verity said, before downing half of her double in one.

To hear her say that gave me more inner warmth than the whisky.

We'd gone to see The Pogues together, up the Uni.

'Better than the Throwing...whatever they're called?'

'Muses, Jarrod. Mu-*ses*. It's different, but... yeah, I reckon. Just about. Though maybe I'll change my mind tomorrow.'

'I don't care if you do. I'm not going to see you tomorrow.'

We rushed through the darkening winter afternoon gloom to the bus station. It was only five past three, but the evening was closing in already.

There wasn't any time for a lingering goodbye. Verity was right, we'd cut it really fine.

'I've got something for you,' I said.

'Well, you'd better hurry up, then.'

I pulled it carefully out of my coat pocket. 'It's the poem I wrote when I was doing the classes I told you about. I copied it out for you last night in my best handwriting. It took me bloody ages.'

She smiled as she put it in her bag, then glanced over her shoulder. The last two passengers were now boarding the bus.

'I told you I'd read you something I'd written one day. Well, I know I didn't read it but...'

'Don't worry, I will try to imagine you doing a recital.' She squeezed my hand and planted a kiss on my lips, really quick, before hurrying off for the bus. Once it was clear that the driver had spotted her, she called to me, 'Whatever happens, you've got to keep it up!'

'Keep what?'

She mimed the action of scribbling on her palm.

I raised my thumb and turned away. Back to reality. Back to all the anonymous faces in the bus station that looked right through me. I had an urge to turn around and blow a kiss to Verity. I was drunk enough, but if she wasn't looking back at me, I'd feel more than just silly. I'd regret it. Better to stick with the memories I had. It had gone well, hadn't it?

So why did my eyes itch, like I needed to cry?

Chapter Twenty-Five

His mask of being in control slipped briefly once he'd realised what he'd done. After I'd taken his queen out of action, Oliver kept his head down and made his moves quickly and aggressively, hoping to harry me into committing a similar mistake. I took every opportunity I had to swap pieces, like I'd seen him do to me; within half an hour, I'd stripped him of everything except his king, and I still had my queen to use against him.

I'd been waiting for forty-odd games to get into a position like this and I was desperate not to fuck it up. But the feeling I might tied a knot in my guts, while at the same time my brain was dancing with excitement.

Check...check...check. You're in check, *mate*.

Oliver crawled away one square at a time, like a half-dead mouse being prodded by a cat.

Check...check...check...

Then he made eye contact for the first time in a while and his pursed lips had curled into a smile.

'Threefold repetition.'

He was looking at me for signs of recognition, but I didn't have a Danny what he was on about.

He pushed out his chin. 'Don't you know the threefold repetition rule? If the pieces on the board have been in exactly the same position three times, it's a draw.'

'I've never heard of it, and I've been playing all my life. I reckon you've just made it up cos you're a bad loser.'

He narrowed his eyes like I was crossing a line. 'Answer me this: how can I be a bad loser when I haven't lost?'

'Cos that *rule* you've come up with sounds like a load of bollocks.' Socio-Ollie-bollocks.

But he'd already turned his back and was on his way to the office.

'Yeah, fuck off with your bullshit rules,' I said aloud to myself. I found out much later that it was a rule, but it only counted if the moves were written down. Now I rearranged the pieces into a checkmate position, as they would and should have been, and went upstairs to get my coat. It was Christmas Day morning, and we didn't have to go out, but I couldn't face being cooped up all day like a turkey.

The park was empty, except for a dad and his toddler who was riding a new bike with stabilisers. I sat on a bench facing the lake and smoked a roll-up, while looking at the ducks and swans gliding slowly between islands of ice. I wondered if they were the same birds I saw when I first came here and got stoned on my own all those months ago.

I remembered Trevor saying that actual birdlime was a homemade glue that hunters used to stick on twigs to trap little birds. Once they land on it, they're completely stuck; I knew how it felt to be stuck. Next week, it would be a year since it all started: six months on curfew in Brightlingsea for shouting abuse at the coppers and six months here, stuck in a Crown Court queue, waiting for a jury to – hopefully – tell me what I already knew. *Not guilty.*

I didn't smash anything then, but I was up for it now. I looked around the bench for a big enough stone to break the ice, but all I could see were poxy little pebbles.

I sunk my hands into my coat pockets and felt for the thick silver bracelet Pat gave me. I turned it over a few times, then took it out to look at the writing engraved on the outside. I guessed it was a message, but the words were full of kays, zeds, and exes, and from a language I didn't recognise. A language that belonged to someone else. On a bracelet that belonged to someone else. A bracelet I'd been willing to palm off on Verity.

I'd assumed my dishonest streak had been there for as long as I could remember but then, when I dug deeper, in the dim light of a very cold Christmas Day, I was able to recall when it started.

Adrian, and a colleague of his from the University, had decided to use me for a bit of entertainment when they were pissed. Adrian fetched a dice and said he would give me 50p if I managed to throw a six. The catch was, he would dock 10p a go in advance from my 20p a week pocket money. I was old enough to work out the odds, but they were egging me on. They made me determined to wipe the pissed grins from their faces, but I didn't get any luck with the dice. I can still remember Adrian gleefully flipping the pages of the calendar next to the fridge, marking off all the 10ps I'd lost. Until he decided that I'd lost too much, and he called an end to their fun. I don't reckon he told me not to tell Mum, otherwise I probably would have done. I took my revenge instead by nicking two pound notes from his wallet when I thought he had enough dosh not to notice. It was the first time I can remember stealing anything.

Adrian may have helped to start me off, but I couldn't blame him for my decision to keep the bob-a-job money when I was a cub. I also hung on to the sponsored spelling test cash when I was at junior school. Dennis had been picking on me for getting too many right and to shut him up I split the proceeds with him. Around the same time, I started to shoplift... if I wrote down everything illegal I'd done, it would be quite a long list.

I thought back to the sorting office, and Pat vaulting the counter with a mail sack. I didn't know it was going to happen, but I had a couple of seconds to make a decision: to run *with* him, or away from him. As always, I ran into trouble. But why was that? What would a normal person have done?

I tried to crush the nicked bracelet in my grip, but it wouldn't yield a millimetre, never mind buckle. I stood up and extended my arm, then chucked it as far as I could into the middle of the lake. There was a 50-50 chance it would land on the ice, but it was only a matter of time before it sunk to the bottom.

Part Three

Part Three

Chapter Twenty-Six

When I clocked Dennis and Sian in the cafe on the top floor of Chelmsford Crown Court, my instinct was to avoid them. It would be better late than never. But after I'd bought a cup of tea and was looking for a place to sit and drink it in peace, Dennis glanced up and caught me.

I forged the most convincing grin I was able; I had no choice but to join them at their table.

'I weren't expecting to see you,' I said.

'Well, here we are.'

I don't know if Dennis was bored, lording it at his aunty's, but he'd definitely been getting fed up. It wasn't only Sian who was carrying extra weight. She was looking at me expectantly as she stroked her bump, so I congratulated them both on the baby. I asked when it was due, though of course, I already knew.

Sian mentioned a date in May. 'I'm really happy for you,' I said. They looked happy too. I wondered how much less happy they'd be if Dennis got put away, and it was daddy not baby who was still inside in May.

My stomach was gnawing away at itself. I couldn't concentrate on anything Dennis or Sian were saying, until: 'Here he is, look. Fuck me, who cut your barnet, Col, the council?'

Dennis was the only one who laughed at his joke. I'd heard him say it more than ten times before, though to be fair, it was more topical this time cos Colin had actually been working for the council.

'All right?' Colin said, but the way he said it, through gritted teeth, showed he was anything but, like the Ouija had told him the world was now ending tomorrow.

'Have you heard about Skully?' Sian asked, like she couldn't wait any longer.

But Dennis wasn't going to allow her the glory of being the one to tell the story. 'Dirty nonce was nicked for picking up boys from the arcades in Clacton and having them stay round his flat above the restaurant.'

'They reckon he was drugging them up,' Sian managed to chip in.

Dennis spoke over her again. 'You must have suspected something, didn't you, Col?'

Colin's shoulders tensed, but he didn't raise his head. He was dragging a dead match around the rim of the ashtray.

'*Come on.* You must have known what he was up to. You were round there all the time.'

Colin sceered quietly, then looked up slowly and stared at Dennis. 'I reckon I know what you've been up to, Snake?'

Before Dennis could answer, a geezer in his late twenties wearing an expensive suit appeared next to our table. He claimed to be mine and Colin's barrister, but this wasn't the lawyer I'd visited in his chambers back in November. That one was thirty years older and had been smoking a pipe as he told me that basically he thought things would turn out all right. This flustered rookie wasn't giving me much confidence. He said his name was Mothersole, and he asked us to join him downstairs for a conference.

In a corner of the waiting area outside Court Three, Mothersole revealed there had been two major developments in the case. The first was that Karen and Terry Grimm had changed their statements to withdraw the claim that they'd been looking after a friend's baby on the night their windows got smashed.

I shook my fist. 'I knew they were lying. I fucking knew it,' I hissed. I looked at Colin. 'I told you, didn't I?'

But Colin's expression was distant, like he hadn't taken it in. I guessed he was still wound up about Dennis and Skully.

Mothersole continued: 'The second development, which you may not find so pleasing, is that the charge against you has been changed from *criminal damage with intent to endanger life* to *conspiracy to cause criminal damage*. What this means in a nutshell is if you were at the scene and didn't intervene to try and prevent the offence from taking place, or you did not leave the scene once you knew the offence was about to take place, then you could be found guilty of taking part in a conspiracy.'

'We've already admitted to being there. But it wasn't like we sat around planning it, did we?' Again, I looked in vain for Colin to back me up. 'We didn't even know what was going to happen, did we?'

Mothersole licked his lips while he waited impatiently for the opportunity to correct me. 'It's a common misconception with conspiracy,' he said, 'that it somehow requires the existence of a pre-determined plot, or plan. But...' He glanced at his watch, 'I'm afraid we're right up against the clock now, so I'm going to need to be brief...'

Lawyers were always saying that. Was that why they called them briefs?

He looked at us slowly in turn. 'Having reconsidered the evidence in light of the new charge, I would strongly advise you both to plead guilty.'

It was his duty to inform us, he said, that an early guilty plea would mean we would qualify for a fully discounted sentence. However, it was also his duty to tell us, that if we decided to plead *not guilty*, and were subsequently found *guilty*, then we would receive a stiffer sentence. This meant that we would be much more likely to be sent to nick than if we pleaded guilty in the first place.

I couldn't believe what I was hearing. Plead guilty to doing what? For the past six months, I'd been telling anybody who'd listen that I was innocent. Cos it was true. 'How can we plead guilty when we're not guilty? Are you saying that it doesn't really matter now whether we did it or not?'

He hesitated. 'Well, that isn't how I would suggest you look at it. But it is true that we need to act according to the new reality.'

'I reckon the real conspiracy is them switching the charge at the last minute to make up for the fact that their main witnesses were lying about the baby. It's a stitch up.'

Mothersole checked his watch again. He didn't have the time to engage with my conspiracy theory. He was only prepared to deal with the new reality. He said that all he could do was to offer his counsel. Ultimately, the decision would be down to us.

'I'm not pleading guilty to something I didn't do,' I said, 'it's as simple as that. No fucking way.'

Mothersole shifted his attention to Colin. 'What about you?'

Colin had spent most of the conference either looking bemused or gawping at his court shoes. 'I don't know,' he said, which wasn't what the man in a hurry wanted to hear. He coughed, then asked, 'What do you reckon the chances are of us getting off?'

Mothersole made up for lost time by speaking twice as quickly. 'Unfortunately, conspiracy is a very complicated and contentious area of law and there are very few black and white cases. However, having studied the evidence, I have concluded that the prosecution does have a strong case here, and therefore on the balance of probabilities, I believe it would be advisable for you to reap the benefits of the discounted sentence offered by an early guilty plea in order to reduce your chances of going to prison.'

'*Reap the benefits*,' I repeated sarcastically.

Colin said, 'It sounds like we're fucked whatever we do.'

He looked down and blew a small spit bubble, as he often did when weighing up a decision, then quickly sucked it in, like he'd finally remembered where we were. 'I'll do the same as him, I suppose.'

We were locked into the dock by a geezer in uniform and made to stand up when the judge eventually showed his face. I was in the middle between Colin and Dennis, who were keeping as far away from each other as possible. The only parts of us that were visible to the rest of the court were our necks and our heads. I sat on the edge of the bench and hung on to the railings. I was keen to focus on the proceedings, but it took a while for the show to get going. It was like a fancy-dress rehearsal for a boring part of a play.

Eventually, the potbellied pig in a wig who was the prosecution lawyer stood up to make a speech. 'Imagine you are part of a young couple,' he said as he gazed along the two rows of jurors, who mostly weren't young at all. 'You've recently married and are saving to buy a house together, so you only go out to socialise on special occasions. On New Year's Eve, you treat yourselves to a couple of drinks at the pub. On the way home you witness a mob of drunken yobs assaulting a policewoman while others scream obscenities at her fellow officers. The next morning, having reflected on what you saw, you decide to do your public duty – as you, the esteemed members of the jury are doing now – and you make a witness statement.

'Six months later, you have moved into your modest first home, a little bungalow in a quiet cul-de-sac. One Saturday evening, soon after moving in, you decide to have an early night because you are working overtime the following morning. You are then woken violently from your sleep by a terrifying noise. A cowardly mob, bent on revenge, have hurled bricks through your front room windows. Members of the jury, please take a few seconds to imagine how traumatic that must be...'

And then, imagine bullshitting that you were looking after an imaginary baby.

When Karen was called to the witness box to speak for herself, she was so nervous and sheepish I could barely make out what she was saying. I waited impatiently for Mothersole's turn, so he could pull her up about her lies. But he didn't even ask her why she'd changed her mind about committing perjury. That would have been my first question.

During Karen's husband's evidence, Dennis released a silent but poisonous fart into the closed dock. It made a stench that caused my guts to curdle, never mind his. He could afford not to take the trial seriously, cos he'd pleaded guilty already. I craned my neck so that my head was leant over the railings. It was as much as I could do to escape. When I finally glanced back, even the dock officer was pulling a face. Surely this counted as contempt of court, or at least contempt for your co-defendants.

As the morning wore on, it became more of an effort to follow the case, in the face of Dennis's farting and nudging and poking; Colin's shifting, sniffing and scraping; and the lawyers and judge playing smart-arse legal games, which only they knew the rules to.

The final prosecution witness was a well-spoken woman I'd never seen before. She said she'd been woken by the "cracked roar" of the van's exhaust as it pulled up alongside the Green.

I heard Dennis chuckling quietly behind me. 'I knew we should have got that fucking thing fixed.'

The witness swore that she saw four people leaving the van carrying bricks. I knew for a fact there were only three. I whispered this to Colin, but he hadn't been listening, which was ironic, cos I'd seen him paying more attention to *Rumpole of the Bailey* on the telly than to the details of his own destiny.

After the morning session, Mothersole asked me and Colin if either of us were willing to be questioned under oath in the witness box. He thought it would be a good idea if at least one of us did, because otherwise the judge could tell the jury they were entitled to hold our silence against us.

Once I was able to get a word in edgeways, I didn't hesitate. Someone had to stick their neck out to stick up for us, and I could already tell it wasn't going to be Mothersole.

Colin said he reckoned that I was the one who was good with words.

Mum had arrived an hour or so earlier and I was chuffed that she encouraged me to take the stand. I reckon I'd learned a lot of my arguing skills from all the arguments I'd had with her.

She took me and Colin to the Wimpy for lunch. Dennis had sloped off with Sian. On the way back to court, I spotted the prosecution barrister through the window of Pizza Hut, as he was about to clamp his jaw down onto an enormous bite. While I was pointing him out to Colin, he looked across and caught us catching him, freeze-framed with his snout dipped in melted cheese. The greedy pig without wig.

Half an hour later, I was facing him from the witness box, and he set about grilling me for his black pudding.

'I suggest to you that you were part of a gang of youths who were hell-bent on causing trouble in the community.'

'I wasn't in a gang. I've never been in a gang.'

'So, you just chose to drive around "mobhanded" in a Transit van looking for trouble?'

'I don't know what you're on about. Anyway, I can't drive.'

'How did you travel to Colchester on the night in question?'

'I got a lift.'

'With whom did you get a lift?'

'With some friends in a van.'

'You mean your van? The Transit van you co-owned with those people you claim not to have been in a gang with?' He looked at the jury like it was one-nil to him.

I glanced sideways to the public gallery at Mum, the one who'd been persuaded to put the insurance for the van in her name. I thought I wasn't doing too bad, but Mum's expression was grimmer than I ever saw her on parents' evenings.

'Can you tell the court what happened later that night, after you'd spent the evening drinking?'

I hesitated, not wanting to say the wrong thing.

'Perhaps you wish to tell us that you don't like to get drunk? You don't drink and you don't drive. You just like to go along for the ride. Is that right?'

'I do drink. You're trying to put words in my mouth.'

'How much alcohol did you drink that night?'

'I don't know. At least five pints.'

'And what did you do when the pubs closed?'

I told him what I'd told the coppers. I was waiting in the kebab shop for my shish when a friend came and told me we were leaving. I understood there had been some sort of fight, but I didn't know the details. Afterwards I thought I was going to get dropped off at home, but the next thing I knew we were parked up by the Green in Brightlingsea.

'And then what happened?'

'Some people got out of the van carrying bricks.'

'And where do you think they got these bricks?'

'They were already in the van.'

'Really? How fortuitous. And who were these people you witnessed leaving your van clutching bricks?'

'I don't want to say.' I looked to the jury, as Mothersole had advised me to, 'I'm worried about what will happen to me if I give people's names.'

'What did you think they were going to do with these bricks? Build a wall, perhaps?'

A burst of sniggering rose from the jury, like schoolkids laughing at a teacher's joke.

'There wasn't time to think, it all happened too quick. If I knew what they were going to do, I would have left.'

'And at what point did you leave?'

'What do you mean?'

'It's a simple enough question but let me rephrase it. Did you leave the scene once you saw these people get out of your van wielding house bricks?'

'No. When they came back, I got a lift home.'

'Ah, I see. You mean once they'd returned from chucking bricks through the windows of a young couple in a vicious revenge attack?'

'It was nothing to do with me.'

I wished I could punch the smirk from his fat face. My fists were clenched, and the skin on my arms was prickling with rage. To him it was a game, just another case. To me it was everything. Shit or bust. I appealed to the jury with my arms outstretched and shouted, 'HOW CAN I BE GUILTY WHEN IT WOULD HAVE HAPPENED WHETHER I WAS THERE OR NOT?'

I stared into the rows of jurors until their faces blurred under the bright lights and they looked as unreal as crowd figures from Subbuteo.

It would have happened whether I was there or not. I thought I had him with that one, but he smiled triumphantly, like he had me. Then he asked for a tape player to be wheeled in.

As the pig in the wig bent down to press play, the look on his face was ecstatic; he was convinced that the line he'd lined up was emphatic.

I neither condemned nor condoned it.

The tape was a bootleg of me. Jarrod Brook Live, at the Clacton Cop Shop, June '85. If I hadn't recognized my own voice with my own ears, I would've sworn I'd never said *condone* in my life. I thought I knew roughly what it meant, but where the fuck had I got it from?

Was it a word that Marshall had used? And I'd repeated it the next day during my third and final interview. Or Arthur Daley, in that episode of *Minder* when he served on the jury? Or did I pick it up from watching too much *Crown Court* on the telly? Or *Rough Justice*? Or *Rumpole of the Bailey*? Or from reading all those criminals' autobiographies? I didn't even realise the word was in my vocabulary. Maybe all that time in the cop shop had sent me a bit loopy and I'd got ideas above my station.

I neither condemned nor condoned it.

'Can you confirm that this is your voice on the tape?'

'Yeah, I think so. It's a bit confusing though, cos you're only playing one line out of a long interview.'

Can you please tell the court, what is this *it* you're referring to? This *it* that you neither condemned nor condoned?'

'I'm not sure. Something to do with smashing the windows I suppose. I don't remember saying it to be honest, it was a long time ago.'

'And how can you have "neither condemned nor condoned" something that you weren't aware of? A criminal act that you claim you didn't know was going to happen.'

'I don't know, I must have meant after.'

'After the damage was done you mean. When you were driven home from the scene in the van you co-owned with the people who committed this despicable act; with these friends you don't wish to name. Is that right?'

'I've told you I didn't do anything.'

'No further questions, Your Honour.'

The next morning, the judge summed up the case for the jury. I didn't understand everything, but it seemed like my *neither condemned nor condoned* had helped to condemn me. He asked the jury to consider whether me and Colin were innocent passengers on the night of this crime spree. The jury clearly thought not, cos it only took them an hour to find us both guilty.

After we were convicted, the judge spoke to us differently. No more benefit of the doubt, and innocent until…we were now convicts, and convicts could be talked to as if they were shit. And locked up for the rest of the day.

Reports were done on us by probation, to help the judge to decide on our punishment. Then around four o'clock, we were brought back up to the dock. Colin and me were sentenced to twelve months youth custody for conspiracy to cause criminal damage. Colin also got an extra three months for stealing money from Skully. Dennis was given 100 hours community service.

The six months I'd spent in the hostel didn't even get a mention. Unlike time on remand, it counted for nothing. When I heard my sentence, I looked over to Mum in the public gallery and shrugged, like *that's how it goes*; shoulders resigned, but expression defiant. I wanted her to think that I wasn't scared. Further down my body, a finger of fear poked me hard in the guts. Gutted.

Chapter Twenty-Seven

'We're going to have to stick up for each other in here, Jarrod, you know what I mean? If someone has a go at you, then they're having a go at me.'

'Fucking right,' I said, 'and vice-versa.'

We were stood together by the open window of a cell in HMP Brixton, listening to other inmates screaming and shouting over each other.

A bloke who sounded close to us kept trying to share how he'd held a woman hostage in her office. *What's wrong, I goes, ain't you ever seen one of these before?* Each time he started up he was heckled and abused.

One geezer was wailing, *Fack off, fack off!* again and again, like a cockney parrot.

Then a booming growl cut through: 'I'll do another ten years for you...CUNT!'

I retreated up to my bunk and rolled a fag. The nicotine-coloured paint on the ceiling was peeling, and there were blue stains of old toothpaste on the walls where pictures had been removed. I lay on my back and took a deep drag, then brushed the ash from my face.

The cockney parrot was at it again. He clearly wasn't sane. I'd heard Trevor talk about the F Wing in Brixton: he said they called it *Fraggle Rock*. It was where the nonces and grasses and nutcases were kept for their own protection.

'I wonder where Skully's ended up. Maybe he's here somewhere.'

Colin kept schtum.

'Nah, he's probably in some cushy nick working in the kitchens. Be his luck, wouldn't it? He only gets nine months for noncing and we end up with a year for nothing.'

'Don't mention that scumbag near me again, Jarrod. I'm warning you.'

'I was only saying it's a joke that—'

'ARE YOU DELIBERATELY TRYING TO FUCK ME OFF?'

'Course not.'

'You had to bring him up, didn't you?' Colin smacked the wall with the base of his palm, '...*you had to fucking bring him up.*'

One of us had to eventually mention the fact that the geezer he'd worked for, and had been convicted of nicking money from, had himself been convicted of...convicted of what? I didn't really understand what *noncing* meant if I was honest. From what I'd heard, it sounded like it covered anything from molesting to rape.

Perhaps Dennis was right, and Colin had some idea what was going on. Now he had a guilty conscience and that's why he was so angry. Maybe the trials bike and new trainers and whatever else Skully had got him were bribes to buy his silence? Was that what Dennis was hinting at in the van on the night the windows got smashed?

Now it was my turn to be silent, cos I couldn't think of anything to say that he might not take the wrong way.

'Are you awake?' He sounded more friendly.

I opened my eyes and saw Colin next to me; his face was lit up by the security lights outside.

'We shouldn't even be here, should we, Jarrod? What have you or me ever done to deserve to be sent to prison?'

'Fuck all. And I still don't understand how we got found guilty.' I sat up with my back against the wall. 'How can they get away with changing the charge at the last minute? So we only had to have been in the van and not go' – I put on an upper-class accent – 'I say you chaps, whatever you're up to looks downright illegal and if you don't drop those bricks at once, I'm going to be left with no other choice but to make a citizen's arrest.'

Colin laughed, or at least snorted. 'I thought you were supposed to be the brainy one. I didn't have a clue what they were going on about most of the time. But I did get the main thing. The only reason they changed the charge was to make sure they could put us away.'

'Yeah. But I still don't understand how we're guilty.'

'I don't know fuck all about conspiracy, but we were there when it happened, weren't we? We had shares in the van, we saw the bricks, we heard the windows get smashed and we wouldn't tell them who done it. So they made sure we copped it whether we deserved it or not. Simple as. You don't have to be a smart-arse, like you, to see that.'

I didn't want to accept what he was saying then, but years later, when I tried to understand the law of conspiracy with law books and legal dictionaries in the library at Uni, I still couldn't work out how we ended up with a guilty. So I suppose Colin's theory was as good as any.

At the time all I told him was, 'I ain't a smart-arse.'

'Yeah, you are. You had to go and give it the big one in the witness box, didn't you? Like you thought you were in *Rumpole* or something, or one of them poxy books you're always reading.'

Colin was acting like the worst sort of smart-arse, the ones who are all clever after the event. Now he was spouting off like a volcano when all the time in court he was dormant.

'At least I had a go.'

'You made it worse. That barrister ripped you to pieces.'

'Fuck off. I went down fighting. What about you?'

He grabbed a plastic mug and chucked it hard at my head. 'You've got an answer for everything, ain't you?'

'Of course I have. Unless you want to try and shut me up.'

His teeth and fists were clenched but I was out of his reach. He'd have to climb up onto my bunk if he wanted a fight. The thought of that made me laugh. And I couldn't take him seriously in his striped prison shirt that was three sizes too big and hung down to his knees like a dress.

'What's so fucking funny?'

'Us arguing. What happened to sticking together?'

'You fucking started it, Jarrod.'

It wasn't the truth, but I wanted a truce. So I kept schtum. Colin carried on loitering, and I rolled a fag, cos it didn't look like I'd be kipping anytime soon.

'I was thinking earlier,' I said. 'If we'd have pleaded guilty, then maybe we would have been let off with community service, like Dennis. But it was different for him, he was guilty, weren't he?'

'They don't give a shit though, do they? As long as somebody gets put away.'

'That's true.' It was also true that if you pleaded guilty, your lawyer could claim you'd learned your lesson and had promised to be a good boy in the future. But if you're *found* guilty, you get treated like you've been caught out lying and have deliberately chosen to waste public money and everyone's time.

'Dennis knew how to play the game, didn't he?' I said. 'Wearing a whistle and bowing his head to the judge when his barrister called him a "proud father to be"; having his pregnant fiancée in the public gallery; getting someone to promise to sort him out with a job. In some ways, I suppose you can't blame him, really.'

'Don't be a mug all your life, Jarrod. That's what he wants you to think, that he's just playing it smart.'

'What was he doing, then?'

'How do you think he got bailed to his aunty's after only a few weeks on remand? How did he get away without being charged for beating up those geezers outside the kebab shop? How comes he ended up in court with us and not with Wayne, Roy and Nutty? How comes he's going to be the only one who don't get sent down?'

'You reckon he's a...' I was wary of using the G-word in front of Colin.

'You were quick to call me a grass cos I was willing to go against Nutty. But to me, that ain't even grassing. This is *proper* grassing. Doing whatever it takes to save your own skin. And it didn't even cross your mind to suspect him.'

'I had my suspicions that he grassed me up for the vicarage, but there was no way I could prove it.'

'He's always been a slippery bastard,' Colin said.

'You're telling me. All those times he bullied me at junior school, and I never said a word. And he's always been the one saying that grasses are the scum of the earth. And then he goes and bricks a grass's windows.

Now look…fucking hypocrite piece of shit.'

'Fucking snidey snake in the grass,' Colin said. 'He's probably in the pub now, laughing at us.'

'Turning over a new leaf,' I said.

Colin sceered. 'Yeah, a fucking tea leaf.'

I laughed bitterly and warmed to the theme. 'More like sliding and sniding around under the leaves. Lower than a fucking centipede.' At least the fact that Dennis was a filthy wrong 'un was something that me and Colin could agree on. 'I reckon you've cracked the case mate, but what are we going to do about it?'

'What can we do when we're stuck in here?'

'We've got to get some sort of revenge, ain't we? We can't just let him get away with it.'

'I'm not going to see him or talk to him again. That's my revenge.'

'I want something horrible to happen to him.'

'Like what? What are *you* going to do, Jarrod?'

'I'll think of something.'

I was awake for a long while afterwards, fantasising about confronting Dennis with various tools from Mick's mate's armoury, making him squeal, like the rat he'd always been.

But it was just fantasies, cos I wasn't capable of that in reality. Despite what had happened in the witness box, I knew my words would always be my most effective weaponry even if it took me years to find the right ones, so that my revenge, like my prison food, would need to be served cold.

I must have fallen asleep eventually, cos I was woken by Colin violently shoving my mattress.

'What the fuck did you say?'

I opened my sticky eyes and saw him standing there like he'd never gone away. 'Nothing. What you on about?'

'Come on you wanker. Say it to my face.'

'Say what? I didn't say anything. Not unless I was talking in my kip.'

He turned away so I couldn't see his face. 'Don't worry about it. It must have been from outside.'

I propped myself up on my elbow and watched him lurking by the cell window, like he was trying to work out where the voice came from.

'What did they say?' But he didn't reply.

We heard the kidnapper kicking off again, broadcasting to F Wing on Fraggle FM. But he was soon shouted down by a young-sounding geezer I didn't think I'd heard from before. I wondered if it was his voice that Colin had got mixed up with mine. He didn't sound much like me.

I closed my eyes, cos I couldn't keep them open, but I didn't think I was going to be able to sleep until Colin got his head down too. I could sense he was still there, trapped in the narrow gap between the bunks and the wall, like a caged bird who was allergic to doing bird: a claustrophobic captive of that human zoo.

We were moved the following evening, into separate cells on B Wing. Colin got lucky with an old lag, who had a decent radio and a supply of teabags. As I walked into my new peter, I clocked a familiar face. It was Ferris, the geezer I was sat next to on the journey from Chelmsford Crown Court to HMP Brixton. He nodded, like he considered me an acceptable cellmate.

On the coach he'd been boasting about only getting two months. Judge Stevens had told him that he was always saddened to have to lock up a fellow ex-soldier, but unfortunately the sentencing guidelines had given him no choice.

I'd learned in the bail hostel not to ask people what they were in for, but Ferris had been so cocky that I couldn't resist. He told me he'd smashed a jeweller's window with a brick when he was pissed. But he was so paralytic, the only thing to get nicked was him.

The cell was colder than mine and Colin's, cos Ferris insisted on keeping the window open permanently to kill the germs and dilute the smell of piss. In the evenings, when we'd been locked up for the night, he told me stories about being on active service in Armagh. He reckoned his best mate and three other soldiers were killed by an IRA bomb at the barracks while he was out on patrol. Now he was trying to live for two people. I didn't have a clue if he was telling the truth, but he definitely knew how to talk for two people.

One thing we had in common was Colchester, cos he'd been stationed there for eight years. But it was like we were talking about two different towns. When he told me the names of all the pubs he used to drink in, I'd never heard of any of them.

After eating my porridge one morning, I lay back on my bunk and retreated into my most nagging worry: when were we going to get moved from here? Mothersole had said we would get transferred to a youth prison "soon" where we'd probably be able to work or do training. In Brixton, all you could do was sleep, think and smoke; I didn't want to think cos there was nothing to look forward to, and I'd already run out of baccy. As I tried to get back to sleep, I heard grunting. It was Ferris, doing press ups in the gap between the bunks and the wall. When he'd finished, I could feel his hot breath on my ear, then he gave my shoulder a rough shake.

'How many press ups can you do?'

'I don't know.'

'Come on, have a go.'

'I don't feel like it. I just want to hibernate.'

'You can't be up there moping all day my old mate.'

I could smell the sourness of his fresh B.O. I rolled over and faced him. 'I'm not really into all that.'

But he wouldn't let me lie. I climbed down reluctantly and managed to do twenty proper ones, after he'd made some corrections to my technique. Then my legs gave way and I lay with my chin on the floor, until he prodded me in the ribs with his bony big toe.

'STAND UP SOLDIER.'

As I got to my feet he was laughing hysterically, then he slapped me hard twice on the back.

Two days later, I managed twenty-five press ups and thirty sit-ups.

I thought I deserved a nap after that, but Ferris was even more hyper than usual.

'You ever boxed, Jarrod?'

'No.'

'Never?' The way he said it emphasised his West Country accent,

205

which had faded after so many years in the army.

'Had many fights, mate?'

'Loads.' It was true that I'd been in quite a few at school.

'Win many?'

'About half and half.' I was roughly mid-table in the league of hardness at Oakbridge, though some kids, like Henry, never seemed to get tested.

'Nobody's going to touch you in here with me about mate. But what about when you get shipped out? You're going to need to look after yourself then, boy. I used to box in the army; come on, I'll show you how to throw a decent punch.'

He began by talking me through how to jab. Then, once I'd punched his palms a few times, he wanted to have a pop at mine. He called it a demonstration, but I had a strong impression that he enjoyed hitting people. Each one of his jabs stung like failing to catch a cleanly struck cricket ball while standing only a few feet from the batsman.

Chapter Twenty-Eight

We were moved from HMP Brixton to a youth custody centre the following week and allocated to one of four huts, which held around thirty inmates in each. Except we weren't called inmates, we were referred to as *trainees* and were given our own room and a key. Compared with twenty-three hours a day bang-up and Ferris, I was convinced this was going to be a piece of piss. Though I was gutted that me and Colin weren't in the same hut.

For a few minutes, while the other trainees were still at association, the hut was quiet. I sat on my bed and looked around my new room: I had a desk, which was fixed to the wall, and a chair where I would be able to sit and write letters and maybe keep a diary. Who knows, perhaps I'd even find time to write rhymes. I noticed the wall between me and the corridor didn't go up as far as the ceiling. I found out later this was so the screws could climb over if a trainee tried to barricade himself in. But it also meant our rooms were never really secure.

When I heard the others piling back into the hut, the nerves piled up in my gut. I knew that early impressions were vital if I was going to avoid being taken for a mug.

A large freckly face peered in through the glass panel of my door, then an overgrown trainee with ginger hair bowled in.

'Lend us a burn, geez.'

I was determined this was going to be a fresh start, so whoever this big lump was had better find himself another fresh mark. 'I ain't got none, mate.'

Ginger plonked his arse on my desk and his massive plates of meat on my chair.

'What's your name, geezer?'

'Brook.'

'Where you come from, Brook?'

'Brixton.' I tried to make it sound tough. *Brixton*. As in: *Brixton jail; Brixton riots; Guns of Brixton...*

Ginger looked surprised, even impressed, like this information was worthy of respect. He raised his eyebrows. 'Brixton, yeah. Whereabouts?'

I was confused. 'The nick.'

'Nah, you plum. Where you from?' Then he spelt it out like he was talking to a Fraggle: 'Where...is...your...manor?'

When I told him, he called me a *fucking bumpkin*, then said his nan had a caravan near Clacton.

'Has she?' I asked, brightly. 'Have you been there?'

'You got canteen in Bricko yesterday, didn't you?'

It was a trick question, so I didn't answer.

He held out his palm. 'Give us a burn, then.'

'I've only got a tiny bit.'

'Why are you fucking lying to me? You got a problem with ginger-haired people or what?'

He kicked my chair out of the way and stood looming over me. 'You're out of order, geezer. We help each other out in here, you know what I mean?'

I bit my lip. What was this, a commune, or a nick? I offered to roll one and give him a twos.

'I don't want a snout that's been in your stinking mouth. I can smell your breath from here you cunt.'

He watched impatiently as I rolled him a fag, while I tried to cover up how much burn I had. Then he snatched the roll-up out of my hand and stabbed a long, freckly finger at me. 'You lied to the wrong fucking person.'

When I walked into the dining hall for breakfast the next morning, I was surprised to see there wasn't much of a queue for the serving hatch.

I walked over and picked up a tray, then a growling Geordie voice called me back.

'Where do you think you're going, Brook?' It was the barrel-shaped chief screw, Slater, who'd given us an induction when we arrived.

'You think you're the only trainee who's hungry, do you? There's nothing special about you lad. Go and sit down and wait your turn.' Slater pointed a stubby finger into the row of tables next to the wall and told me to sit there every mealtime for the rest of my sentence.

The further I walked down the aisle, the more I wanted to cry. The only empty place as far as I could see was next to Ginger. *Every mealtime...* every mealtime was going to be a concurrent mini sentence. Ginger was smiling when I reached his table. Was this really a coincidence? Or had he somehow engineered it so that I had no choice but to sit next to him?

He scraped his chair back to make it more difficult for me to squeeze past. My other two tablemates were bogging me out with contempt, like Ginger had already told them what they needed to know.

'Well, look who it ain't.' Ginger said.

I trapped myself into the chair next to him and leaned away against the wall. Had he been telling the truth last night when he said he could smell my breath? Or was it a general insult? Maybe he'd already spread the word: that new geezer, Brook, fucking *reeks*. I hadn't used shampoo or toothpaste in the ten days since I left the hostel. Slater said we needed to get money sent in for 'private spends' which we could use to buy toiletries. There weren't any phones, so I'd have to send Mum a letter. It was going to be a while before my hygiene got better. I didn't even know where I was. My best guess so far: Hut Four, HMYCC Harewood, at least an hour on a coach past Reading, middle of Fuck-knows-where-shire.

Ginger stood up and the rest of our table followed him. When I came back with my breakfast, his hot morning breath invaded my face, but I couldn't smell anything as nasty as him. 'You don't want that, do you, Brook?'

Before I could ask *Want what?* my chipolata had gone from my tray. Ginger's big gob wasn't full though, cos he still had enough room to say: 'I told you you shouldn't have lied to me, Brook.'

After breakfast, it was pissing with rain, and we were ordered over the Tannoy to go to the car park for work parade. I was sent to line up with the Generals Brigade, along with the other new recruits. As I looked around at the ranks of dripping identical brown macs, I felt the emptiness in my chipolata-less guts. This was us. This was us for at least the next six months.

There were a few trainees between me and Colin, so I couldn't attract his attention. I stepped slightly out of line so I could see him in case he turned around. After what had happened with Ginger, I wanted a reminder that we were in this together. Or even just to give him a look to say, *Fuck this for a game of soldiers.*

But Colin was standing as stiff and stoic as a squaddie while the rain flattened his Brixton-butchered barnet. I reckon he was as ready for graft as he'd ever been.

At least we'd be working together, so there was bound to be a chance to sneak a quick word. But after we were led by two screws into the woods, me and Colin were put into separate groups. Mine was taken to clear a patch of brambles without gloves. It seemed like us Generals were treated like the biggest mugs.

At lunchtime, my new tablemates wheedled out of me everything they wanted to know: *What for? How long? Where's your Co-ds?* And then used my answers as ammo against me.

They took the piss cos I didn't even throw a brick. As if they'd done something heroic to be in the nick.

By dinnertime, I'd been sent to Coventry. I realised this when they were talking about the weekend's football fixtures and both times I tried to chip in, they ignored me.

Ginger asked the others if they could hear something.

'Like what?' said Chilvers, a thick-necked south Londoner who talked quickly out of the side of his mouth.

'An annoying whining noise; like a fucking little gnat.'

I didn't say a word for six meals after that.

Most of us didn't work at the weekends, but in the mornings, we had to prepare for inspections. The Saturday hut inspection was done by Slater alone; on Sunday he was joined by the Governor. I was reminded of the full boot and shoe inspections we had every Thursday at Oakbridge, but this was even more like the army. We had to fold pieces of newspaper into every piece of our clothing so that they had a straight edge. I tried for hours, but this was too fiddly and confusing for me, so I had to beg help from another trainee, which put me a tailor-made cigarette into debt. For the Governor's Inspection, we also had to put on a crisp dickie dirt. I'd never been able to get the hang of ironing, and that's why I'd never voluntarily worn a shirt. It was also partly why I never wanted to work in an office.

At breakfast time on Sunday, while I was still in Coventry, I had no choice but to listen in to my tablemates having a debate about which hut was going to win the big inspection that morning. I'd already been told by Ginger, who was the number one in Hut Four, that I'd be scrubbing the corridor with soap and a stiff brush. When it was dry, it would need to be buffed, and now Ginger was claiming that nobody could get a floor as shiny as a geezer in our hut. Chilvers also fancied himself as a champion buffer. As they went on and on, I worked out that the prize for winning a Governor's Inspection was to be the first hut allowed to go to ablutions and association. Big deal. Call that a conversation?

I was relieved when Ginger finally got the nod from Slater and rose to lead his men to the serving hatch.

As I passed between the rows of tables, I clocked trainees eating cornflakes instead of porridge. This was an unexpected Sunday treat; maybe they served up Frosties at Christmas.

When I spotted the fried egg and bacon, I eagerly thrust out my tray. I'd had a hard-boiled egg on Friday – though like the weather it was cold and grey. On Saturday we got another chipolata; Sunday was looking like the breakfast of the week, even for the persona non-grata.

I stopped at the urn and filled my blue plastic mug with the stewed brown liquid they called tea. It had an oily rainbow on the surface and sugar wasn't provided, but when I returned to the table, I was still able to fantasise for a few seconds that I was sitting down to a fry-up in a caff. Mealtimes should have been the best times of the day, even if the food was nothing to write home about: at the very least you could sit in the warm and have a chat, but these petty bastards at my table were determined to deny me even that.

I was eating my cornflakes with my arm curled around my tray to protect my grub when Ginger made me jump by elbowing me. 'Oi, Brook, your Co-d wants you.' I twisted round to get a view of Colin's table, but he wasn't even looking my way. I turned back to my tray, and of course...both slices of bacon had vanished.

Chilvers was grinning with his mouth stuffed with loot, the end of a greasy piece of streaky was dangling down his chin. I felt my rage rise; I snapped inside; my fist tightened to give him a clump. I couldn't punch him with screws about though, so instead I just called him a cunt. Twice.

'You fucking slippery cunt. I'm going to fucking have you, you cunt.'

Ginger's eyes were alive with anticipation. My train had arrived at the station. I was about to be whizzed back from Coventry on the Inter-City. 'Only one thing for it,' he said. 'Up the washrooms after.'

Chilvers was waiting for me when I arrived, patrolling in front of the first row of sinks and smacking his palm with his right fist. I'd clocked he was stocky, but I hadn't noticed how well-built he was before; perhaps I'd bitten off more than I could chew. He was older than me too. Like Ginger, he looked like more of a man than a youth. Now it was too late, and anyway, you can't get more provocative than robbing bacon from a prisoner's plate. I wasn't going to let it go just cos he probably did weights. Otherwise, he'd be taking liberties forever.

Trainees arriving to wash their cutlery were realising that something was occurring. A crowd was building; a ring was closing in; I looked around for Colin, but I couldn't spot him. A gangly geezer with an afro, who looked about twenty-five, had appointed himself the referee. Now he was telling us to get on with it quickly.

I didn't have time to remember Ferris's training in jabs; I just rushed in instinctively, the way I always had; head down, and lashing out blindly with my fists. When that didn't stop him, I switched tactics and went for the trip.

As I tried to force a leg behind his, he was pounding my back and sides with punches. Still, he couldn't bring any power to his swing, cos I had him where I wanted him, pinned against the sinks. But my arms were getting lead-heavy already and it was a struggle to cling on: the bacon thief was all meat and too strong. I lost my grip, cos my strength was almost gone; then he shoved me to help me along.

I managed to stay on my feet though and staggered back towards him. This time he was ready and got a hold on my neck, then he yanked me around and flung me down on the deck.

As I scrambled away across the damp washrooms floor, the geezer with the afro got between us.

'You had enough, mate?'

I was reluctant to give up, but as I cowered on my wet arse with my back against the radiator, the throbbing pains started to kick in; the bruises of a loser were swelling under my skin. My mouth tasted of metal teaspoons, which was weird, cos we were only allowed plastic cutlery.

'Come on geezer, you've had a go. You don't want to end up on a Governor's Report, do you?'

He was showing me the way to an honourable exit. I reached up for the windowsill and nodded to accept it.

Chapter Twenty-Nine

There was no possibility of studying English, or anything academic, so I got a place on the P&D course. I hoped it would lead to my first qualification: City & Guilds, Basic Painting and Decorating Skills. Soon after starting with the P&D, I found a copy of *The Ragged Trousered Philanthropists* in the library. The two went together like panes and putty. This time I was determined to finish the novel, even if it took me the rest of my sentence.

My room in the P&D workshop had only recently been completed by the previous trainee and my first task was to strip off his freshly pasted woodchip. I'd already learned that when the wallpaper was tougher than Ginger to remove from your room, you needed to score it with a scraper, while imagining that you were striping Ginger's boat, then use a wide brush to soak it with water. After practising this technique for almost a week, I still had two walls and the ceiling to go.

The teacher was an old geezer with a starched white coat and dyed black hair called Mr Henry Stringer, but we were allowed to call him H. His other concession was the car speakers in the ceiling in the corridor, which meant we could listen to music on the radio while we worked. Other than that, he was strict. Any infringement of his many rules meant going "in the book" and being docked 10p a pop from our £2.20 a week wages. This included entering each other's rooms or talking across the corridor. I spent most of my time daydreaming, which is what I'd always done at work.

While I waited for the water to soak in, I went over and looked out of my basement window. There wasn't much of a view though, just a brick wall slap bang outside with a flower bed on top which didn't contain any flowers. I was hungry. Like at boarding school, the nagging in my stomach was a regular reminder of who held the power.

By fronting up to Chilvers, I'd saved my pride and my Sunday bacon, but my tablemates still left me out of their conversations. I'd assumed that having food nicked was a ritual that most trainees had to go through until they snapped, and a scrap was the logical conclusion. It was only after I'd been there for a few weeks that I realised fights were actually quite rare. Nobody wanted to risk getting put on a Governor's and losing remission. As it stood, if I stayed out of trouble, I would only have to serve half of my twelve-month sentence.

After my scrap with Chilvers, I was no longer in Coventry, cos my tablemates didn't actually ignore me if I tried to join in; it was more like self-censorship, cos I didn't feel like talking. But I was listening.

They thought they were getting things past me by talking fast and using London slang. What they didn't know was that I collected new slang words and enjoyed the challenge of trying to work out what they meant.

Ginger had got a knockback on his jam roll, and now he'd have to serve at least another twelve moons in the shovel. Unless he decided to have it away on his Bromleys. Even Chilvers didn't know that Bromley-by-Bows was rhyming slang for toes. So, when he asked Ginger for an explanation, I was given a new word for free which was handy, cos I'd never even heard of that place.

Losing out on his parole made Ginger more dangerous than usual, but at least by overhearing this news at the table, I'd had a warning that I needed to be extra careful in the hut. Apart from Chilvers and a few others, the rest of us were either sys or saps or plums. Anyone who couldn't be written off as an idiot would be accused, at least at our table, of thinking they were Jack the Biscuit.

I amused myself by trying to remember all the new slang I'd learned as I forced myself to put more effort into scraping off wallpaper. H had a habit of sneaking about, like Misery, the foreman in *The Ragged Trousered Philanthropists*, trying to catch us not working. He'd already told me twice that I was too slow: the second time, when he nabbed me standing under the speaker listening to news about pit closures, he put me in the book. I may have been slow, but I was also impatient, cos once I'd stripped off all the wallpaper and sanded down the gloss underneath, I'd finally be allowed to start using my paintbrushes. Then I could feel like a proper apprentice.

Perhaps if I was more normal, I would have started learning a trade as soon as I left school. That's what most people did in Brightlingsea. If they were ambitious or entrepreneurial, they grafted for someone else for a few years, then eventually got a van with their name on the side and bought an ad in the *Yellow Pages*. I didn't want to be bossed about, so I planned to start straight away on my own by putting up postcards in the corner shops and newsagents. Once I was established, I'd take on a labourer to do all the sanding and scraping, then I could just turn up like a tradesman with my kettles and brushes. But I swore I'd always pay my workers properly and treat them with respect.

Aside from a snatched chat if he was working at the serving hatch, I usually only saw Colin in the evenings when he was watching TV in the dining hall which doubled up as the association room. He was usually with Palmer, a mucker from the kitchens, which meant it was difficult to talk to him openly. Depending on what was on telly, I risked getting into an argument with somebody by talking at all.

I knew Colin was proud of his job cos he was often still wearing his kitchen clobber in the evenings, and he was super chuffed that the screw was impressed with how fast he was able to chop veg. He was studying for a qualification in basic food hygiene and had gone back to dreaming aloud about having his own caff. Unlike me, he appeared to be prospering on the safari park wing of the system.

One Thursday evening in February, I clocked Colin watching *Top of the Pops*. For once he was on his own.

'What's happening?'

Colin had always tried not to miss *Top of the Pops*, especially if he thought Madonna might be on, but now a particularly drippy ballad was playing, and he was prepared to indulge me with an answer more elaborate than *nothing* or *not much*.

'I got a letter from The Snake. He's asking what we want to do with our share from the van. Thirty-five quid each.'

'Is that his way of saying sorry for being a scummy wrong 'un?'

'He's never going to admit to anything. That's part of being a snake.'

'What else did he say?'

'Some old bollocks about a fight outside the Chinese in Brightlingsea.' Colin chuckled sarcastically, 'Oh yeah, he's asking if he can come up and visit with me old man in a couple of weeks.'

I lowered my voice. 'Get him to bring some hash, then.'

I thought he'd be game, but Colin pulled a face like I was expecting him to plug smack up his arse.

'I already told you, I don't want him anywhere near me.'

'Nor do I. But once he's paid us what he owes us we don't need to speak to him again. If we wait until we get out, we'll never see a penny.'

'Why don't you get him to bring it to you if you're so bothered?'

'I would if I could. My old dear won't have him in her car.' Mum hadn't forgiven Dennis for talking her into putting the insurance for the van in her name, which led to her getting hassled by the coppers.

Colin sneered, 'It's all right for you. I don't want anything to fuck up my parole.'

All right for me. Like it was my fault he'd got an extra three months for nicking money from Skully and so had to apply for parole. Though if he did get his parole, he'd be out on the same day as me. I lowered my voice to a whisper and told him that Ginger was still on my case. If I could get him stoned, then he would probably leave me alone. And I doubted he'd give so much of a toss about winning inspections.

Colin shook his head and said he didn't want to smoke that shit anymore. He explained that he was also going to give up baccy cos it was too expensive a habit in the nick, and he wanted to get fit so he could try and get into the Harewood football team.

Same old Colin. All or nothing.

'You could sell your share, couldn't you? You'd be set up for the rest of your sentence.' I knew from Wayne and geezers in the hostel that puff was pretty much the most valuable commodity inside. According to

Trevor, most kangas turned a blind eye.

Colin didn't take his eyes off the telly. 'You're not fucking listening. I'm not risking losing my parole over anything. I want to get out of here as soon as I can.'

'So do I ...' Didn't we all? But I also wanted to serve better quality time, otherwise it was going to drag worse than double maths; double maths if I was forced to sit next to a psycho who enjoyed jabbing my thigh with a compass. I thought we were supposed to be helping each other out in the nick. Now Colin had conveniently transformed himself into a model prisoner; basically, a lick. He'd be going jogging with the Governor next.

But I didn't say any of this: I was lacking his killer instinct for manipulation, rewriting the history of old favours, playing the best mate card.

A big cheer went up from the studio audience, then Madonna appeared, high-kicking and twirling and pleading with her baby to set her free.

I wasn't in the mood for it, so I got up and left.

Chapter Thirty

Ginger decided to have it away on his Bromleys and judging by the rush of activity in the corridor, half of our hut was intending to join him.

He was stood in the doorway of my room, his brown nylon mac stretched tightly across his wide shoulders, a packet of Bourbons stuffed in each front pocket. He was puffed out, like he was wearing all his kit at once.

'Are you coming, Brook, or what?'

I hesitated for a second and Ginger moved on to the next room. I looked around for what to take. I didn't have any biscuits, so I settled for my Walkman and a couple of tapes. Fuck it. I didn't deserve to be there in the first place.

There were at least ten trainees gathered at the front of the hut, all geed up like footballers in the tunnel, waiting for Captain Ginger to blow the whistle. One of them, Taylor, my next-door neighbour, greeted me like I was one of the chaps by slapping me hard on the back with his good hand. The lower half of his left arm was prosthetic and had metal pincers on the end which he used for gripping. He was here cos he'd taken it off and used it to knock someone out. The judge warned him that next time it would be confiscated.

'Top man,' Taylor said now. 'The more the fucking merrier.'

The front door was only open wide enough for one trainee to peek out and keep bogeye, but the freezing wind seeping in made me cough and was a reminder that we were still in the thick of a lingering winter.

Taylor turned away from me to a geezer I knew was his mate; I still didn't have any mates in this place. Apart from Colin, obviously, but I hadn't sought him out since he let me down with the hash and he hadn't come looking for me either.

For the first time, in my time, there was a buzz about the hut; now we were all in it together. But how long would the unity last? Surely, once we'd legged it past the washrooms and the football pitch and the quarry into the darkness of fuck-knows-where-next, we were bound to get split up and I'd have nobody to stick with. I couldn't imagine me and Ginger stopping for a breather and splitting a packet of his biscuits.

Where was Ginger? Was it because of him we were all still waiting?

As I looked back down the corridor, my thoughts had an unfamiliar and immediate clarity: I didn't need to go anywhere; with Ginger gone I really could have a fresh start. When I reflected on this moment later that night, I thought I might have experienced what other people called common sense. All my life, I'd been told I didn't have any.

I was the only one left from our table at breakfast the next morning when Slater gloated that fifteen of the nineteen escapees were already banged up in Marshton. In the second it took me to look round at Colin's table, I found myself hoping he'd gone. I don't know why, cos when I clocked him, swigging his tea, I was actually relieved and then I felt a little bit guilty.

By dinner time, another three had been captured. Slater never mentioned the last escapee, though a rumour went around a couple of weeks later that Ginger had made it to Amsterdam, from where he'd sent the Governor a telegram. Maybe I was right, and he'd just needed to get stoned after all.

One lunchtime, soon after the new recruits arrived, I was half-listening to lame synth-pap and crap chat on Radio 1, when my ears were alerted to something much rougher and more exciting blasting across the corridor. It was coming from the room of a new trainee, Atkinson who'd moved in directly opposite me.

I was wary that it could come across as clichéd, to start a conversation with a black geezer about reggae, but I was intensely curious to know what he was listening to. When I looked through the glass panel into his room, he was lying on his bed reading *Papillon*, another reason why

I thought we'd get on. But when I knocked, he lowered the fat paperback and cursed, *raasclaat*. Then he asked loudly if I'd clocked that his door was shut. I didn't know there was such a thing as privacy in the hut.

By the weekend, a new number one had emerged from the fresh batch of trainees. With his inhaler and thick glasses and overlapping front teeth, Barratt didn't strike me as a typical hard man, but he definitely had all the chat. It was Barratt who shortened Atkinson's name to Ackee, cos he was so into reggae, and ackee and saltfish is the Jamaican national dish. He also had a *joey* to make up his bed pack each morning and iron his shirt.

On Sunday morning, Barratt sent his joey to fetch me. He wanted to know how long I'd been at Harewood and what chores I'd done lately. I had nothing to lose by telling him the truth: Ginger had taken a dislike to me and made me scrub the corridor every weekend for six weeks, even though I was hopeless at cleaning. Barratt laughed wheezily, and easily, like he actually wanted to have a laugh, then said he'd get some of the new bods to do the shittiest jobs. I left his room with a bounce in my step and congratulated myself, yet again, for not being a sheep and following Ginger across the fields.

The following day, Ackee's door was open after lunch and I clocked him leant over his desk, fiddling with the back of his radio.

I hovered in the doorway. 'What's that you're listening to, mate?'

He glanced up with a scowl, like, not *you* again, then he snapped, 'Sound, man.'

This time, rather than ignore me, he'd chosen to answer cryptically, which threw me slightly. I said, 'It sounds blinding. I really like a bit of reggae and I wondered what it was.'

I noticed he'd managed to connect his Walkman to the speaker of his Roberts Rambler. Colin's old cellmate in Brixton had told him that Roberts Ramblers were the best radios you could have in the nick. I begged Mum to send me one up, but the radio I actually received was less dandy; some brand I'd never heard of, that she'd bought cheap from Tandy.

'Who's your favourite sound?'

'I don't know.'

'Cha! What do you mean, you don't know, man?'

I didn't know what he was on about. 'I ain't an expert, I just like a lot of the reggae I've heard.'

'Name some of the artists you check for. Directly.'

'Like Bob Marley, Smiley Culture, Yellowman. Erm…UB40.'

'*UB40*.' He widened his eyes and stared at me incredulously. Then he dismissed me with the back of his hand. 'Piss off, man. Don't fuck me around.'

I was being serious, so I stood my ground. 'Have you heard UB40's *Baggariddim* LP? It's a bit like what you're listening to.'

He sucked his teeth and waved me away again, this time more violently. 'LEAVE. YOU HAVEN'T GOT A CLUE, MAN.'

I wasn't going anywhere. I'd been waiting for months to have an interesting conversation. 'Okay, what do you think of Tippa Irie?'

'Cha! Every bandwagonist boy think they know 'bout Tippa and Smiley; just cah dem man went on *bloodclaat Top of the Pops*.'

'I ain't jumping on no bandwagon, I honestly like the music.'

'Tippa chats pon Saxon, man. Saxon a my sound, you get me?'

I worked out later that *sound* meant *sound system*. 'How come? Are you one of the owners of it?'

'Piss off with your stupidness man.'

He looked back down at his homemade sound. When he glanced up again, I was still there.

'Saxon are my sound, man, directly. But listen keenly: that don't mean the sound belongs to *me*. You understan'? Me and my bredrins dem used to go raving to Saxon every week. Saxon are like Liverpool, man. Top of the league. You get me?'

I did, sort of. But he'd jumped quickly to Advanced-Level Reggae, while I was still cramming for CSE. 'What you're listening to sounds pretty wicked to me. 'What is it?'

We were interrupted by the Tannoy: *Bing bong: All trainees report for work parade immediately. All trainees report for work parade…*

'Why do the kangas always have to repeat everything?' I said.

'Cha! I ain't even ready, man.' Ackee looked at me like this was my fault.

'What work group are you in?'

'The general dogsbodies, ta raas. Digging frigging ditches and ting. Better than bang-up in Marshton though innit?'

I nodded. I knew what it was like to do bang-up. Directly. Marshton was the closed part of the nick, about twenty miles up the road. Ackee must have been moved here for good behaviour when the failed escapees were shipped the other way. 'You should try and get on the P&D course, man. At least it's in the warm.' He clearly liked to keep himself to himself, so: 'You have your own room to work on as well, and the teacher mostly leaves us to it. And we get to listen to the radio. I know there's a place going at the moment.'

Ackee was nodding, and even hinted at a smile, 'Yeah man, I might do that, bredrin. It sounds like my sort of ting.'

Chapter Thirty-One

Visits and letters are the highlights of life inside, but if I didn't get anything for a few days, I made an effort to take it in my stride. I'd seen supposedly tough geezers, like Ginger and Chilvers, go visibly downhill if they didn't hear from their girl. Sometimes it was better not to be in love. I wasn't in love with anybody, but there was still no one I'd rather get a letter from than Verity. The opposite was true of Dennis.

When he wrote to me, he managed to spread his words so thinly that he only averaged about four to a line. The sum of these 200-odd words was a waste of both our time, cos he didn't say anything of interest. I replied with a letter as empty as his, plus interest. Meaning: I revealed even less, so that what I wrote was pretty much meaningless. I was glad that he never came back to me; I didn't want to be owing him words while he still owed us money.

He asked me what was wrong with Colin, but even if I'd known that I wouldn't have told him. He said Colin hadn't replied to his letters. What I could have said, is that by this point, Colin wouldn't have replied to anybody. He'd told me one night that he wasn't going to send out any more Visiting Orders, and he probably wouldn't even read any letters he received. Though I did find that last part a bit hard to believe.

I was chuffed to get a letter from Lucy. I reckon she said more on two-thirds of a page of A4 than she'd ever said to me in one go before. She told me which subjects she'd chosen to study for GCSE; about seeing Curiosity Killed the Cat in concert, up the Uni; and the big fight outside the Chinese in Brightlingsea. She was a bit vague about the scrap and said *apparently*, though I'd already heard Colin's account of Dennis's account and Dennis was there on the scene throwing punches.

Verity's letters didn't mention the Chinese. She wasn't really into gossiping, never mind about fighting. She wanted to know how they filled our days doing time. I thought it would be too dry to write it down normally, so I decided to tell her in rhyme. I was also inspired cos she'd said that she really liked my poem about the dole. But this time I struggled to get on such a creative roll. Well, the rhymes did flow freely, but when I read them back, they sounded too obvious and forced; even twee. A bit *de dum, de dum, de diddly dum, de dum de dum de dee.*

I was reading the poem for Verity yet again on a Sunday afternoon, and hoping it would improve, while waiting for Mum to turn up for a visit. Verity had told me she was starting a band and had already written some songs. I hoped she was having better luck with couplets than me.

I jumped up with a start at half past two. *Bing bong: Brook to the visiting room. Brook to the visiting room.* The carrot-crunching screw with the bad attitude made it sound like a threat when in the nick it was the best news you could get. Fuck you, kangaroo. I'll be out of here in ninety days and a breakfast. How about you?

I jogged down the path next to the lawn that we trainees weren't allowed to walk on, then across the car park to the Portakabin they called a visiting room.

Mum stood up and gave me an excited wave as I walked in, like I was severely short-sighted. When I got closer to her table, I could see she was delighted. She leaned over and embraced me for as long as I'd let her, which wasn't very long. I was already embarrassed, and I knew the screws were on the lookout for any lingering contact.

When I sat down and looked around, I clocked Barratt at the next table. Even more reason to feel self-conscious. Visiting him were two good-looking young women who I guessed were slightly older than us.

Mum said she was sorry she was late, but the car had got a puncture on the motorway. She'd spent half an hour on the hard shoulder, waiting for the AA.

I would have expected that to have really pissed her off, but she was still beaming. She asked me how I was doing, and I said, *not bad, the usual*. Then I thought I'd better make more of an effort, beings as she was going to spend seven hours in a car on her own just to see me, so I told her I'd passed another test for my City and Guilds. I didn't admit it took me three attempts though, cos I wanted her to pay me to paint the house. When I suggested the idea now, without bringing up money, she started fidgeting, like she was distracted.

'Do you fancy a cup of tea? And some chocolate?'

Nobody turned down sweets on a visit.

When she'd gone, I glanced sideways at Barratt, just as the woman directly opposite him lent forward and clasped his hand. The other one, who was tall and had wavy black hair streaked with highlights, was sat upright, her deep dark eyes on the lookout for screws.

We both pretended not to notice as Barratt stuffed his hand down his trousers. Then her lips curled into a slight smile to show me she knew I was looking at her.

I glanced down at the table and a flush crept up my cheeks. But two seconds later, my curiosity drove me to have another peek.

Barratt, and the woman I assumed was his girlfriend, were laughing now that the deed had been done. The other one was smiling at them, but then she tilted her head slightly towards me as I looked across, like she was expecting this to happen. Her smile slowly widened, and her eyes were dancing for me.

My heart started thumping like I was the trainee who'd just plugged some drugs. I decided I wouldn't look down unless she looked away first, or Barratt turned around. Then Mum returned, all too quick, and unstuffed the chocolate bars from her cardigan pockets.

'I may as well tell you my news, Jarrod, now that you've brought up the house.' She was staring at me with cautious determination.

Oh no, here we go. Sweetening me up with chocolate, like she did when she gave me a Mars Bar in the kitchen, before revealing I was being packed off to boarding school for five years. I guessed she'd been renting out my room cos she needed the cash. What did it matter though? As long as I could have it back.

'I've decided to move to Brighton.'

I tore open the Kit-Kat with my teeth and snapped it in two, but not vertically, the way people usually do. 'What do you mean, Mum?' But she couldn't have put it more clearly.

'I need a change. Bill and I spend most weekends together anyway and ...' She shrugged and smiled, then sipped her tea.

'But what about me? Where am I going to live?'

I must have said it loudly cos the whole of Barratt's table looked over. But I wasn't able to catch her eye again.

Mum said, 'Well, you don't need to worry, because I'm not going to be selling the house for at least a year.' She told me her friend, Shirley, was going to live there and she'd agreed I could let my old room if that's what I wanted.

'What about Lucy?'

'She doesn't want to move away from her friends.' Mum added, all sarky, 'and apparently Adrian has promised to decorate her bedroom.'

'He's probably bribed her with a microwave and fridge in there as well. Then she'll hardly have to see him.'

'It's different for Lucy. You're eighteen now, Jarrod, it's time to take responsibility for yourself. When I was your age, I was already responsible for you.'

That was a fact, so I couldn't really argue. But bloody hell, she'd thought it all through. Well, she had just spent three hours in a car with nothing else to do.

'Come on, don't look so glum. I'm sure I can help you with a deposit if you need it. Or there's a spare room at Bill's. You can come and live with us for a while if you like, until you get yourself back on your feet.'

'Why would I want to do that? I've never even met him, have I?'

I thought I was only stating the obvious, though if I'm honest, there was an edge to my voice. She looked hurt, like I'd lobbed litter on her fresh bed of roses.

'Don't tell me you want to go back and hang around with all those petty criminals in Brightlingsea. And then end up here again. Or somewhere worse, serving a longer sentence. Is that what it's going to take for you to finally learn your lesson?'

Mum had raised her voice to an excruciating level. I could hear them all giggling at Barratt's table. I stared down at the horrible charcoal school trousers they made us wear for visits. I'd gone from flirtation to humiliation in the space of a Kit-Kat and half a stick of Twix; now I didn't want to face any of them.

Eventually, I looked up at Mum, slowly and self-consciously, 'I've already learned my lesson.'

'What *are* you planning to do, then?'

'I'm going to be a self-employed painter and decorator,' I said, then repeated aloud, without conviction, a variation on the spiel I'd told myself many times in my head. 'I'll start off with small jobs, then, when I've got a bit of money, I'm going to do one of those things where you can learn to drive in a week – a crash course, or whatever they're called – and then I'll save up and buy a van.'

She was looking at me sceptically, like none of this was ever likely to happen.

'You don't believe me, do you?'

'It's not that I don't believe that's your intention, I'm just not sure if I can imagine you driving around in a van decorating houses.'

I wanted to upend the table. Or throw it through the window. Instead, I dared to glance over, but this time her eyes were focussed on Barratt, as he made them laugh with one of his stories.

Mum leaned across and placed a hand over my tightened fist. 'I'm just not convinced that painting is the right occupation for someone with your lack of…for someone with dyspraxia.'

I wished I'd never told her. 'I haven't even been diagnosed yet.'

'Why don't you think about going to college instead?'

'It's too late for that. I need to earn some money.'

'Don't be silly, it's never too late. Look at Tony. He's training to be a teacher now.'

'Good for him.' I meant it too. Maybe she had a point, but I wasn't going to admit it there and then. I'd rather find a way to contradict her, especially after she'd destroyed my dream.

A screw walked between the rows of tables, letting us know that visiting time was over.

'If I go back to college, I'll have the same problem I had in my mocks. They won't be able to read my writing.'

Mum was saying something about it being possible to get extra time in your exams if you were diagnosed with dyspraxia when I heard a scraping of chairs as other visitors got up to leave. I became distracted by an urgent need to say goodbye to *her* with a smile.

'There's someone Bill knows who–'

The screw hovered by our table and told us to finish. His uniformed beer gut was blocking my view of Barratt's visitors leaving.

Mum glared up at the fat kanga. 'Let me finish my sentence, will you. We heard you the first time.'

I lay on my bed and tried to doze off the chocolate and post-visit comedowns. All I had to look forward to now was dinner, and Sundays were usually the worst. I supposed they were balancing the fact that it had the best breakfast. I tormented myself by imagining my tray: curling luncheon meat, cold processed peas and hard mash that had been spitefully flecked with swede.

And then *her* smile came back to me. Nobody had ever smiled at me so promisingly, apart from Verity. I wanted to think that she was trying to tell me: in different circumstances…then, maybe.

I was exactly halfway through my sentence, and although I didn't know how many J Arthurs I'd had, I was confident the count, like the deed, could be done with one hand. I'd begun to wonder if the rumours were true, that the screws were putting some powder in the tea urn to stop us feeling horny. Now Barratt's gorgeous visitor had stirred something inside me.

It had been nine months since I'd last kissed Verity properly; nine months since I'd snogged anybody. All my sexual memories were locked in a box, and I'd rarely been in the mood to fumble for the key. It started in the hostel when I was sharing with Ted. I wasn't able to get aroused in that room, didn't matter whether he was in there or not. Even in the bath I'd found it hard to stay hard; there always seemed to be voices on the landing disturbing me.

There was no privacy in the hut either. Not with a big window in our doors and a front wall that didn't reach the ceiling. At boarding school, I'd developed techniques, to go undercover, under the sheets, but here every movement in bed resulted in a creak.

I guess that after a while I'd stopped having more than passing thoughts about sex. Until that Sunday. It may have only been looks and smiles, but her dancing eyes had got under my skin. Now I felt compelled to imagine what was under her clothes. And what we could get up to under her sheets. But I would have to wait until tonight. Was it possible to do it lying *under* my bed?

I was unpleasantly surprised by a knock at my door. When I opened my eyes, I saw Barratt's joey at the glass. The main man wanted to see me immediately. I told myself it was only a smile. She smiled at me first and I was just being friendly. A churn of nerves stirred in my chocolate-stuffed guts, but at least I didn't have an erection.

Barratt was stood by his window smoking a joint; his number two, Henderson, was sat on the bed. They'd first met in a detention centre a few years earlier.

Henderson was smirking. 'How's it going, Brook?'

'All right.'

'How's your old dear?'

'...Okay.' Was that a trick question?

Then Barratt attempted an impression of Mum, as if Mum was a bossy posh woman in a sitcom. 'Oh, *Jarrod*. I do hope when you get out you're not going to hang around with those *dreadful* criminals again.'

I had to grin and bear it, but inside I was mortified. Insulting each other's mums was a verbal sport in the nick, but I thought I was above getting too wound up about that stuff, cos it wasn't like any of them actually knew my mum. But now Barratt did. Sort of. Still, the woman I'd been lusting after could easily be his sister.

'I'm only teasing you geezer. The way your old girl shut that screw up was fucking wicked mate.'

I was pleasantly surprised when he offered me the joint. I took a pull, which burned my lips, then instantly turned them upwards into a grin. I'd already recognised the pungent sweet smell. 'Squidgy black, ain't it?'

'Gold seal. You puff a lot on the out, do you?'

'All the time: buckets, hot knives, pipes, the lot.'

He looked at Henderson. 'I thought so. You must have an idea who the puffers are in the hut.'

'Yeah, I reckon.' I had chatted with a couple of stoneheads. One of them, Barber, was there for intent to supply.

'Fancy selling a bit of this?'

I hesitated, but only cos I was shocked that he'd asked me.

'I ain't a complete cunt, you know. You can have a good little earner if you screw your nut. There'll be more an' all if you don't fuck it up.'

In this place, you were either a fraggle, or a sap, or one of the chaps, and I'd had enough of being kept awake by hunger pangs every night and roasting cos I'd run out of burn three days before canteen.

Occasionally, if he was feeling sociable, Colin would call round for me and we'd walk together to supper, which consisted of a couple of biscuits and a stewed oily cuppa. Ackee always had a bag of sugar, and I'd beg him a bly. He didn't mind giving us a spoonful as long as it weren't every night.

I told Colin about the gear on the way to the dining hall. I guess I was seeking his approval as usual. But I also wanted to make sure he heard it from me.

His first reaction was: 'Why the fuck would he give it to you of all people?'

I knew Barratt was good at *delegating*, though it wasn't a word I was familiar with at the time. He had Henderson to organise the inspections, a joey to make his bed and clean his shoes, and various trainees to keep bogeye for screws. But Colin had a point, I was also confused: why would Barratt delegate the sale of his hash to me? Maybe he'd made my chances of success the subject of a bet. I'm not sure I would have bet on myself. The only thing I'd ever dealt was a pack of cards, and I'd never stored anything at all up my arse.

But I weren't going to come out with all this to Colin. 'Why not me? He guessed I was a smoker; he don't want to do it himself. We get on all right…'

'And if you get caught, you'll end up in Marshton. What's going to happen to you then?'

'I'm going to be careful.'

He checked over his shoulder that nobody was close to us. 'You want to watch your back, Jarrod. I reckon they could be setting you up.'

Colin had got para without even having a puff. Though if he'd asked me, I would have given him a blim for free. Maybe that would've put the smile back on his face.

Chapter Thirty-Two

'Make sure you keep it plugged,' Barratt had said, before biting me off a chunk. 'You just need to stick it up far enough so it can't fall out.'

That night, I practised plugging and unplugging in bed. After each plug, I got up to squat and shake my arse to make sure it didn't come loose. Early the next morning, as soon as it was light, I sat at my desk and rolled the sticky black hash into thin strips, each one long enough to make a single skin spliff, and then I squeezed them all back together in the oily cellophane and replugged. Luckily gold seal was as malleable as Blue-Tac and nestled not too uncomfortably when pushed into my crack.

The rule of tick in the nick was that anything borrowed had to be repaid double on canteen day. It couldn't have been any more cutthroat capitalist but then it weren't me who made up the rules. I was reminded of something I'd recently read in the *Ragged Trousered Philanthropists* which was that until we get socialism, or in my case freedom, then we had to do what was needed to survive.

There was no such currency as cash, and I didn't know the exchange rate for hash, but Barratt advised two spliff's worth for a half-ounce packet of burn and I made this the gold seal standard. He wanted two ounces, so anything I sold over eight spliffs would be profit in my pocket. Or up my arse, depending on what I chose to do with it.

The first trainee I approached was Barber, the stoner, then Palmer, Colin's best mucker from the kitchens. After a few initial enquiries, the punters came to me. I wasn't expecting it to be so easy.

Each morning, I went through the ritual of dividing the lump back into strips to make sure I was still on track. Once it was down to the size of a pea, I had to clench my buttocks constantly to make sure I could still feel it.

On Barratt's next visit, he 'came through' with a jagged rock of Moroccan, which was much harder to break into deals and gave me a sore bottom. The piece I had to sell was the size of a small bird's egg, and after having it plugged for a day and a night, I decided to find a new nest. It wasn't only the discomfort, I started to get para that I could be mugged, and therefore it was better not to keep all my eggs in one basket. I divided half the rock into small pieces, which I stashed in a matchbox and stuffed behind the radiator in my P&D room.

This time, word got around quickly, and I was being approached by more trainees than I would like to have been. Many of these geezers who now knew my name were from outside my hut, Hut Four; some of them I'd never had any sort of dealings with before.

I had customers waiting for me after meals outside the dining hall; approaching me during association; I was even hassled at work.

One afternoon, I came out of the shower and two strangers backed me into the corner of the washrooms like an endgame at chess and kept up the pressure until I bit them a blim under duress.

It seemed like the rest of the nick had gone dry, and everyone was now begging me for a spliff and a bly. I'd always found it harder to say no directly than to lie, but to do either convincingly I had to push myself to look at the desperados hard in the eye, until they gave up and walked away with a screwface, cussing me and sometimes muttering threats under, or even over, their breath. I didn't tell Colin about any of this, cos he would probably have told me that he'd tried to warn me. And I'd already made him proper para and angry, cos he'd been pestered a few times about whether I had any, just cos he happened to be my Co-d.

A hefty geezer from Colin's hut, called Silvestre, came to Hut Four to find me. His shoulders were almost as broad as the corridor.

'Why are you disrespecting me, Brook?'

'I don't know what you mean.'

'Why are telling everyone you won't let off a ting to me?'

It wasn't true, but he didn't wait for an answer. He lifted me above his head by my chin and pinned me to the corridor wall. 'Don't ever take my name in vain.'

I'd never spoken the word *Silvestre* in my life. Not even after I'd clocked him snorting a line off the back of his girlfriend's hand during a visit.

Barratt didn't come through for a month and I was relieved to have a break from the grief. The final consignment he gave me, though I didn't know it was the last one at the time, was an eighth of sticky gold seal which carried a stink that lingered on my fingers. I'd already built up a sustainable burn habit, and I could now afford to pay a trainee to iron my shirt and fold my clothes for inspections, so this time I decided to smoke the profits. I went to tell Ackee the news.

If you judged a tape by its cover, then Ackee was a lover of soul and country and western. At any one time, we were allowed to have six pre-recorded cassettes in our possession, and his half a dozen collection had been taped over with sound system selection. He was playing one now, on the system he'd strung up by connecting his Walkman to the speaker of his Rambler. A speaker that was vibrating with distorted bass.

'Is that Saxon you're listening to, Ackee?'

'Nah man, a Jaro dat. Directly.'

'Who?'

'Kill-a-man-jaro, the champion clash sound from back a yard.'

'I don't think I've heard of them.'

Ackee pulled in his chin and grinned, 'You don't know nutten 'bout sound, Brooky. Your sound is the tin pan sound, man. Directly.'

Whatever. Ackee may have been reggae-clever, but what he didn't know was that my arse was the champion arse, with an eighth of prime gold seal freshly parked.

'I might have a lot to learn about sound systems,' I said, 'but I do know a little bit about puff.' I was the one grinning now. 'You wait. We're going to have a proper session tonight, mate.'

He gestured to the door, so I came in and closed it. 'It's top gear,'

235

I said quietly, then whispered, 'gold seal.'

He pressed a finger to his pursed lips and nodded thoughtfully, but I could see from his eyes that the news had made him happy. 'I don't know nutten about the hash, man; strictly sensi me smoke on the out yuh nuh, star.'

'And I don't know anything about sensi, but I do know we're going to be licking a buzz for Miss P. It's the best, mate, I'm telling you. That's why they call it gold seal.'

I'd never heard him laugh, like *really* laugh before. It was a low rumbling sound, like the bass on his tapes, and it made the top half of his body shake. When he stopped, he shoved me playfully. 'Yes Brooky, big up yuh chest now, star.' Then he lowered his voice, 'Anything we need, I've got it covered. Cigarette, Rizla...munchies and ting.'

Ackee could always draw on a stash, probably cos he didn't smoke fags. He wasn't a baron exactly, but nor was he averse to an opportunity; like when it snowed, and he bought himself an extra blanket for two tailor-mades and four custard creams.

One day he let me into a secret, something he said he hadn't told anybody else at Harewood: the reason he was so keen to keep his nose clean, was that his earliest date of release was the day before Notting Hill Carnival. Any fuck-ups and he'd be missing the biggest gathering of sound systems in the world for a third year in a row. Still, I was confident he wouldn't say no to a smoke.

I'd picked up from Wayne but had since heard with my own ears that reggae, not Elvis, was the real jailhouse rock. On Sunday nights, at eleven o'clock, everybody in our hut was listening to reggae whether they liked it or not, cos half the radios were tuned into the Ranking Miss P. At least they were under Barratt's regime. Ginger had made sure that everyone except him and his mates were silent by whatever arbitrary time he decided; and if you didn't get the message the first time, there'd be threats to come and batter you with a PP9 battery in a sock.

Now it was only ten o'clock, and I'd already dealt the last of the gold seal I needed to sell and rolled up a few spliffs for later. By quarter past, I couldn't wait any longer. I wanted to block it all out for a while;

the bantering, bartering and begging, and enjoy a buzz with some tunes on my Walkman.

It was a pity I didn't have any reggae to put me in the mood for the show. I'd thought about asking Mum to send me the Bob Marley tape I had at home, but Marley was his parents' music according to Ackee. I asked him once what the new type of electronic reggae was called, that Miss P often played. 'It's ragamuffin, innit,' he curtly explained.

Dear Mum, please could you send me some ragamuffin music? And she'd be asking herself, what is this *ragamuffin*? I spluttered on my spliff now as I remembered she'd told me once about a conference she'd been at, where her tutor had looked through the programme and asked: *Who is this chap, Reggae?*

At three minutes to eleven, word spread that the doddery old night screw, who patrolled hourly, was on his way after leaving Hut Three. We would have to hold tight before starting the party. He paused outside each of our rooms with his torch beam pointed at the ceiling while all of the trainees pretended to be sleeping. We're all present and correct, I believe, sir, now hurry along. There's nothing to see here. *We've* got something to hear though, *see*, when you've finished dawdling. You get me?

I knew he'd gone when a radio came on, then another and another and another. I got up to turn on my transistor and snatch up my matches; doctor, I think this reggae fever is catching.

The Ranking Miss P was talking between records, a husky and intimate mix of patois and BBC. *This one's dedicated to the roughneck posse.* The electronic snares rat-a-tatted like machine guns, followed by a simple keyboard melody. I beamed with recognition, *I know this one*; then the vocals came in and a woman MC was bragging that she couldn't be tested. I was confused: last week I'd heard a gruff geezer cussing President Botha over the same tune. Ackee told me later that when a rhythm was hot, it got versioned again and again and again: sometimes by different producers.

Afterwards, Miss P went into a section of lovers; still wicked rhythms, but some of the lyrics were corny, I had to admit. I stepped across the corridor to deliver Ackee his spliffs. We bumped fists, then he gave me half a packet of Bourbon biscuits. There was too much excitement fluttering in my guts to be hungry, though once I calmed down, I'd be craving with the munchies.

I was still stood in his doorway when we heard: *Trouble double dah-ah-bull, trouble double dah-ah-bull.* I knew this tune even before I knew Ackee. No false alarm this time, it was Barrington Levy, 'Here I Come'. When the music kicked in, it was greeted with cries of appreciation and extra percussion; fists banging the doors and the walls. Ackee climbed onto his chair and was pounding on the ceiling: *Lick wood*, he bawled out, *lick wood*.

Trainees rushed spontaneously from their rooms and the cloying scent of gold seal became thick and almost sickly in the narrow corridor. The recess in the middle of the hut was transformed into a dancefloor. I laughed uncontrollably with the joy of release. I didn't want to dwell on this thought, but I knew: the nick would never get any better than this.

Chapter Thirty-Three

I'd never seen anybody playing chess in the hut, so when Barratt suggested a competition, I couldn't believe my luck. We only had one board, but another was swiftly knocked up, by felt-tipping the black squares onto the seat of a wooden chair.

My first match was over in twenty minutes, half of which were spent teaching my opponent how a knight moves. The quarter-final was as easy as taking biscuits from a baby. In the semi, I drew Barber, who I thought could be a dark horse cos he didn't fall for any of my traps; once I'd managed to pin him back, I gradually turned the screw and got him on the rack.

The final was played on a Sunday, in the dorm at the end of the hut. Two beds were dragged into the middle of the room and the board placed on a locker between us. The entry fee for the competition was a packet of biscuits or three tailor-made cigarettes. These were displayed on top of another locker next to the players. Winner takes all.

My opponent was Wilson, a trainee so fresh he still had a decent haircut. He also had clear skin and rosy cheeks, like he'd been eating decent grub up 'til the end of last week. I hadn't seen him play before, but I was still convinced I would win. In the early stages we appeared to be evenly matched and then Wilson pieced together a multi-pronged attack. I felt stung, cos I hadn't seen it coming.

I didn't see Colin coming either, but when I looked away from my troubles on the board, he was stood in the dorm doorway with a manic expression on his face. Barratt moved quickly to have a word, but whatever he said he allowed Colin to stay. Later, he asked me, 'What's wrong with your Co-d? He was acting like some sort of fraggle.'

I wanted to blame Colin for making me lose my concentration; truth was, he didn't help, but Wilson had got me already. Luckily, for the final, we'd agreed best of three.

In between games I went into the corridor with Colin, and he said he really needed my help. I didn't give him a chance to explain. It was really bad timing I told him, though I was also aware that in Harewood, *help* could only mean one thing: being hassled to hand something over. I promised I would come and find him later.

In the second game, Wilson got better; almost from the off he had me under heavy pressure. Barratt warned me twice about taking too long with my moves. Maybe he knew, like I did, that even if I took all the time in the world, Wilson would always be at least one move ahead. I'd assumed I was the same player who'd beaten Oliver; in reality, I was just a rusty amateur.

The prize slipped further and further away until finally it was too late; the last time I heard *check*, it ended in mate. I cursed myself for being a greedy fool, cos it was me who'd called for the rule of winner takes all.

But it turned out that the winner didn't take all at all. Wilson split his nine packets of biscuits and twenty-one tailors with the promoter. I should have guessed: Barratt had even delegated his hustling.

The next day, on a sticky afternoon in the middle of June, the sun's rays had even found a way down to my P&D room. I was brushing paste onto a length of woodchip when I clocked Colin's flushed face at the open window. His forehead was glistening with sweat like he'd been running.

'You've got to help me. I've got people threatening to slice me.'

I hadn't gone to find him like I'd promised. 'How comes?' I asked, though I couldn't really afford to hear him out. If H caught me talking my wages would be docked.

'I owe out four ounces of burn.' He glanced over his shoulder, like his debtors might be coming.

Four ounces. Did he think I was Harry Grout or something? 'I thought you'd given up smoking!'

'What's that got to do with it?'

'Well, four ounces is a lot of burn.' But it was such a lot of burn, that if he was lying, he would have come up with a less ridiculous amount.

He was shifting from foot to foot now, like a restless jogger waiting for the traffic lights to change. 'I lost it at cards, all right. If I don't give them two ounces by Friday, they're going to kill me.'

To be down four ounces at cards, he must have been chasing his losses like he used to do on the fruities. Double or quits; shit or bust. Bust. *Shit, I'd better go and find Jarrod.* But I didn't have any baccy to give him.

'Who do you owe it to?'

'I don't want to talk about it.'

'Not Silvestre?'

Then I remembered Barratt telling me that a new lot had taken over Colin's hut. Barratt had got into a ruck with one of them in Marshton. Maybe they'd sussed out Colin was a gambler and marked his card; taken him for a mark and marked the playing cards. Now he was a marked man. But what could I do?

'I've got to get back to the kitchens in a minute. Are you going to help me out or what?'

'I can't give you what I ain't got. I can only afford half ounce a week with my wages from here.'

'I thought you were supposed to be a baron.' He said it sneeringly, like I reckoned I was Charlie Big Spuds, and if he chose to, he could expose me as one of the saps.

'Not anymore, I ain't. It's all dried up, mate.' This wasn't quite true, cos I was still selling a little burn to feed my own habit, but Barratt had stopped giving me hash to sell yonks ago. If I'd won the chess competition, it might have been different...but I didn't.

'Come on, Jarrod, I'll sort you out, won't I? You know me. Even if you can only give me half ounce.'

I knew him too well, at least as far as coughing up debts was concerned.

'Don't you trust me? I'll pay you back when... I've already written to Dennis to tell him to bring down some... thingy.'

Four months after I'd had the idea. If he was me, he would have sceered. 'It's a bit late for that, mate. I'm getting out of here in three weeks.'

'I've never said no to you, have I? Remember when you were skint in the bail hostel?'

I did. He gave me two quid and I was able to buy half ounce of baccy.

'We promised we were going to help each other out in here, didn't we?'

At the start of my sentence, I would have agreed. But when I needed him, he didn't help me. My experience of selling hash had forced me to learn to repel almost every attempt at manipulation, but I was still surprised that I was able to be so militant with Colin, cos he knew my weaknesses better than anyone. I'd put up a barrier that even he couldn't penetrate, whatever guilt trip he laid about us being best mates. Looking back, I can see I'd lost my empathy; I was treating my old friend like he was just another trainee.

I heard H's footsteps and gestured frantically for Colin to get away from the window.

'How's it going, Brook?'

'Really well. I'm just about to start on the ceiling.'

'Well, stop dawdling and get cracking.'

H moved on and I chuckled to myself cos he was an unlikely saviour. Then I folded the wallpaper in the way that he'd shown me.

I didn't have much sympathy for Colin gambling and losing. I'd seen it untold times before. I'd watched over his shoulder as he poured all his money into fruit machines, like he'd been hypnotised, and I always knew that he'd soon be tapping me up for a loan. But if prison had taught me anything, it was how to say no.

His head popped back up above the window ledge. 'You think it's fucking funny, do you?'

I didn't answer.

'Don't ever ask me for anything again, Jarrod.'

'I won't.'

And I never did.

Chapter Thirty-Four

My pillow was yanked out from under me while I slept and pushed down hard over my face. When the pressure eased and I was able to breathe, I was punched three times in the head.

Clammy fingers with jagged nails forced a ball of paper into my mouth. My attacker slipped quickly from the room without having spoken a word.

I lay there for a few moments, breathing heavily and unable to think clearly, then I pulled the wet paper plug from my mouth and dropped it over the edge of the bed. I knew that turning people down when I was selling hash had made me a few enemies, but that was months ago now.

I got up and stood in my doorway, listening for any coughs or creaks that could give me a clue as to who wasn't asleep. My room was next door but one to the recess and I often woke in the night and heard people getting up for a piss. Sometimes I heard more than one pair of footsteps creeping about and I wondered what they were getting up to. All I could detect now was snoring and pipes rattling and a voice mumbling angrily like he was arguing in a dream.

Very early the following morning, I clocked sunlight glinting on the foil of my baccy, which had been knocked to the floor during the break-in. The screwed-up ball of paper was next to my bed, and I leaned down to grab and unravel it. In block capitals, on a scrap of blank prison issue letter, it said: *YOUR CODEES DETT IS YOUR DETT YOU MUG. GIVE OZ OF BURN TO TYLER NEXT TWO CANTEENS OR WI'LL CUT YOU.*

*

By the time I'd caught up with Colin a couple of days later, I already had a plan for how to pay off the debt. Though I wasn't going to tell him yet, I wanted him to sweat. And for him to see that I was scared too, and angry that he'd dragged me into his mess.

He was sat slumped at the side of the dining room during association. There were two empty chairs either side of him, like he was carrying an infectious disease. Even I left a gap between us, though that did mean I could see him more clearly.

'How's it going?'

I wasn't particularly interested in the answer, which was just as well, cos all I got was a grunt; then he lifted his head, but he didn't turn around. I leaned in closer, and lowered my voice to a whisper, 'They're after me now. One of them punched me in the face when I was asleep. They reckon they're going to cut me up if I don't give Tyler two ounces for them.'

He finally turned to me, and I could see the scabs and sores around his mouth and the dark grooves under his miserable eyes. 'Who was it?'

I glanced around as if searching for the answer. We were sat close to the table tennis table and heard a trainee cussing when his smash hit the net.

'I don't know. I fucking wish I did though. It happened too quickly.' Though I was pretty sure he wasn't hefty enough to be Silvestre.

'I'm sorry, Jarrod.' He sounded croaky, like his voice was rusty. 'I know I fucked up really bad.'

I reckon Colin's sorries were as rare as him walking past an amusements arcade on the out.

'I've got a plan,' I said.

'What?' The croak had gone. I thought he might even crack a smile.

I'd told Barratt about the attack cos I needed to tell someone, and I didn't think it was fair to involve Ackee. I also wanted Barratt to confirm that a line had been crossed, that a summit of hut leaders would be hastily set up and an amnesty and truce put in place. But Barratt's initial response was a slap back to reality. The only ones who were in it together were Colin and me. Barratt said it was considered legit in the nick that if the inmate who owed you wouldn't cough up, you could try and pursue their Co-d. But I didn't tell this to Colin, I cut straight to the deal.

'The top geezer in our hut said if I go and pick up a drop-off for him tomorrow night, then he'll give me two ounces of burn.'

Colin's narrow eyes scanned the room. 'What geezer?'

I checked that nobody was listening to us. 'Barratt.'

A flicker of recognition brought a subtle change to his expression, and he seemed to be reassured that the drop-off would happen.

'You'd better be careful though, Jarrod.'

'I know. It's got to be done though, ain't it?' Well, that's what I'd been telling myself. Ideally it would be Colin who risked losing twenty-eight days, but even if that could be arranged, he clearly wasn't in a fit state to undertake this mission. His arm was shaking now as he tried to hold down his leg to stop it from moving. The whole left side of his body was trembling.

'I'll pay you back, Jarrod. You know that.'

I didn't care anymore whether he did or not, but I couldn't quite bring myself to let him off. Particularly as I hadn't actually risked anything yet. 'The main thing is that we both get out of here in one piece.'

Colin grunted. I guessed in agreement.

Chapter Thirty-Five

I had no choice but to expose myself to the security light on the veranda, and to the risk of being seen by a kanga, from the screws' office on the other side of the lawn. I crept down the creaky wooden steps and around to the side of the hut, then ran to the back of the washrooms where Barratt said the torch would be.

I crawled on my hands and knees in the damp long grass until I found it, then stood up and tightened the shirts around my waist. I turned on the torch, and although the beam was sickly and pale, I could make out the path which led into the woods. Once I'd passed where I remembered gathering brambles with the Generals, I stopped to try and get my bearings. This was the furthest I'd been from the hut since arriving at Harewood more than five months earlier. I could hear Ferris, my ex-army cellmate in Brixton, giving me orders in my head. *Remain calm, soldier. Check your compass.* What compass? All I had was the vague memory of a crap map drawn by Barratt.

He'd told me a drop-off mission usually involved going to collect a parcel that had been left in the woods. This time was different, cos the drop-off merchants were expecting something in return. Barratt had heard that our blue and white striped prison work shirts were now fashionable on the out and were selling for thirty quid each on Camden Market. He gave me three, one of which I was wearing, the other two were tied around my waist.

I was conscious of how loud my footsteps sounded crunching on dry twigs, as I crept past the garden walls of screws' houses. It was ironic that one of them had a bathroom light on, cos it helped me to see where I was going. I had a brief sense of déjà vu as I recalled quickening my step past the houses of teachers when we sneaked out from Oakbridge two years earlier. It had seemed like a laugh at the time, but...*Keep focussed, soldier*, Ferris said, *distracted minds cost lives*. He'd actually said that during one of the stories he'd told me in Brixton.

I had lost focus, thinking about all that, and I realised I'd wandered into a clearing which didn't lead anywhere. I could hear birds chirping from high up in the branches, then when I looked up I saw the full moon. It took me by surprise, like I'd never seen it before, and I was confounded by the way it loomed just above me; like if I climbed to the top of a tree, I could hit it with a stone.

I turned on the torch to retrace my steps and drained the last from its batteries. Eventually I saw a glimmer of light in the distance. I followed it to the top of the bank above the road and looked for a spot to plot up. Some of the trees I clocked were skinny and covered in ivy; others had thick trunks and gnarly roots, which I could feel through the soles of my shoes. Perhaps one day our plimsolls would be fashionable too, and it would be trendy to eat porridge for breakfast.

I was still choosing a tree to hide behind when a car passed below me, and I wasn't quick enough to react. I waited in vain for it to return, then sat down on one of the shirts. As time dragged on, I became increasingly gloomy and knackered. What if they didn't turn up at all? Barratt hadn't spoken to his mates directly, the arrangement had been made through another trainee, who worked in the town and had access to a phone box. They were meant to arrive about three, but the specifics of time didn't mean much to me cos I didn't have a watch. After a while, I was able to see my feet and I assumed it was getting light. Or was it just that my eyesight was adapting to the night?

A car approached slowly, and my bowels loosened. Shit or bust - either I was about to get nicked, or I was finally in luck. I clambered down the slope and flagged the motor with a shirt. It pulled over, then the driver wound down his window.

'How many you got?'

'Three.'

He sucked his teeth. 'He's fucking done us up, ain't he?'

I passed him the shirt I'd been waving, then the one I was wearing, and finally the one from my waist.

The passenger was as pasty as a prisoner and had a big boil on his neck. He was building a joint on the door of the glove compartment. 'That Barratt's a slippery fucker,' he said.

As the driver reached over to the backseat, I tuned into the reggae coming out of the stereo. I recognised the rhythm but the song I didn't know. Though I would have bet another shirt that the singer was Gregory Isaacs.

I heard a clinking of bottles and then the driver opened his door and handed me two heavy carrier bags, which had Marlboro logos on the side. 'Here you go, man, have some duty free.'

As they pulled away, the passenger called after me to *be lucky*, then, 'Oh yeah, tell him I couldn't get hold of no caviar.'

On the way back, I tried to work out what he meant. Maybe caviar was slang for cocaine: rich man's food equals rich man's drugs. Surely he didn't mean *actual* caviar. Though I didn't even know what actual caviar looked like, or where it came from. It occurred to me that I didn't know a lot of things. Like the fact there were birds that chirped in the night, or how and why the moon changed size.

Somehow, I knew that the drop-off motor was an XR3, but that sort of knowledge was fuck all good to me. I didn't give a toss about cars.

248

Chapter Thirty-Six

It could only be canteen day, cos the whole place reeked of fresh burn. A hundred blocks of Golden and Old Holborn: cellophane ripped off with teeth; foil packets pulled apart with relief. The hut also smelt of liquorice and biscuits and penny chews. Everyone was in a better mood on Friday afternoons. Unless they owed their canteen to a baron. Or had to pay off someone else's debt, like me.

I needed to get it over with and move on. One more canteen and I'd be gone; nine days and a breakfast to be precise. And then at last I'd have paid their price; I could go out into the world and get on with my life.

Entering Hut Three, which was the hut of my enemies, was like déjà vu gone askew; same old scenery but different faces. I knew a few of them, but that didn't mean I was welcome; nobody had a bly to roam these places. Still, Smithy, from P&D, nodded from his doorway as I approached, the rectangle of a Drumstick lolly bulging in his cheek. Conan the Librarian was doing pull-ups on his door-frame – he knew me from the library, but I never found out his real name.

The screwed-up message had said give the burn to Tyler, but I'd found out he was just a sap they were using to stay anonymous. 'Do you know which one is Tyler's room?'

Conan pointed a strong arm across the corridor.

I was relieved I didn't have to go too deep into their territory.

I guessed Tyler had heard me, cos he appeared in his doorway. I followed him into the room and handed over four half ounce packets of burn.

As I was leaving, I heard a commotion behind me. I looked around and saw somebody being dragged out of their room by two geezers and slammed against the wall of the corridor.

Nobody else at Harewood had a barnet as bright as that.

I ran at them instinctively and shoved one of Colin's attackers hard enough that he toppled back and almost went down on his arse. Almost. He recovered quickly and rushed towards me, eyes blazing and fists at the ready. I knew I had to hit him first, cos he definitely wanted to hit me.

I lashed out with my left when his head was in reach. I thought I'd caught him cleanly with a corker on the cheek, but then he unleashed a whirlwind of fists like he'd knock me into next week. I knew it wasn't the time to be meek, but if I wanted to avoid a humiliating defeat, I'd have to cling on to stop him letting rip; get a leg behind his and go for the trip. I pushed into his chest with my head and managed to drag him round against the corridor wall.

For a moment, everything stopped still in a deadlock. If only I could get him into a headlock. If only.

My grip slipped, then a sickly thud, as a knee crunched into my chin. I staggered backwards and covered my face; a follow-through punch and I was all over the place. What happened next, I couldn't be sure; the next thing I knew I was pinned to the floor. Looking up at a geezer I'd seen but had never spoken to before.

Was this the cowardly bastard who broke into my room and stuck a pillow over my face?

'You had enough, Brook?'

I said, 'Yes', but I meant no.

I groaned as his weight lifted from my chest; when I looked around, I was surrounded by a forest of legs. Conan the Librarian yanked me to my feet, and I walked away slowly as if I was finished, then suddenly turned and charged back like I was Popeye on spinach. I saw it in his eyes that I'd caught him by surprise, but then he caught me too, with a well-timed thump that stung and rung and echoed in my ear.

I grappled blindly to get a hold of his shirt, but I was dazed, and he was alert. He got me into a headlock and threw me to the floor, then took a run up in prison shoes that were as tough as old boots.

It was like a bomb had gone off in my head: a bang and a flash, then an explosion of pain, which thumped through my skull and rattled my brain.

Chapter Thirty-Seven

The screw who accompanied me to A&E turned over the epaulettes on his shoulders to cover up "HMP". But with my trendy work shirt now ruined by dark pools of blood from my broken nose, there was no hiding what I was or what I'd been doing. When we got back to Harewood, I was surprised to be given a choice: spend my recuperation in the sick bay or in the hut with the boys. I chose the hut, cos I was eager to know what everyone had been saying about me.

As it turned out, most trainees were content to gawp through the window in my door and smirk at the splint covering my nose. Recovering was boring, so I tried sleeping as much as possible, but it was uncomfortable to get my head down with half a mile of padding stuffed up my left nostril.

It wasn't only my nose that was blocked, my thoughts were clogged up too. I couldn't concentrate on anything until Sunday afternoon when Ackee offered to lend me a couple of his precious sound system tapes. The next morning, while the rest of the hut was at work, I listened to them both straight through on my Walkman. Then after lunch, I played them again.

I became hooked on one track in particular which appeared on both recordings. It had a repetitive bassline which got stuck in my head. Ackee told me it was called the Answer rhythm. It acted as a bed for the MCs to toast their lyrics over.

On the second day of studying those tapes, some rhymes of my own had begun to take shape. It wasn't even a conscious decision; a couple of the lines floated fully formed into my mind, others I invented and reworked as I rewound the cassette and replayed the Answer rhythm again and again.

I hadn't written anything in Harewood, apart from letters, and Verity's poem, which I binned. It may have taken a kick to the head to get my creativity flowing again, but now I was even fantasising about leaving Harewood on a high by performing my rhymes on my last Sunday night, as a warm-up for the Ranking Miss P. Maybe I could namecheck Barratt and Henderson to get them on my side.

I was practising aloud when I heard a knocking of knuckles on the glass panel in my door. Colin was pulling a face like I'd gone mad in isolation.

I sat up in bed and bent my legs to enable him to sit down. He mumbled an apology about taking ages to come and see me.

I told him not to worry about it.

He looked at me directly for the first time. 'I got turned down for my parole the other day.'

'No way. How comes?'

He chewed his top lip for a while. 'The kitchen screw stitched me up with a snidey report.'

'Bloody hell. Is that all?'

He lifted a foot to stare at his shoe. 'And I got caught outside the hut during the night.'

'Doing what?'

'Nothing.'

'To rub it right in, the fucking pie and liquor came to see me. He tried to say that maybe God hadn't meant for me to get parole.'

Now *I* bit my lip, to stop myself from grinning. Or worse. Pie and liquor was my favourite piece of rhyming slang, but I'd never had the opportunity to use it naturally. Until now. 'Why would the pie and liquor bother saying that to you?' Colin believed in UFOs and ghosts, but as far as I knew he wasn't religious.

'Fuck knows. Fucking wanker. Now the earliest I can get out is November.'

But he wasn't the only one who'd be serving extra time. I still had to go in front of the Governor for fighting. When I brought it up now, he got all defensive.

'You didn't have to get involved, did you?'

'Why were they starting on you anyway?'

Colin admitted he was still half an ounce short of being able to pay them off. If he didn't cough by Friday, they would double the debt. In that moment, I didn't feel like jumping in to help him again. 'I've retired from the ring mate. I've finally learned the hard way that I'm no good at scrapping.'

'Sometimes it's got to be done.'

'Yeah. I suppose.' But I wasn't really sure that I believed it anymore. Of course, there could be circumstances when I might have to defend myself, but most people went through their whole lives without needing to get into a physical fight. I'd been battered twice in a few months, and I wouldn't know until after my operation tomorrow if my nose would ever be straight again. What if I had to spend the rest of my life looking at a loser in the mirror?

Colin came to see me again the next day. We sat in silence for a while as he bit his nails. I knew there was something he wasn't telling me. I could have tried to get it out of him, but I didn't have the energy.

Eventually he revealed he had a secret about Skully.

They were in his flat above the restaurant after work and Skully said he'd been experimenting with some cocktails but needed a second opinion. Colin could remember drinking a couple, then the next thing he knew, he woke up in an armchair with his trousers around his ankles. Skully was kneeling between his legs. Colin tried to kick Skully in the head, but his feet got caught up in his trousers. When he tried to lift himself out of the armchair, his legs felt really heavy, but at the time he just thought he was pissed. Now he was convinced that Skully spiked his drinks.

I didn't know what was more shocking: Skully's behaviour, or the fact that it had taken Colin so long to tell me. He said it happened a few days before my party, and that's why he'd lost it with Lucy's mates after he fell asleep, and they put make up on his face. A few days later, I was on my way round to his to make sure he was all right, when I bumped into Dennis robbing the vicarage.

Colin swore that if he'd known for sure what Skully was up to, he would have gone to the coppers. But he didn't, then Skully went to the coppers about him. It was the extra sentence for theft that meant Colin had needed to get parole. Now he'd been turned down, he couldn't get out for at least another four months. I reached under my pillow and gave him a sealed packet of Golden Virginia. At least he'd be able to clear his debt.

He promised to pay me back, but I said it was a present. Then I told him how I'd awarded myself a bonus from the drop-off.

After I'd hauled the heavy bags back to where Barratt had told me to stash them, I couldn't resist having a rummage inside. There were bottles of booze, untold packets of burn and Bensons, slabs of Dairy Milk, even a big lump of cheese. When I stuck my hand down into the bottom of one of the bags, I'd felt a wooden handle, then serrated metal. There was a blade about four inches long. I didn't feel right about bringing in a knife, especially after those bastards had threatened to cut me. But what choice did I have? Barratt must have been expecting it. I helped myself to an ounce of his burn to feel better.

'What did he want with a knife?'

'I don't know. He never said anything, and far as I can tell he ain't used it.'

Neither of us spoke for ages and the room fell still. Even the dust particles floating in the sunlight above our heads had seemed to stop moving.

'There's something else...you'd better not ever tell anyone.'

'Course not. You know you can trust me.'

He picked at the scabs around his mouth.

'I keep getting these voices in my head and they're driving me mad.'

'What sort of voices?'

He shifted and twisted his body. 'I don't know how to explain it. They just turn up out of nowhere and start criticising everything I'm doing, calling me useless.'

'You're not useless. I sometimes hear like an inner voice telling me

I'm an idiot and I should have done things differently. It's normal.'

'Not like this you don't. This ain't my *inner* voice, as you call it. This is like…other voices. I don't even know who the fuck they are or where they're coming from.'

When he said *other voices*, I thought of the Ouija and how he'd told me the world was going to end in 1993. Neither of us had brought it up since. When I mentioned the Ouija now, he shot me a look like I could be taking the piss.

'This is actual voices. I can hear them in my head. It's not dead people.'

As he looked at me now, I could see the fear and sadness in his eyes. It reminded me of when he came round to mine during the curfew and said that he thought his brain was going to explode. This time I realised I was out of my depth.

'Are you going to tell someone? I mean, like ask to see a doctor.'

He sceered. 'What, and get sectioned in a loony bin like my old dear?'

This was something he'd only hinted at before.

'I went to see her a few times, Jarrod. But in the end, I told my aunty I couldn't take it anymore. I remember seeing Mum with all this white foam around her gob,' – Colin rubbed the scabs above his upper lip – 'at first, I thought it was toothpaste. But it was what the medication had done to her. She didn't have any choice about taking it. She didn't have any choice about anything. She didn't even know where she was.'

'I'm sorry, mate.'

'There's no way I'm going to let them put me in a straitjacket. Or on pills that turn you into a zombie.'

He stared at me defiantly. 'I'm telling you, Jarrod. That ain't happening to me.'

Two days later, the Governor told me he was dead.

Chapter Thirty-Eight

The whole nick was gathered in the dining hall and hushed, then the Governor made an announcement. Afterwards he called for a minute's silence.

I shut my eyes. Colin was no longer my responsibility, and he couldn't think I was his. The thought made me feel guilty. Like: what kind of a best mate did that make me?

I peered around the tables before the minute was finished and clocked Barratt looking over. He seemed to be telling me to wait for him afterwards.

Outside the dining hall, I flinched instinctively when Barratt lifted his arm, but he only wanted to put it around my shoulders. For a couple of long seconds, he gripped me tightly, then as we walked through the car park he asked if I'd heard how it happened. I told him the truth: the Governor wouldn't say.

Barratt checked that nobody could hear us.

There was a quiver in his voice. I would never have expected him to be affected.

'He stabbed himself in the chest, up the washrooms.'

This took a moment to register, then I decided it didn't make sense. Not unless... I pictured the knife I'd brought back from the drop-off. Barratt's knife. Was that how he knew? But it didn't seem feasible either. 'I didn't even know that was possible?'

'He must have sneaked a blade out of the kitchens.'

*

The Governor had told me I could take a day off work, but I didn't want to be alone with my thoughts. I also needed to complete the last test for my City and Guilds: stripping and repainting a door.

I soon realised that it wasn't enough to be busy. I couldn't think straight, and I needed to talk. I turned off the blow torch and went for a walk, down the corridor to Ackee's room. I didn't care anymore whether H docked my wages, but in the circumstances, I was confident he would give me a bly.

Ackee was sanding his window frame when I called his name. He turned around and I clocked all the white dust that had stuck to the sweat on his face. I told him I couldn't focus and had already burned a black mark on my door.

I don't know if he'd heard the details of how Colin had done it, but he didn't ask any questions. He was angry at the system for not looking after us properly. A good mate of his had hung himself on Christmas Day in Feltham. 'How come they're always ready to spin a boy's cell over nutten and don't notice when he's losing his mind?'

He warned me not to do anything that could fuck up my release. On the out, I'd be able to get over it in peace. I nodded along because it made complete sense, though I didn't know for sure how long I had left; the disciplinary for fighting was still looming.

'Whatever happens, at least I'll be out for Carnival.' Ackee had offered to show me what it was all about. We still meet there on the same corner every year.

He swiped his forehead and grinned. 'Fifty-one days and a *bloodclaat* breakfast, bredrin.'

I was stirring my kettle of paint when the Governor sent for me. In theory, I was there to face a disciplinary, but the first question he asked me was how I was coping. I didn't think he'd be interested in the fact that I'd hardly been sleeping. 'Not too bad, thank you, sir.'

The Governor could barely muster the conviction to lecture me about fighting. He was tripping over his words and rambling. Maybe he was genuinely upset. The end result was a suspended sentence, which we both knew was as close as he could get to letting me off.

On my last night in Harewood, I dreamt I was sat in Colin's kitchen while he experimented with recipes to serve in his caff. He was crouched down, with a folded tea towel over his shoulder, peering through the glass door of the oven at his pie. I had a strong intuition that it wouldn't turn out well, but in the dream I didn't know why. The whole caff plan was just pie in the sky. As he talked about his ambitions, I didn't have the heart to tell him they were never going to happen.

When I woke, it hit me like another swift boot to the nose. Colin would never be going home.

I yanked the sheets and blankets away from my body and sat up on the edge of the bed.

Suddenly, the prospect of going to Colin's funeral made me retch. Having to face his family: looking his old man and his brother in the eye, and not being able to tell them what I knew.

Truth was, even if I told them everything, it still wouldn't be the whole story. How could it be?

I didn't know how long I'd been sat there, but the vague shapes in the room were now becoming clearer. I leaned over and picked up the letter from my desk. On the back, below Mum's familiar neatness, was the uneven scrawl of some rhymes. I would find it hard to decipher my lines, even with the light on, but I could remember the rush I got from writing them down.

Then, with a clarity more powerful than I'd felt when I walked away from the breakout, I knew now that this is what I believed in: the infinite pleasures of working with words. I didn't need to try and live Colin's life; I could do justice to his memory by writing down what had happened to him. What had happened to us. It took me a while, but I did it.

I understood that I would always be struggling with my clumsiness and crap coordination to be anything greater than a poorly rated decorator. Why would I put myself through that, just cos it was currently the only qualification I had? The qualifications I wanted to take were in English Language and Literature. I didn't know yet where they would lead me, but that wasn't the point. For the first time ever, I felt certain I knew what was right.

I stood up and ripped off the sheets and blankets and chucked them on the floor, slipped into my prison issue slippers and slipped out the door. I needed to escape from that room.

Outside, a tiny robin was hopping on the top step of the veranda. I stood completely still and watched as it stopped a few times to bob down and pick up crumbs in its beak. The robin took off, and my eyes followed it across to Colin's old hut, Hut Three. I wanted to believe his was a merciful release. That he'd only done what he needed to, to bring himself peace.

Above the screws' office and dining hall in the distance, the sun had started to rise; soon it would shine on the world beyond the gatehouse and drive. The dawn breeze reached my face and was delicious to breathe. I promised to live every moment on my day of release.

Acknowledgements

Duncan Campbell for his generosity and enthusiasm. Kim Cope for all her assistance in the lead-up to publication. Susan Hunt for her support over many years and proofing early drafts. Catherine Doran for proofreading the final version and going beyond her remit.

Kit Caless at Influx Press for his honest assessment at a critical stage. Ray Robinson and Rodge Glass at TLC for their editorial feedback. Anna at SilverWood for helping the publishing process to run smoothly.

Elisa Vasquez-Walters and Kieron Corless for always being ready to champion the cause.

Martin Newell, Mick Barry and Alec Turner for help with research into the miners' strike in Essex.

Thanks to friends and family in Berbinzana, Hernani and Lasarte-Oria (Basque Country), in whose homes some of this novel was written. Also, to Julian Davey, for the writing retreat home swaps in Ottery St Mary.

Ollie and Bernice for providing work security and believing in me. Alice Clark for bringing a youthful eye to the penultimate draft.

Most of all, to MariJose, whose ideas and constant encouragement helped spur me on to give it my best shot.